RUNNING IN PARALLEL

RUNNING IN PARALLEL
BOOK 1

RUNNING ᴵᴺ
PARALLEL

WRITE
ON GIRL

KARA O'TOOLE TREECE

RUNNING IN PARALLEL

Write on Girl books are available from your favorite bookseller or from www.KaraOTooleTreece.com

Paperback ISBN: 978-1-7371380-1-3
Ebook ISBN: 978-1-7371380-0-6

Library of Congress Control Number: 2021912434
Cataloging in Publication data on file with the publisher.

Layout Design: Rachel Thomaier

Printed in the USA

10 9 8 7 6 5 4 3 2 1

For my mom

PROLOGUE

United States
Fourteen Years Ago

The woman worked in her lab while her daughter sat quietly coloring in a coloring book. Somewhere in the back of her mind, the woman knew it was past dinnertime, and her daughter had to be hungry. But she was so near to finishing this last batch of tests. She just needed a few more minutes. If this experiment worked the way her calculations predicted, the results would be the biggest the scientific community—hell, the *world*—had seen in more than a generation. Those government guys just might start taking her seriously. Just one more minor adjustment to the experiment, one more test, and they could go. She would pick up pizza on the way home, a partial apology to her daughter and husband for her tardiness.

She attached probes to the object and entered the calculations into the computer. She had performed variations of this experiment multiple times, to no avail, but this time was different. She was positive her hypothesis was right. So, one more test, then pizza.

She looked at her daughter and smiled. She sat so quietly that sometimes the woman would get lost in her work and forget she was even there. The woman knew that bringing her daughter to the lab was not ideal, but with the hours she was spending on these experiments, this was the only time she was able to spend with her. "The sacrifices of a working mom," they said, usually with a sneer. Luckily, her daughter didn't seem to mind coming to the lab.

The woman powered up the computer and punched in the calculations, double- and triple-checking the numbers to make sure they were correct. Once she was satisfied, she took a deep breath and pressed *Enter*.

And nothing.

Nothing happened—not even a spark like the last time. Disappointment threatened to overwhelm her; she had been so sure that this time it would work.

"Momma?"

The woman did not look up from her computer, checking her calculations again and again. "Hmmm?"

"Momma—what's that?"

"What's what?"

"That!"

The woman looked up to find the object of her experiment glowing with a bright white light. The light steadily increased, until the woman could see the cracks of the object from the inside. The object started to vibrate, and the woman ran to her daughter, instinctively throwing herself on top of her to shield her from the light.

As she cradled her daughter in her arms, she squinted into the blinding light at the object. Next to it and hovering in midair, she could make out a small square of darkness, stark against the light the object was emitting. Before the explosion, the women absently wondered what was causing the small patch of darkness, and then everything went black.

FARA 1
United States, Present Day

I awoke with a start. Panic gripped me as I fought with sheets tangled around my legs, my T-shirt drenched with sweat. I had been running away from something or someone. Breathing hard, I sat straight up in bed. I had to get away, I had to . . . I stopped and looked around. It was just a nightmare, just a nightmare, I said to myself again. But it felt so real. I could still feel my legs pumping. I took a deep breath and curled my arms around my knees, telling myself it was just a dream and to calm down.

I took another deep breath and tried to stop my racing heart. I'd had nightmares all the time when I was a kid, but I hadn't had one in ages. I remember my mother rushing into my room in the middle of the night and lying next to me in my small bed, smoothing the damp hair off my forehead. It was the same every time I had a nightmare; she would come in, lie down, and say soothing words, or sing a song. She'd stay until I was no longer afraid. She did that even when I was in high school and asked her to stop—convinced I could take care of it myself. But she always came, until they died.

I stopped that train of thought right there; now was not the time to dwell on their deaths. I put that sadness away into a box and pushed the feeling deep down.

In an effort to calm myself, I looked around the room. Dawn was slowly seeping through the worn curtains of my tiny bedroom. The walls were the same beige as the carpet, which was threadbare and stained from god knows what.

The light fixture was dangling precariously—left over from the days when shoulder pads were in style, all brass and frosted glass. The closet door was off its rails. My shitty little slice of home.

Beck was asleep on top of the covers. His brown hair stuck to his forehead, mouth slightly open as he softly snored, the stale stench of booze lingering on his breath. I remembered him coming home last night from the bar, pinballing off the walls as he drunkenly made his way to my bedroom. I guess I needed to start thinking of it as our bedroom, since he moved in last month. Now this tiny slice of home was ours, and while I was happy to share it with him, he seemed . . . indifferent. I hoped in time he'd change his attitude and grow to love living with me. If we were to make it work—well—I'd think about that later too. Thankfully, he hadn't woken up with all my thrashing about. I blearily looked over at my cell phone; the alarm would go off any minute, and I wanted to savor the quiet. I put my hand on his arm, and he rolled away from me.

With a sigh, I slid out of bed, turned off my alarm, and shuffled into the bathroom. I let out another sigh as I turned on the light; this room was more pathetic than the tiny bedroom, if that was even possible. Maybe someday I would have enough money to get a better place, but until I landed that "dream job" (whatever that was), this would have to do. Maybe once Beck got back on his feet, we could find a place together that didn't have a chipped sink or an olive green shower. This entire apartment would be retro chic if it weren't so sad.

I looked at my reflection in the mirror and grimaced. The natural wave in my long blonde hair had flattened on one side, and the dark circles under my blue eyes reached my cheeks, which made me look older than twenty-one. That was to be expected; I had been working double shifts at The Grill to

KARA O'TOOLE TREECE

cover our expenses for the past month, and sleep had been a luxury. Beck promised that he would pitch in as soon as his business was up and running, but for now it was up to me. I had been on my own since my parents died when I was seventeen, so I was used to the feeling.

I peeked around the corner to see if Beck was stirring, but he was still passed out. Eventually we would have to talk about a beer budget, but not yet. He was going through enough with starting his business that he didn't need me nagging him. I would bring it up when the time was right, hopefully before our rent was due.

I got ready quickly, as I wanted to hit the gym before work. I felt guilty at the expense of it, but my trainer, Millie, insisted that I go, and even gave me a discount to stay a member.

"Kickboxing," she would say, "is better than homicide." I think she was only half kidding.

My car was a black POS. Its nose was bashed in from my last wreck and held together with a bungee cord; I had disdainfully named it Voldemort. The money it would cost me to give Voldemort back his nose had ended up going toward groceries last month, so Voldemort he would remain, for now. He had been a present from my parents on my sixteenth birthday, and for that reason alone, I didn't want to get rid of him. Call me sentimental. Beck joked that I would keep Voldemort until he fell apart, to his last nuts and bolts, but he didn't understand—his parents were alive, and he was able to talk to them whenever he wanted. All I had left of my family was this car.

"You're a POS, you know that?" I said as I opened the door. Voldemort seemed to roll his eyes at me. Cheeky bastard.

The day was typical of early spring in the Midwest—chilly, overcast, windy, and with just enough light rain to be annoying. The rain became increasingly annoying when

5

one of Voldemort's windshield wipers started going really fast on its own, like it was throwing a spontaneous dance party. It was another thing that I would need to get fixed when I had the funds.

It was early enough in the morning that most of the commuter traffic was headed into the city; the roads heading into the suburbs were only just starting to be dreadful. The gym was in a strip mall, in a typical office park, with the usual chain restaurants and coffee shops to keep the office workers happy. I parked out front and took a deep breath before walking in. Although I loved going to the gym and, if I was honest with myself, kicking the crap out of things, people and crowds gave me anxiety. I had been told since I was little that I was too quiet, and although I tried to engage in normal human interaction, I usually just felt awkward. My fear of saying the wrong thing and hurting someone's feelings or making them angry won out over my desire to engage in social circles. I did everything in my power to avoid being awkward, and to avoid confrontation, for that matter, and that was easier when I didn't participate in life. I only listened, unless not responding was more awkward than responding.

Adora had promised she would be here this morning, which gave me the boost to get out of the car. I met her almost four years ago when I started waiting tables at The Grill. My first day of work she took one look at me, sized me up, and said: "I think I'm going to like you" and that was that. She took me under her wing, and we became fast friends.

I walked into the building and was immediately accosted by her full-body hug. I laughed, trying to extricate myself.

She held me at arm's length, looking me over with a critical eye.

"You look like shit."

"Well, you look good." And she did. She was tall and lean, and her brown skin glowed against the vibrant pink of her tank top.

"No, seriously, Fara—you look terrible. Are you OK, honey? Did you get into a fight with Beck or something?"

"I'm fine. Really. I just didn't sleep well, and I've been working doubles for an eternity."

She rolled her big brown eyes. "Ah, yes. Doubles to pay for that asshat's car. And rent. And beer. And god knows what else."

"*Beck*," I emphasized, "is having a hard time right now, so I'm picking up the slack. He would do the same for me."

"I'm not so sure about that, Fara. He doesn't deserve you."

"And *I* don't deserve to have this conversation before coffee."

As if on cue, Millie walked out of the back room. Built entirely of muscle and bone without an ounce of fat on her, she was compact power. Her long, graying braid hung down her back. She stalked into the room and waited for us to get into our places.

Her stern gaze landed on me. "Fara, I'm starting to see your shoulder muscles. Nice work."

I beamed. Although I would never be built like her, I wanted to lose weight to get a swimsuit body for the summer, so I came to the gym most days. Adora thought I was nuts (I had a body and a swimsuit, what more did I need?) and swore that men checked out my curves more times than not. Adora once told me that she would sell her left nipple to have an hourglass figure like mine, and I said that I would cut off a limb to find a pair of jeans that fit both my waist and my butt. Women, it seems, are rarely happy with what we are given.

Class was an hour long and, as always, it was brutal. By the time we were done, I was a sweaty mess and looking forward to going back home to shower. The rain had turned into a light mist, and I wondered if Voldemort's windshield wiper would work again.

And there was a stranger leaning against a black sedan next to my car.

He was dressed in slacks and an open sport coat, and his dark blond hair was cut close to his head. I stopped and stared at him—trying to figure out if I knew him, somehow. He was an attractive guy, so much so that I would have recognized him if I knew him. Fear started in my stomach and made its way to my throat, my fight or flight response kicking in. I turned to go back into the gym.

"Miss Bayne?"

The man was walking toward me. How did he know my name?

"Miss Bayne? I need a minute of your time."

I stopped, my heart pounding. How did this guy know who I was? And how did he track me down here? The man seemed to sense my rising panic and stopped about twenty feet away.

"My name is Agent Hanlon," he said, as if it would answer my questions. I stood there, not moving. I wasn't really sure how to respond; was there a proper etiquette for this sort of situation? Was there a handbook for when you are randomly approached by someone with "Agent" in front of their name?

"How can Fara help you?" I heard Adora say. She must have been in her car and come over when she spotted this weird vignette.

Agent Hanlon cleared his throat and took a step closer, keeping his eyes trained on me. Even from where I stood, I could tell that his eyes were gray like a wolf's, completely clear and bright. As I took a better look at him, *wolf* was not an inaccurate description. His suit strained against the muscles of his arms and back, and every step toward me screamed *predator*. Like his body could barely contain him. I backed up a pace.

"Ah, you must be Miss Connors. I was hoping to talk to your friend for a moment." He smiled, but it didn't reach his bright eyes; those remained unnervingly focused on me.

Adora was apparently having none of that. "How do you know my name? And what do you want to talk to Fara about? What agency are you from? Why are you ambushing her outside of her gym?"

Agent Hanlon chuckled and held up his hands in a placating manner. "I'm really not trying to ambush anyone. I think she has some information my department would be interested in, so I was hoping that we could meet. Would now be a good time?" He posed that last question to me.

"No, it's not," Adora said, folding her arms. "She has other obligations that will last all day. Why don't you give her your card, and she can contact you when she has a minute?"

Even though Agent Hanlon kept the smile plastered on his face, I could see annoyance in those icy eyes. I was relieved that Adora was running interference for me; my anxiety had reached almost a full panic attack.

He pulled out a business card, which he handed to me with a nod. With the movement of his arm, I could see that a gun was holstered under his coat.

"I will look forward to your call, Miss Bayne," he said, and with that, he turned on his heel and headed toward his car.

"What in holy Hannah was that about? Who was that guy and what could he possibly want with you? I mean, he has ticked every government agent stereotype box he could have: piercing eyes, amazing body, sad clothes, unmarked car—"

"Yeah—if he's even an agent," I interrupted. "He could just be some weirdo. I'm absolutely positive that I have no information on anything important, unless he wants to know The Grill's dinner specials from yesterday."

I looked at the card and read it out loud to Adora.

Agent J. Hanlon

United States Department of Weapons Technology

I didn't recognize the division, but that didn't mean it wasn't legitimate. The whole situation was super strange. On top of that, I was now going to be officially late to my first shift. I shoved the card into my purse, gave Adora a shrug and a quick hug, then ran to my car to try to make up lost time.

BLU 2

Midwest Territory, Present Day

I was running out of time. Plans or no, I would need to leave soon to avoid detection. Though I wasn't ready to give up, it had been over an hour with no sign of the Second Counselor leaving his office. Styx had only been able to loop Jurisdiction's surveillance video feed for two hours; I was officially pushing my luck.

I cracked my neck and rolled my shoulders, willing myself to relax. According to intelligence, Jurisdiction was planning to build a facility of some sort, and the blueprints were in the possession of Jyston, the Second Counselor. He was supposed to be heading to a dinner party any minute, creating an opportunity for me to grab the blueprints. However, the Second Counselor was dawdling, and my perch from across the street was becoming increasingly uncomfortable. No one warns you that rebel reconnaissance is literally a pain in the ass—yet it is, and here I was: running out of time, with rubble digging into my backside.

I looked through the binocular program of my palmbox one more time and sighed. Through the window, I could see that the Second Counselor was as he had been for the past hour: sitting behind his desk, feet up, reading some sort of report. He must have been the slowest reader ever, since the report was only a few pages long. Maybe instead of overseeing Jurisdiction building projects, he might invest in a reading tutor? Just a thought.

I rolled my shoulders again but didn't stand to stretch; I had to make sure I stayed hidden. Even though Styx had the surveillance video on a continuous loop, and even though we had chosen this spot for its concealed location, Jurisdiction had eyes and ears everywhere. I couldn't risk anyone catching my whereabouts; after my last mission, the price on my head had doubled. I just had to wait a few more minutes until the Second Counselor decided to go to the party. Then I could make my move.

Why blueprints? It sounds cliché, but the Team was concerned because we hadn't been able to find out anything about this specific project. With its heightened security and the secrecy surrounding it, something nefarious was afoot. The bigger the secret, the worse for the population it is. You don't need to hide constructing an office or a sandwich shop. Anyway, the facility must have been important if Jyston himself was personally overseeing its construction; he normally didn't stoop to such mundane tasks. With his involvement, the Team figured the building had to be something terrible, and we needed to figure out what flavor of terrible we were dealing with. Now, if only he would get his ass in gear and go to the damn party.

I scanned the rest of the area, checking to make sure no one was out and about. I was outside of the city center, in what would have been the suburbs before the war. Most of the buildings around me had either been destroyed by Jurisdiction's weapons or sat abandoned. The weapons Jurisdiction had unleashed on the population had demolished most of our city, and they hadn't bothered to rebuild this area because it didn't profit them; it was too far out from the city center where they had their headquarters. Unfortunately, that meant whoever used to live and work here was left to find different accommodations.

There were burned-out buildings, toppled financial towers, and rubble littering the dilapidated streets for as far as my eye could see. The only intact structure housed Jurisdiction's satellite office, in what had once been a library. Jyston, himself, had requested this location for the office—for what purpose, one could only guess, and my guess was that its remote location made it more difficult to snoop on. I looked again through my palmbox. This man was thwarting my plans.

Styx chirped into the comm in my ear, standard mission gear. "Any sign of His Assholeness?"

She was back at the Compound, presumably trying to keep Jurisdiction from recognizing that their security video feed was on a loop.

"Yeah. He hasn't moved an inch since the last time you checked," I replied. "If he doesn't get moving soon, he'll be late to the party."

Styx snorted through my earpiece. "I'm sure that the High Governor will delay the festivities on his account. His Royal Prickness could be three hours late and the High Governor would still lick his ass."

"Probably."

Rumor had it that the new High Governor of the territory was trying to establish himself with the Jurisdiction elite. Inviting the second most powerful person in the world to his estate was the High Governor's next political move. I wasn't sure why the Second Counselor had accepted the invitation, but that wasn't my concern. What I needed was for the tyrant to get out of the office so I could do my job. Fifteen minutes to go before I had to abort the mission.

I searched the surrounding area again, sighed (again), and then filled my time by checking my supplies for the hundredth time, such as they were: a dagger strapped to each thigh, and a palmbox attached to my belt. I'd left my sword at the Compound; I needed stealth and speed, not brute force—or so I hoped. I hadn't needed many other tools since Styx had promised that the added tech in the palmbox could get me in and out of the office building without alerting the whole city. Useful things, these palmboxes—the technology could be loaded with any sort of program Styx could come up with, from lockpicks to tasers. This time, she'd kept the programs simple because this should have been a quick snatch-and-grab job. It was late enough that the security would be minimal, and the only people left in the office would be the bureaucrats who were trying to impress Jyston by working late. They would scatter like the rats they were once he left. There was no use in working late if you weren't getting political credit for it.

A sleek sports car pulled up, and a tall woman with shoulder-length blonde hair got out, her heels clicking on the pavement as she walked to the front door.

"Shit."

"What?" Styx asked, although it was muffled like she was eating something. Good to know she was on her toes.

"Dagna just pulled up and is entering the building. What the fuck is the Counselor's head spy doing here?"

"No idea, Blu, but you need to get the hell out of there. That bitch is a nasty piece of work and would love to get her hands on you, especially after your extra credit activities during the last mission."

"She deserved what she got."

"You burned down her house!"

"Don't be so dramatic. It was her summer cottage, not her house. She wasn't even in the cottage when I set fire to it, which would have been even better. She's obviously overreacting."

"Obviously. But seriously, B, get out of there! Abort the mission."

I turned down my ear comm while Styx was still yelling in it. I had ten minutes before I had to abort the mission, and I was going to see it through. I hadn't spent my entire life training to overthrow Jurisdiction just to give up at the first sign of trouble. Not that I would take unnecessary risks, but as of right now I didn't have enough information to abort. Maybe Dagna was just picking Jyston up for the party? Now that was a thought: two of the most horrific people in history dating each other. I shuddered and refocused.

I heard gravel shift from behind me and felt that familiar *tug* of my instinct that said that I was going to be in trouble. Shit. Carefully, I grabbed a dagger from its sheath and took a deep breath. A cold, metallic smell wafted on the air—the smell that I associated with Jurisdiction's minions. I slowly shifted my weight to get better balance. The first decision I had to make: do I run down the fire escape for an extraction, or do I just kill the minion quickly and hope there is enough time left to continue the mission? As I turned to make my move, the minion spoke.

"Stop right there! Don't move. You are to come with me."

Slowly, slowly, I started to stand. My body had been trained for so long, my muscle memory kicked in.

"I said, don't move! Dagna wants you unharmed. At least for now."

Shit. Shit! How did Dagna know where I was? Change of plans: I was going to have to fight this idiot and hightail my ass out of here.

I spun around, shooting my leg out as I did to take the minion's legs out from under him, and I hit his forearm at the same time so he would drop his palmbox. Minions might be the mindless grunts of Jurisdiction, but their palmboxes had enough power in them to incapacitate me. I could live with stitches from a dagger, but I couldn't live with being dragged, unconscious, to the cells where Jurisdiction took its prisoners.

I grabbed my palmbox and shoved it into the neck of the prone minion, sending a shot of disabling power through him. I would have liked to take him with me for questioning, but I couldn't carry him down the fire escape, and throwing him off the building seemed like it would defeat the purpose of keeping him alive for questioning. I stared at him for a second, wondering if I should just kill him, and turned my ear comm back on.

"What's happening, Blu? For fuck's sake!"

I took one final look at the minion and decided I wasn't going to kill him today.

"Jeez, Styx, it's almost like you care," I said, starting down the fire escape, taking rungs two and three at a time. "Things went a bit to hell, so if you could send in an extraction team, I'd be really grateful." I hung off the last rung and dropped, sprinting down the alley as soon as my feet hit solid ground.

"What happened?"

"The mission was compromised. Somehow Jurisdiction knew I'd be here, and Dagna personally sent minions after me. I need to check to see if anyone else is around. Please tell me someone is close. Dammit!" Minions were patrolling at the cross street at the end of the alley. "What are they doing there? Someone set me up. Get me out of here, Styx!"

"I'm sending in the cavalry. Ink is almost there."

"You're the best."

"Yes, yes I am. Head south toward Harney Street and he'll pick you up."

I sprinted the other way down the alley, jumping over debris and piles of garbage. Vagrants flattened themselves against the walls as I raced past them. I absently wondered why they were this far outside of the city center, but I couldn't dwell on that. My legs and lungs started to burn. Skipping daily training with the Captain seemed to be taking its toll; I'd keep that in mind the next time Styx woke me up at dawn to go running. Maybe.

I kept running, dodging behind rubble that used to be an office park and some sort of chain restaurant that no longer existed. I looked around. I seemed to have lost the minions. Now, where was Ink?

"Need a lift?"

I whipped around to see Ink in his car, looking at me with that perma-smirk. He opened the door as I raced toward him.

He peeled out before I could even get the door closed.

"Thanks" was all I could muster. I leaned into the leather seat, equally glad to be out of that mess and pissed that it had all gone to hell. Ink started the drive to the Compound, checking his rearview mirror to make sure we hadn't been followed. Jurisdiction's minions had yet to find the Compound, and we wanted to keep it that way.

We sat in silence until my breathing finally slowed enough to speak. He handed me a bottle of water.

"Want to talk about it?"

I took a hard look at him and realized that he had to be really angry if he wasn't giving me shit about the aborted mission. Normally he'd be calling me a fuckup and giving me a hard time, but right now he was glaring ahead at the road, clenching and unclenching his fists around the steering wheel.

I had known Ink since we were kids; we had grown up together in the Compound and joined the Team at the same time. His tattoos stood out starkly against his pale neck, where a vein looked as if it would pop out of his skin. Yep, he was pissed. His dark hair always had that purposely disheveled look, like he'd just gotten out of bed—his or someone else's. His green eyes were surrounded by eyelashes that I could only dream of having. Bastard. Everything about him screamed, "I'm bad and you like it," but we had been there, done that, and realized it wasn't for us. We were definitely better off as friends. Right now, he looked like he wanted to bludgeon someone.

"Dagna knew that I was there," I said after I caught my breath. "The orders were to take me alive. We need to get back to the Compound and talk to the Captain." Ink grunted in agreement.

He floored the accelerator and we headed north in the direction of the Compound, which was our home, training facility, rebel base—our everything. After the war, the Captain and some other rebels had started helping kids who had been affected by the war (like me), mostly orphans (also like me). They'd created a safe space for us to grow up. She brought us in, gave us a place to live, teachers to train us, and food to eat. We always had the choice to leave if we wanted, but once we decided to stay, she gave us nicknames as an initiation, of sorts. She said that the new names came with a new sense of purpose. Every one of the kids she brought in decided to stay, which says everything you need to know about the Captain.

She named me Blu because when she found me, I had been begging on the streets and was so dirty that all she could see was hair and big blue eyes. Ink got his nickname from drawing all over the wall by his bed in the Compound the first night he was there, although now with his tattoos it seemed as if he'd taken the nickname to heart. Styx once told me that her nickname came from being built like a stick, but my guess is there's more to it than that.

None of us remembered much of our lives before the Compound. I didn't even know how old I was, although I guessed I was in my early twenties. What we did know is that we'd spent our entire lives training to defeat Jurisdiction and to return democracy to our world.

Today we'd been thwarted, and that made me want to kick someone's ass.

Ink finally pulled in to the long, tree-lined drive that led to the series of buildings and open spaces that made up the Compound. It had been a college or university of some sort before the war, but now you were more likely to see someone carrying a sword than a book. There weren't any colleges anymore, at least not for anyone other than the Jurisdiction elite. Most of the campuses had been repurposed. My adrenaline dropped: I was home, and I was safe.

The entire series of Compound buildings was set over a mile away from the main road, behind a thick forest of trees far outside of the city center. The Compound was nearly impossible to find unless you knew exactly where it was, which was the reason the Captain and the Team were able to stay hidden for as long as we had.

Ink continued up the drive, past the first building, which had "Admin" in faded letters on the door, and to the open green space between two dormitories. As I made my way out of the car, he grabbed me by my elbow, stopping me. He hadn't said two words since he saved me, and I had let him have his space, but from the look on his face, he was about to explode.

"What the fuck, B? There were only a few people who knew about this mission—someone must have talked to Jurisdiction."

"I know. Someone sold me out."

3 FARA

I ran into the apartment, shedding my clothes as I went, and jumped into the shower. I didn't spare a look toward the bedroom, although I could hear the white noise machine whirring and deduced that Beck had yet to wake up. I thought he was supposed to go meet with a possible business prospect, but maybe it was cancelled. I would ask him later.

I sped through my routine, pulling my hair into a bun that bordered on slovenly, but I put on enough makeup to avoid a work uniform violation. The Grill's dress code was simple: black pants and black T-shirt. The atmosphere was casual, but my manager was very particular about appearance—especially with the girls. Why he insisted on makeup was beyond me, but my guess is that it came from the same place as his desire for all the waitstaff to be "attractive." He probably thought I should feel flattered that I passed the "attractiveness" bar that he set. Maybe I should be flattered.

Makeup and uniform on, I raced to The Grill. Despite the rush, by the time I ran in through the back entrance, I was ten minutes late.

"Look who bothered to show up."

I ignored the comment and began putting on my apron, trying to speed through the routine to start my shift.

"Were you late because that boyfriend of yours kept you up all night screaming his name?"

He walked up behind me and whispered into my ear. "I bet you like it. I bet you would like it even more if I took you to bed. I could show you what a real man could do."

Adora came up to my side; she had beaten me to work. "Oh for god's sake, Hewitt, get your dumbass filthy mind out of the gutter and leave the girl alone."

Hewitt traced my jawline with his finger, his hot breath in my ear. I was frozen in place, panic overriding my senses. I wanted to turn around and punch him, or run, or scream, but I couldn't move. All I could do was stand there and try not to cry. His hand slid down my neck, down my shoulder, and toward my waist . . . and then he was pulled away from me with a grunt. I whirled around to see Calum pinning Hewitt up against the wall, holding him by his neck.

"Don't. *Ever*. Touch. Her," Calum said with deadly calm. Hewitt was struggling against Calum, but with his legs dangling above the ground, he was losing the battle.

I met Calum's eyes both in thanks and a plea to stop. I didn't want to make a scene—didn't want confrontation. I just wanted to get my shifts over with so I could go home. Calum's broad shoulders shrugged as Hewitt slid down the wall, landing on his ass with a satisfying thud. I gave Calum a slight nod and a smile of thanks, and he walked back to his station at the grill. We'd been friends for so long that looks and nods were all it took to communicate—and both of us being as shy as we were, we had mastered that art. We had been friends since he punched a bully in the jaw for taking my lunch money in kindergarten, and he'd been my silent protector ever since. He went back to grilling burgers but gave me a small smile as I walked away, one that didn't reach his eyes.

Adora pushed Hewitt with the toe of her shoe. "I'll nail your nut sack to the wall if you get anywhere near her again."

She then put her arm through mine, and we walked out into the restaurant to start our shifts.

"Don't worry about Hewitt," she said quietly. "He only messes with you because he knows you won't fight back. Sick bastard."

Shame clamped down on my chest; I wanted to fight back, but I didn't know how—I wasn't raised that way. I wasn't even sure how to begin.

Adora continued, "One day, I want you to roundhouse kick Hewitt in the nut sack, spit on his face, then walk away."

"What is your obsession with nut sacks today? Anyway, one day I'll figure out how to stand up for myself so that you and Calum don't have to fight my battles for me. I really hate that you have to." I tried a lighthearted smile, but by the look on Adora's face, I knew I wasn't fooling her.

"Girl—let me tell you something. First, my obsession with nut sacks may or may not be because it has been way too long since I've gotten any. But really, don't ever feel bad that I stand up for you—it is my right as your friend. And Calum, well— if I were you, I'd love having that brooding hunk of tattooed meat throwing men around for me."

I rolled my eyes even though Adora was correct—Calum was gorgeous and had punched more than one person on my behalf. I turned around and saw Calum watching me quietly, his eyebrows raised at the comment. Feeling awkward, I didn't know what to do, so I started my shift.

The Grill itself was casual enough that we turned tables over quickly but nice enough that the tips were worth it. The décor was understated, with low lights and high-backed booths. When I complained once that the low lighting made delivering the food difficult, Adora joked that the low lights made us much more attractive, and we should be grateful for extra tips. She had a point, and right now I could use all the tips I could get, both monetary and verbal.

This was the only job I'd ever held, having gotten it after my parents died. Their estate covered the costs of their funeral, bills, and paying off their debts but didn't leave anything for me, so at seventeen I was left to fend for myself. I applied for dozens of jobs, and the former manager of The Grill took a chance on me, brought me under her wing, and taught me how to make ends meet waiting tables. She mentored me, helped me get through high school, and stuck around long enough to help me get established. She died a couple of years ago from cancer, but I didn't want to think about that now.

Once she left, she was replaced with the new manager. Everyone on staff called him "Douche" behind his back. Or maybe to his face too—he was so self-absorbed he probably wouldn't notice. In fact, I'm not sure I even remembered his real name, because Douche was how I saw him.

He immediately instituted all these new rules regarding appearances, fired most of the older waitstaff, and hired a bunch of new staff who looked like they'd walked straight out of a Hollister advertisement. Worse, he allowed a culture that permitted people like Hewitt (whom he'd hired) to harass the waitresses without repercussions. One girl had complained to Douche about Hewitt's behavior, and she was fired. So, I put up with Hewitt and the others. I needed the money and had nowhere else to go. Sometimes, I daydreamed about punching Hewitt and Douche in the boy parts and walking away in slow motion to some theme music—like a movie. I knew I would never do it, but it was nice to dream. Not that I planned on waiting tables my whole life, either, but going to college or applying for other jobs was off the table for now, at least until Beck got his business going. I wasn't going to think about that now either.

The shift was slow, and Adora and I spent most of our time avoiding Douche and catching up on gossip, which is fun but not useful in paying the phone bill. Eventually the hostess let me know that she'd seated someone in my section. I brushed myself off and rounded the corner only to see Agent Hanlon sitting alone in the booth, looking down at what appeared to be an ancient BlackBerry. I was surprised to see him but more surprised to see the BlackBerry. I didn't realize they even made those anymore, and I absently thought that if the world was in the government's hands, and those hands held ancient technology, we were all doomed.

I really didn't want to talk to him, so I told myself it was just a coincidence that he was here, and he really just wanted a sandwich. Taking a deep breath and plastering a smile on my face, I walked to his table, cataloging the details of him. "Great tips," my old manager used to say, "come from great observation—knowing what the customer needs before the customer even knows that they need it." I fell back on her sage advice as I assessed Agent Hanlon. The jacket was gone and had been replaced by a blue polo that was snug against his broad shoulders and chest. His skin was tan, even though it was early spring in the middle of the Midwest. He was clean-shaven, and his full mouth was turned downward in a not-quite frown. If I had to guess his age, I would place him in his late twenties, although he could have been anywhere from twenty-five to forty-five. I also noticed that he had stopped looking at his ancient technology and was intently staring at me with those icy gray eyes, as if he was allowing me to catalog him in that predatory calm. There was no humor in the eyes at all, like it would be easier for him to punch through a wall than laugh at a joke.

"Miss Bayne, what a pleasant surprise," he said, although his face said just the opposite. I got the distinct feeling that I had done something wrong, but considering I had just met the man and I needed cash, I wouldn't worry about it. Maybe he was always this grumpy.

"Agent Hanlon, right? Welcome to The Grill. Can I get you something to drink?" I kept that smile plastered on my face, thinking *tips, tips, tips* over and over.

He paused, quickly looking over the menu.

"I could give you more time—"

"No," he interrupted. "I'll have the prime rib sandwich, medium with a side salad and iced tea. No dressing on the salad."

I nodded and walked away, grateful that we were able to conclude our business in less than a minute. Hope started to bubble—but I should have known better.

I grabbed the iced tea, walking past Hewitt on my way back into the dining room. He followed me, making lewd comments under his breath about my backside as he did. I approached Agent Hanlon's booth, trying to ignore Hewitt's horrible commentary as best as I could, but he walked right behind me and grabbed my ass—which made me jump— sending iced tea cascading across Agent Hanlon's table. And right at that moment, I wished desperately to disappear, which had to be less painful than the embarrassment of throwing iced tea at a federal agent. Hewitt kept walking as the agent stared at me, and I mumbled apologies, grabbing whatever napkins I could to stop the iced tea from dripping from the table.

Agent Hanlon excused himself and got up, and just like that my anxiety took over with all the worst-case scenarios running through my head. I started to panic—I was sure he was going to find Douche and complain about me. I was going to get fired. I was going to be hauled into the department of god only knows what for accosting an agent with iced tea (would that be an accosteaing?). My name would be in the paper as a felon, and I would end up living in a van by the river. How was I going to pay my bills? Would another restaurant even hire me if I got fired? And all because of that jackass Hewitt. If I wasn't so pathetic and spineless, I would explain myself to Agent Hanlon, tell him that the Iced Tea Incident was due to Hewitt being a creeper, but I couldn't convince myself to go after him.

Tears lined my eyes as I turned around to get a dish towel, only to see Agent Hanlon standing in the middle of the restaurant about three inches away from Hewitt's face. Agent Hanlon was at least six inches taller than Hewitt, and forty pounds of pure muscle heavier—and whatever the agent was saying to the little weasel was making Hewitt turn pale. It was like seeing a blade of grass trying to stand up to a giant brick, which would have been funny if I hadn't been so mortified. I rushed back over to the booth, dish towel in hand, and wished with all my heart that the ground would swallow me up so I could hide for fifteen years, until everyone forgot about the time I threw iced tea at a federal agent.

Agent Hanlon made his way back to the booth. "Are you OK?" he asked.

I nodded, afraid to speak just in case the tears started again.

"You shouldn't have problems with him anymore," he said. I looked up at him, and he met my gaze. "I saw what happened. Does he do that to you often?"

I shrugged. "I've gotten used to it. He just startled me this time, is all. I'm really sorry for spilling on you."

"Why are you apologizing? He should be over here apologizing to you, and if I had my way he would be. You shouldn't have to get used to something like that. Do you want me to talk to your manager?"

"No! I mean, no, thank you. My manager handpicked Hewitt to work here, so that conversation would not go well for me."

Agent Hanlon nodded, understanding flashing across his face. "Well, the offer is there. Just so you know, I explained to . . . Hewitt . . . that the delivery and service of iced tea was a sacred rite in many southern states, and desecration of that right was intolerable." I stared at him for a second, and I swore that there was humor in his eyes. Did he just make a joke about me spilling the iced tea?

When I didn't say anything, he sighed. "In other words, I told him that what he did was felony sexual assault, and since I'm a federal agent, I'd make a very convincing witness, should you decide to press charges—which I would encourage you to do. I also told him that you had my card and could call me anytime he decides to interrupt iced tea service again."

I bit my bottom lip to keep the tears from leaking onto my cheeks. "Thanks."

He caught my arm as I wiped down the table once more but then quickly let it go. "Hey—don't give that jerk another thought, OK?"

I nodded.

"I still need to talk to you, but I can see that you are busy. Would you have time, tomorrow possibly, to talk to me? I can meet you at a place of your choosing."

I thought about it, and it occurred to me that my anxiety would keep me up all night worrying about what he wanted to talk about tomorrow.

"I have a break in about forty minutes," I said. "We can meet in the back booth, in the corner, if you want."

*   *   *

"What did that hot agent man do to Hewitt?" Adora asked as I ran through the kitchen to beg Calum for some food. I had already delivered Agent Hanlon his sandwich without throwing anything more at him.

"Why—did Hewitt say something to Douche?"

"No—I just saw that hot agent man towering over the scumbag, and I've been waiting for you to come back and tell me what happened. So spill it!"

I grimaced. "If you only knew how accurate that statement was. Hewitt grabbed my ass right in front of Agent Hanlon, causing what I will now only refer to as the 'Iced Tea Incident,' and it appears that Agent Hanlon was not pleased with the outcome of said Iced Tea Incident, or Hewitt's grabby hands."

Adora raised her eyebrows. "Hewitt got his ass handed to him by that hot agent man?" I rolled my eyes and snorted. "Serves him right."

I shrugged, although I couldn't disagree. "Can you please stop referring to him as 'that hot agent man'? I have to talk to him in a few minutes and I can't take him seriously if that is running through my head." Calum rolled his eyes and sighed, the pain of the long-suffering. I giggled.

"I am only speaking the truth," Adora said with a grin. "He is an agent, and he is hot—like, melt-my-underwear hot. Let me know what he says. And if he needs someone to test out his handcuffs . . ."

"You really need to get laid."

Agent Hanlon was already sitting at the booth when I got there, so I slid into the other side and set my plate down. He raised an eyebrow at me and motioned to my giant plate of food.

"Sorry," I said. "I have to work the next shift, and this is the only time I get to eat today."

"Do you always work two shifts?"

"Money doesn't grow on trees, and bills continue whether I work or not."

He nodded, took a breath, and looked at me. I waited, expectantly. He stared at me some more, and I took a bite of my cheeseburger, which was delicious. It felt like Agent Hanlon wanted me to start talking and was using the quiet as an interrogation technique. Unfortunately for him, that wouldn't work on me. I might not be good at a lot of things, but being quiet was something I excelled at. I ate in silence for a few more minutes and waited. Little did he know that all I ever really wanted was quiet and a good cheeseburger. Sitting here, I had both and could wait a long, long time.

When he eventually realized that I was not going to break at his brooding silence, he decided that he needed to start . . . whatever it was that he needed to start.

"I should probably explain my role with the government, just so you know I have some legitimacy."

I shrugged. Since I had no earthly idea what he needed to talk to me about, he could start wherever he wanted. I popped a french fry in my mouth.

"I work for a division of the Department of Weapons Technology that specializes in new and unusual weapons and technology."

I had no idea where this was going. New and unusual weapons and technology? What did that even mean?

"We received a report recently that you might have information that could lead us to one of those unusual weapons. That you either have a component of the weapon in your possession or know someone who does."

I gaped at him and waited to see if he'd give any indication that this was an elaborate hoax. He didn't laugh.

"What?"

ceived a report indicating that you have, or know who has, a component of an unusual weapon."

I heard you the first time, but I had to make sure I wasn't hallucinating. Are you sure you have the right person?"

"Yes."

I laughed. I couldn't help it—thinking about my life and my utter lack of anything that worked. My phone would still be a flip phone if my carrier hadn't forced me to upgrade. All the appliances in my apartment could be sold in an antique shop if they actually worked, and my car was held together with a fucking bungie cord. How could the government be so wrong? I didn't even have a blender that would blend, and he was questioning me about whether I had a piece of some sort of weapon?

"Well, I obviously don't. I didn't even know that you all existed until this morning."

"I trust the report, Miss Bayne. You might not realize that you have this component, or it could be your boyfriend's. But we are certain it was traced to your apartment."

"Agent Hanlon, I don't mean to be rude, but I think there's been a misunderstanding. I live in a shitty one-bedroom apartment. It's about five hundred square feet. It's not like I can hide a missile in my linen closet. I don't even have a linen closet."

He gave me a hard stare. I guess joking about missiles was not something you did with an agent of the government.

"Our scanner picked up the component's signature coming from your apartment at approximately three o'clock this morning. What were you doing at that time?"

I sat there, dumbfounded. I had been sleeping, and Beck had been . . . I wasn't sure when Beck got home, but there was no way Beck was involved in any of this.

"I was sleeping."

"Where was your boyfriend at the time?"

"Home."

"Do you care if I ask him a few questions?"

"I'm not his keeper."

Agent Hanlon raised one perfectly arched eyebrow at that, and I shrugged while I took another bite of my cheeseburger. He could talk to anyone he wanted, but it wouldn't change the fact that I wasn't hiding some sort of weapon of mass destruction with my old underwear.

Something else that I realized as I sat there: while I usually panicked with new people—I wasn't scared of Agent Hanlon at all. It seemed weird that I wasn't tongue-tied around him, especially since he'd just insinuated that I was keeping a weapon in my shithole apartment. Maybe the ridiculousness of his questions was overriding my anxiety? Or maybe the worst had happened during the Iced Tea Incident and my brain couldn't be bothered to worry more? I'd have to think about that later.

He was looking at me expectantly, but I had already finished my food and was gathering my dishes. He stood to leave. I looked up at him, realizing just how huge he was. He had to be at least a foot taller than I was, and it was like staring at a very attractive, solid wall.

"Thank you for your time today. You have my card, so if you think of anything at all, please let me know." He said the words, but it was like his mind was already on to the next thing.

I smiled out of habit, nodded, and took my dishes back to the kitchen. As I walked past, I noticed there was a $100 bill on the table.

It wasn't what I expected, and I felt almost dirty taking the money. But, considering he had just accused me of being in possession of some sort of unusual weapons thingie, I shoved the money into my apron and smiled. Maybe today was not going to turn out to be as shitastic as I'd thought.

After the longest, slowest second shift ever, I finally pulled back into my apartment's parking lot. I was dead on my feet and ready for bed, although I was looking forward to cracking open a beer and talking to Beck. I wanted to see if his business meeting had been postponed, and to fill him in on my crazy day.

I walked into the apartment and realized that Beck was gone again. My stomach started to knot; a familiar combination of anger and dread. Of course he wasn't home—he was never home when I got off work—so why was I surprised? Since living here, he had gone out with his buddies for beers every night, coming home late and usually hammered. It wasn't much different than before he lived here, except now I was living with it. He never once asked if I wanted to go. He told me that none of his friends brought their girlfriends, so I would be intruding. I believed him, but that didn't make it hurt less, especially since I really could have used a beer after the day that I'd had.

I checked my phone, but I knew there wouldn't be a text or call from him. Just like there wasn't one the night before or the night before that. Or the week before that. I always asked him to let me know if he went out, not because I kept tabs on him but because I cared. He always said he would, and he never did.

"Everything OK?" I texted.

I plopped down onto the futon and waited for his response. I wouldn't be able to relax until I knew he was all right, so I started looking around my apartment, taking inventory of my home for lack of anything else to do. The Formica was peeling from the edge of the kitchen counter. There was a dead bug stuck in the ceiling light. There was the stain on the carpet from previous tenants. There was the button that had been missing from the futon since I inherited it. The cupboard door was barely hanging on. Everything I owned was worn and sad. Sort of like me.

"Yes. Out with friends. Be home later."

Although I tried to stop it, my eyes started to sting with the tears that I wouldn't let fall. Was it really that bad that he had gone out the past few weeks while I worked? I tried to be empathetic; he was probably bored since I was working all the time. Was it that big of a deal that he didn't think to let me know, even though I had asked him to? I knew what Adora would say, that it was not my responsibility to "teach a grown-ass man common courtesy," and she was right. But the thought of having the conversation with him about how his going out, without telling me and when money was tight, and how his lack of communication with me made me feel unappreciated. It left me feeling empty. I knew he would say I was making a big deal out of nothing—that I was overreacting—since that was what he always said. Then he would promise to do better, and fail. I knew he wouldn't change, so what were my options? Was it really so bad? He was funny and sweet; was going out with his buddies worth the fight? I pushed the feeling away. I would think about it later, after I had some popcorn for dinner, then sleep. Sleep: the thought of it put a smile on my face. I would even risk the nightmares just to end this weird and horrible day.

4 BLU

Worry flashed across Ink's face at the realization that someone had alerted Dagna of my whereabouts, but just as fast as the worry came, the look was gone. He got out of the car and walked toward the Quad, his shadow cast long across the open green space by the setting sun behind him. The Captain was in the middle of training some trainees, and as we walked toward them, most of them looked awestruck at the sight of us.

I theoretically understood it—we were what they were working tirelessly to become: the principal members of the Team. We had completed more missions than any other Team members in the Compound's short history and had caused Jurisdiction more setbacks than we could count. Our pictures were on wanted posters throughout most of the territory. Each of us had a price on our heads—mine being the largest since I'd burned Dagna's summer cottage down (she deserved it). But, as with most things, the stories of our exploits were usually blown out of proportion, with the odds against us exaggerated and our actions miraculous. The more the trainees and others talked, the bigger our reputations became, and the more uncomfortable I was with the attention. Today was no exception, especially considering what a complete fuckup my mission had been. I was not in the mood to deal with their misplaced hero worship.

Not that I really had to worry—most of the trainees' attention was focused on Ink, which was the usual way of things. He milked every ounce of his bad boy image as we headed toward the Captain, his confident saunter making the girls swoon and the boys want to be him. He didn't *try* as much as he oozed a sense of sexy danger. I was impervious to it; I'd known him forever. He was tall, his abundance of lean muscle showing through his skintight T-shirt. He had multiple tattoos covering each arm and swirling up his neck, and he walked with a casual swagger that came from knowing he was gorgeous. The sword on his back caught the last rays of the sun, as did the daggers on each thigh. He was a picture-perfect assassin.

The older girls whispered and giggled as he walked their way. He winked at one of them, and she almost fainted. I shook my head; how was she going to dismantle Jurisdiction if she couldn't even handle Ink's wink? He saw my look and his grin widened. I punched him in the arm; he did that on purpose. Asshole. The Captain took one look at my face and turned toward the trainees.

"The last part of your training today is a three-mile run. Starting now."

The trainees groaned, but one look from the Captain and they started off on their jog. I didn't envy them.

"Blu, I should make you join them," the Captain said. "You have been neglecting your training."

I was going to reply with something undoubtably witty, but the fact that I got my ass handed to me running away from an aborted mission made me keep my mouth shut. I could be smart, sometimes.

The Captain indicated that we should follow her, and she took off at a fast pace through the Quad. I scrambled to keep up with her, my short legs already tired from my near escape. Perhaps I really should join the training. Tomorrow. Maybe.

We were heading toward the Captain's quarters, passing

buildings on our way. They were in various states of disrepair and were connected by paths of broken brick, which added to the Compound's crumbling veneer. If it weren't for the people who lived and worked here, it could be seen as a bit creepy. I loved it, but then again, not much creeped me out.

Lights flickered on in the windows of the two dormitory buildings, Team members undoubtably trying to corral little kids for bedtime. While most of the Team members lived on the other side of the Compound, the other inhabitants lived in these two dorms. I wasn't sure how many residents the Captain had living here currently, but it was a lot.

The Captain never turned anyone away from the Compound, and she never made a big deal about taking in all these people. She fed us, clothed us, gave us homes, and made sure we were educated in basic classes. But since we lived in a war-torn world, that wasn't all; as soon as we were strong enough to pick up a dagger, she made sure we were trained in weapons and combat. I could throw a dagger before I could tie my shoes, and that skill had saved me more than once.

The air took on a chill as the last remnants of sunlight dipped below the trees, and the smell of dirt and pine mingled with the upcoming buds of flowers. Trees in bloom lined the path as we walked uphill, careful not to trip on the broken bricks. People were out, walking to and from buildings in small groups or alone. Wood smoke from the armory drifted on the air, as lights lining the path flickered on. I loved the Compound in spring.

The Captain's quarters were in an old redbrick building that was covered in vines so thick they had broken through windows on the top floor and grown into the rooms beyond. The middle and bottom floors were in better shape, meaning only that the windows were not broken, and the vines were held somewhat at bay.

We entered through a nondescript door in the side of the building and walked directly into the Captain's office. Although Styx was forever trying to convince the Captain to add security measures to her office door, the Captain refused. She said that an open-door policy was contingent upon the fact that anyone could actually open the door. I tended to agree with Styx, but there was no use arguing with the Captain once she'd made up her mind about something.

The office took up the entirety of the first floor of the building and had battered dark wood floors and peeling paint. The large table in the middle of the space could seat at least twenty people, and a smaller table was pushed up against one set of windows on the right. Opposite them was a small reading area with a worn couch, chair, table, and some bookshelves that were overstuffed with books. The whole place felt lived in and welcoming.

I took in the familiar sight of the Captain as she maneuvered around her office. She wasn't that much taller than I was, and was all muscle. If it weren't for her short gray hair, she would look like she was in her twenties from behind. Her eyes, however, told a different story; they showed that she had done enough and seen enough for a thousand lifetimes. They gave her away as a warrior.

Ink and I sat at her desk, across from her. She steepled her fingers and waited for me to begin my report, and without preamble I told her what had happened. After I had finished, she let us sit there in silence while she carefully considered the situation. After a moment, she spoke.

"Dagna knew where you were, and wanted you brought to her alive?"

I nodded.

"Well," she said, "that confirms my theory. Dagna now considers you her personal enemy."

"Because Blu torched her house?" Ink said with a smirk.

The Captain rolled her eyes at Ink's irreverence but continued anyway. "Yes. Before then, Blu was just another member of the Team, bothersome in a general way. However, Blu deciding to take matters into her own hands made it personal."

"But how did she know where I was?"

"Dagna is the Counselor's spymaster, and we know that she has spies everywhere. It's always surprised me that we've never caught a spy trying to infiltrate the Team. The minions' actions today confirmed that she has someone on the inside: we have a mole."

"No fucking way," Ink said. We looked at each other in disbelief.

"My theory is that they have been lying dormant, just gathering information but yet to divulge anything important. Maybe because they are unwillingly spying for Dagna. Maybe she has information on the spy and is blackmailing them. Or maybe Dagna gave the spy orders to lie low. Whatever the reason, they haven't been an issue, until now."

As much as I didn't want to admit it, it made sense. "Do you think that if I hadn't burned down her summer cottage, she would've left the spy dormant?"

"I don't know, Blu. Something else would have eventually set her off."

"You know that I didn't just give in to some random pyromaniac whim, right? She was torturing kids in that house, Captain. She was hurting them just to see if they knew anything about their 'traitor' parents' supposed actions against Jurisdiction. *Kids!* I couldn't just walk out of there. She had to pay. It was like when I . . ."

I was breathing hard now, my eyes stinging, panic starting to rise into my throat. The Captain's gaze softened as I took a deep breath.

"I know," she said softly. "I know."

Ink put his hand on my shoulder, but I shrugged him off. I didn't want his pity; I could fight this panic attack on my own. I dug down to that part of me that was made of fire and lightning. I remembered who I was and who I had become, and after a couple of deep breaths, my panic slowly slid away. It had happened so long ago.

I was only a child when I was taken by Jurisdiction and tortured because Dagna thought I knew more than I did about the Compound. But I was a different person now, and they weren't dealing with that child anymore. I would do whatever it took to make sure that they would never be able to do something like that again, to me or anyone else.

I'd known that burning down Dagna's summer cottage would have consequences. It had been just another reconnaissance mission; the Team had intelligence that Dagna was running some of her spy operations out of this specific building. My orders were to watch the building and report back to the Team. But, when I began my surveillance, I realized more was happening than we originally thought. When I saw those kids there, starved, beaten, burned, and god only knows what else, I got them out and burned the place down. I wasn't kidding when I told Styx that my intention was to burn Dagna down with the building. One day I would kill her. That might not make me a good person, but I would take that over one more kid being hurt.

"So, to sum up this disaster," Ink said, "burning down Dagna's house has royally pissed her off enough that she has a personal vendetta against Blu; we have a spy—which is going to colossally screw us—and all the while, Jurisdiction is building something heinous, and we missed our opportunity to get the blueprints. Is that it?"

The corner of the Captain's mouth turned up in an effort not to smile. I couldn't help but laugh.

"I believe so."

"Oh good. I thought this was going to be hard."

"There is some good news, though," the Captain said. "We know that Second Counselor Jyston still has the blueprints. We also know that Jyston did not attend the High Governor's party tonight, for whatever reason. Not to be deterred, the High Governor has invited the Second Counselor to his lavish masquerade party, which he is throwing to celebrate our territory's history and Jurisdiction's accomplishments, as clichéd as that sounds. According to my sources, Jyston will be loaning the High Governor the blueprints to display at the party as part of his collection. Blu will get them there."

Ink interjected. "Not that Blu can't handle herself, but is she the best candidate for this mission? Now that the price on her head is so high, there's no way she'll get out of there without someone turning her in. Not to mention that the Queen of Sadism wants to capture her."

"I won't get caught."

"Like today?"

"Bite me."

"Children! Please focus," the Captain said, exasperated. "The party is in three days, which will give us time to plan. If the Team decides that Blu is not the best option, I will leave that up to your discretion, although my guess is that you will have to handcuff Blu to the table to keep her from going. Because of the spy, we'll keep the details of this mission between you two, Styx and Jackrabbit. We can't have another leak. The five of us will meet in my office after training tomorrow to start the planning. Blu, I'll expect you at training first thing in the morning. Understood?"

FARA 5

I woke up with a start, the remnants of another nightmare slipping away. It felt so real, more than a dream. Something tickled my memory, just out of reach. What time was it? I wondered how much more sleep I could get before my alarm went off.

As I was snuggling back into my bed, I felt a breeze on my face and smelled men's cologne. The fragrance was unfamiliar. Had Beck started using a new aftershave? The breeze ruffled my hair, and I cracked open my eyes.

I sat straight up. A light the size of a business card was hovering about a foot in front of my eyes. I stared at it, and I realized that it was not a light itself, but that light was coming through the space, almost like a tiny window. I would have thought I was still dreaming, but I felt the breeze again, and on that breeze was the smell of the cologne, stronger this time. I reached my hand out, not quite knowing what I was doing. Then I heard the door to the apartment open. Beck was finally home. When I turned back to the weird space window thing, it was gone.

Where did the window go? I must have imagined it. I snuggled back down into bed and waited for Beck to come into our room. After a minute, I heard a large crash, followed by Beck giggling, and I jumped out of bed. I opened the bedroom door to more crashing pots and pans in our small kitchen. Beck had apparently had too many cocktails. Again. It was just after three in the morning and I really needed to get some sleep, but that wasn't happening until Beck decided he wasn't going to play chef tonight.

"What are you doing?" I asked him, stooping to grab an errant strainer.

He blinked up at me from the floor, where he was picking up the pots he had dropped, his hazel eyes blurry.

"Making ramen noodles." He giggled again.

I struggled to keep from rolling my eyes. "Come to bed, Beck."

He stood and looked me up and down, a slow smile lighting up his face. I took his hand, and he lurched a bit as I dragged him into our bedroom. As I shut the door, Beck pushed me up against it and kissed me hard, tongue darting into my mouth, and his hand on my ass. He tasted like Jägermeister and cigars, which was not my favorite. Although I really wanted to go back to sleep, this was the man I loved, and I wanted him to be happy. And right now, what would make him happy was sex.

He continued kissing me, and I took his shirt off as we tumbled back into the bed. He crawled on top of me, slipped off his shorts, and slid my underwear to the side.

"It's been too long," he said as his hand crept under my T-shirt. In less than a minute, he had collapsed on top of me, a smile playing on his lips. We lay there, Beck breathing heavily and his weight making it hard for me to catch a breath, but I was enjoying our closeness. With one final breath, he kissed me on the forehead, rolled off me onto his side, and pulled the covers up. I stared at his back for a minute, my feelings pushing their way into the open. That was it? It wasn't like the other times we had sex were much different, but I always held out hope that he would at least hold me when he was finished. He only did that when I asked, and usually reluctantly, like I was asking the world of him. I probably was.

Was this what relationships were supposed to feel like? The other boyfriends I'd had had never lasted this long, so I was in uncharted territory. I pushed the feelings down—I would deal with those later, when I didn't need more sleep.

"I love you," I said.

"Love you too," he mumbled. I went to the bathroom to clean myself up.

"Was Calum here earlier?" Beck slurred, half asleep.

"No, why?"

"Because it smells like cologne in here."

"He could smell the cologne?" Adora asked as we were leaving the gym the next morning. "Are you sure that's what he said?"

"Yes—it freaked me out! I couldn't go back to sleep after that. I was just waiting for that weird window thing to reappear. But it didn't. I'm starting to think I'm crazy."

"So sex with him was so bad it made you hallucinate?"

"I didn't say it was *bad* sex."

"It was with Beck. It couldn't have been great."

I glared at her. "What's that supposed to mean?"

"Look, Beck is inherently selfish. Inherently selfish people are terrible in bed because they only think about their pleasure, and not yours." She looked at me over her sunglasses, one perfectly shaped eyebrow raised. "Tell me I'm wrong."

I thought about it, about how we didn't have sex very often, and when we did, it was like it was last night . . . short and to the point. I shrugged.

"That's what I thought. It is bad enough that he's mooching off you and you're working your ass off so that he can go out drinking with his buddies, but at least he should be good in bed. Like, rock your socks off as payment for allowing him to be a professional couch potato. Believe me, I've had my share of loser boyfriends, and I know one when I see one."

I continued to glare at her, although it didn't have much heat behind it. Her words only hurt because they hit so close to home.

"He loves me, you know."

She squeezed my shoulder. "I know he does, but does he love you more than he loves himself? Only you can decide that."

I didn't want to think about it. "What do you think about the cologne thing?"

Adora shifted her gym bag to her other shoulder. "I'm not sure what to think. Of all the weirdos in this world, you're one of the most honest and most grounded people I know—so I have no reason to doubt your sanity. I might think that you were still dreaming, if Beck hadn't smelled it too. But shit like that doesn't happen in real life, right? Weird visions, lights, breezes?"

I popped the trunk and tossed my bag inside. "Maybe it just means that I need more sleep?"

"Or maybe there's some paranormal shit happening." Adora pushed the lid of the trunk closed. "I read a book once where someone's house was haunted, and the homeowner would feel a cool breeze and smell roses every time the ghost appeared. Maybe your apartment is haunted by a hot man who smells good?"

I laughed. "With my luck, it's someone like Hewitt, who only haunts me so he can be a creeper while I'm taking a shower." I shuddered at the thought.

"You just described Hewitt's perfect afterlife—eternal creeper."

A car door closed, and we both looked up to see Agent Hanlon walking toward us.

"What is this dude's deal?" Adora said under her breath.

"I don't know, but I've got a bad feeling about this."

I watched him approach: sunglasses on, sleeves rolled up over his muscular forearms. The sun reflected off the gun clipped to his belt, and in that moment, with the sun gleaming in the desolate wasteland of a strip mall parking lot, he reminded me of a modern-day Wyatt Earp. He exuded the sort of stillness you can only get when your mind is completely focused. It must have been the confidence that he was doing his job to protect the population from bad guys . . . even if his focus was mistakenly on me. I had to admire someone with such a clear sense of who he was and what he did, since I didn't have that. At all. All I managed to do was pay the rent, put food in my fridge, and make sure Voldemort didn't fall apart.

He nodded at us as he took off his sunglasses. "Miss Connors, Miss Bayne."

"Agent Hanlon, if we're going to keep meeting like this, please call me Fara."

Adora looked over her sunglasses at me with a smirk that let me know she'd caught me flirting. Was I flirting? Maybe I was, but I was terrible at it, so it didn't matter.

"I can't do that, Miss Bayne. I'm here on official business." And just like that, my unintentional flirtation seemed ridiculous.

"Agent Hanlon, I have to work another double shift."

"Unfortunately, I can't let you do that. My orders are to speak with you now. We can make time for you to call your supervisor and let him know that you won't be in today."

"You mean, right now in the gym parking lot?"

"No. You'll need to come with me."

"You don't understand. If I don't go into work today, I'll be fired. I won't be able to pay my bills. You might not live on the brink of homelessness, Agent Hanlon, but that doesn't mean that I don't. I have to work."

I didn't know what my rights were regarding being questioned by agents of the federal government, but I had a feeling that if Agent Hanlon wanted to speak to me right now, there wasn't a lot I could do about it without getting a lawyer, which I couldn't afford. And, more than likely, I would lose my job.

"You can't just drag her ass down to the station or whatever without a reason or a warrant!" Adora pointed her finger at him.

"When it is a matter of national security, I can."

"I'm not getting in that car until you tell me what is happening," I said.

Adora looked at me in surprise, and I realized that this was probably the first time she had ever seen me stand my ground. Come to think of it, it was probably the first time I had stood my ground in as long as I remember. I even surprised myself a bit.

Agent Hanlon was not deterred. "I'll explain in the car, but we really need to go now."

"Agent Hanlon, I will happily go with you when you tell me *why*. I told you yesterday that I am not harboring a weapon in my kitchen cabinets, so I'm not sure what else we need to discuss."

"We received another weapons reading coming from your apartment early this morning."

I gaped at him, and my brain was instantly abuzz with a million questions. What were these readings and why were they coming from my apartment? How did the department get these readings? Unfortunately, even if their technology was malfunctioning, it was still leading them to me, and I needed that to stop. The sooner I could get this figured out, the better—especially if I was going to have random government agents show up on my doorstep willy-nilly. Plus, I wanted answers, if I could get them, and Agent Hanlon was holding all the cards right now. I was going to have to go with him, even if I didn't like it.

"You OK with this, Fara?" Adora asked. I nodded, reluctantly. "OK," she said. "I have no idea what is happening, but it's my day off, so I'll cover for you until you can make it back to The Grill. I don't want Douche canning your ass because of Agent-No-Fun."

Agent Hanlon stiffened at that, but Adora ignored him. I hugged her hard.

"Thank you," I whispered.

"You can thank me when I see you in a couple of hours."

"It might take more than that," Hanlon said, walking toward his car.

"And you," she directed at Agent Hanlon. "If she comes back with even a scratch on her pinkie toe, I am calling all the news stations and painting you as Public Enemy Number One. Do I make myself clear?"

Agent Hanlon didn't even flinch. He was like a brick or boulder or something. He must have been used to having people threaten him, or things must have not bothered him. Maybe he just didn't care.

She continued. "Be careful, my friend. I don't like this at all."

I gave her another hug. "Call me crazy, but for some reason I trust him," I whispered. "I may not like him, but I trust him. I'll tell you everything when I get back, and will text you as soon as I can. I promise."

"You also trust Beck, and he's a goober. Stay safe, OK?" She squeezed my shoulder, then headed to her car.

"Ready?" Agent Hanlon asked.

"As I'll ever be." I got into his car. "Where are we going?"

We pulled out of the parking lot, and I waved goodbye to Voldemort, promising him I would pick him up as soon as I could. He might be a POS, but it felt weird leaving him there. I would probably need to bum a ride to get him.

"Did you just wave at your car?"

"Voldemort gets lonely."

"You call your car Voldemort?"

"Yes, he's currently without a nose, so it seemed fitting."

A muscle in his jaw twitched. At some point I would need to figure out his nonverbal cues if we were to spend any more time together. Neither of us was exactly a chatterbox.

"You didn't answer my question," I said. "Where are you taking me?"

"We are headed to your apartment. I thought you might like to shower and change."

"And in the meantime, it would give you a chance to look around for my weapon of certain doom."

Agent Hanlon stopped the car and glared at me. "Miss Bayne, you might find this all very ridiculous, but believe me when I tell you that people's lives are at stake."

"Did it occur to you that I might take this more seriously if you just told me what the hell is going on? This whole thing is crazy! If you stopped playing Mr. Secretive Agent Guy and just told me what was happening, I might be less inclined to think the government has lost its mind."

Agent Hanlon looked at me long and hard, and I realized that was the most I'd ever spoken to him. It might have been the most I had ever spoken to a stranger. Ever. What was it about this situation, or Agent Hanlon, that made me feel braver (and chattier)? Was it so absurd that it didn't register as "real life" in my normally anxiety-filled brain? Or was it just that I was listening to my instincts? As much as I wanted to think that he was wrong about all this, I trusted him.

He started to drive again. "There is only so much that I can tell you, Miss Bayne. What I can say is that my department has acquired some technology that alerts us when the weapon is activated. I had it tested yesterday after our meeting, and I can assure you, it is functioning properly.

"It's possible that someone is trying to misdirect us. I need to verify that. The only way I can do that is by scanning your place."

"But why would they choose my apartment?"

"I don't know."

I shrugged. "Fine. Be my guest. Scanning my entire apartment will take less time than it takes me to shower."

I directed him to park in my normal spot. I sat in the car for a second, a sense of dread coming over me. I wasn't fearful for the scan. I knew he wouldn't find anything to worry about. But now that I thought about it, I didn't want Agent Hanlon to see my shitty apartment. And more than that, I didn't want him to meet Beck. If I was completely honest, I was embarrassed by my apartment, by the fact that my boyfriend was probably still sleeping off his hangover, by the fact that my car was held together by a bungee cord. I knew it was irrational to feel that way, but I did.

I took a deep breath and tried to calm down; the sooner he could scan my place, the sooner I could be rid of him and go back to my normal life, whatever that was. But was that what I wanted? The past two days had held more excitement than the entire previous year. Was the dread more about Agent Hanlon not finding anything, and then I would have no more reason to see him? And what was I doing, thinking about another man like that?

Agent Hanlon opened the car door. "Are you getting out anytime soon?"

I sighed, got my keys, and headed toward the building's front door. Agent Hanlon beat me there and opened it for me.

"Thank you, but there's no need to do that."

"Chivalry's not dead."

I raised my eyebrows at him.

"Also, it keeps you in front of me."

"So I can't push you up the stairs?"

"Or stab me in the back."

"With what? My apartment key?"

"You'd be surprised."

"I'm sure I would be."

We reached the second floor and walked down the dimly lit hall to my apartment. The paint was peeling, and there was a slight smell of mildew coming from the communal laundry room. As we walked past the closed doors of the other apartments, I could hear my neighbor and her boyfriend screaming at each other, their words muffled but the hostility clear. Agent Hanlon slowed, as if he were trying to decide whether to get involved. After a moment he continued on, listening to the loud television show blaring through the door of the next apartment.

"How do you sleep with all this noise?" he asked.

"You get used to it. And white noise machines. If you think the fighting is bad, the making up is even louder."

I took my time unlocking my door, wishing that my fairy godmother would emerge and clean the place up, while giving me a smaller butt and more manageable hair. None of those things happened. Agent Hanlon walked into my tiny space, his face unreadable. He gave my apartment the once-over and didn't comment on the bedroom door being closed. Beck was still sleeping, although I hadn't expected anything else.

"Can I get you something to drink?" I said, trying to play like he was a guest, and this was a normal thing happening.

"No, thank you. Please go do whatever you need to. This should only take a minute."

I hurried through my routine as fast as I could, anxious to see what he found. I left my hair loose, and it hung in blonde waves past my shoulders. I would probably end up putting it back up during my shift, but keeping it down made me feel prettier. I put on some makeup and looked at myself in the mirror. Other than the dark circles under my eyes, I didn't look half bad, and I wondered if Agent Hanlon would notice. I stopped myself. Why should I care if Agent Hanlon thought I was attractive? I probably wouldn't see him again. Plus, I had a boyfriend who was sleeping just outside of this door, and even though he wasn't perfect, I was his. Agent Hanlon was probably married with a perfect wife, and they lived in a gorgeous loft in downtown. Whatever my subconscious was trying to tell me, it needed to STFU right this second. I pulled myself together and walked out of the bathroom. Agent Hanlon didn't even look up from his ancient BlackBerry.

"Find anything?"

He looked up, startled. I blinked and repeated myself.

He stood up abruptly. "We need to go."

Beck, of course, chose that very moment to come out of our room in his underwear, and I cursed the fates for the timing of it all. If he had stayed passed out for just two more minutes . . . Awkward did not even begin to cover this. Beck looked at us blearily, then his eyes popped open.

"Oh—hey. Company?"

"This is Agent Hanlon from the department of something-or-other. He had some questions for me, but we're done now. He's going to drop me back off at my car, and I'm heading to work before Douche can fire me. I won't be home until late. I'll send you a text when I can, OK?"

I knew I was rambling, but every instinct I had was to avoid confrontation, smooth this over, make everyone happy, and get out of the apartment before any sort of pissing match could start. But Beck was already heading back into the bedroom. It was like he couldn't be bothered to figure out what was going on. I called after him, "See you tonight?"

"Maybe—heading out with the boys again."

I clamped down hard on the anger that rose from my stomach. Now was not the time to have this conversation, not while Agent Hanlon was here, looking at me with that unreadable face again. I took a deep breath, letting it out through my nose and releasing the anger.

"Ready?" Agent Hanlon opened the door for me, standing back so I could make my way through.

BLU 6

It was still dark when someone yanked the covers off me.

"Blu, wakey wakey! It's time to train!"

I grabbed the covers out of Ink's hands and pulled them over my head. He was way too chipper for this time of the morning.

"I brought you coffee."

I uncovered just my eyes to be sure that it was not a trick to get me out of bed. Yes, Ink had brought coffee—and a donut. Maybe I only partially hated him for waking me up. I sat up and held my hand out, hoping that the coffee would magically appear there. Or that Ink would hand it to me. Neither happened.

"Nope. Get up and get dressed and then you get your coffee."

I slid out of bed, gave him the one-finger salute, and padded across the room in search of my gear. As I was contemplating ways to make his life hellish, I realized that Ink was quiet—too quiet—for his normally chipper morning disposition. I turned around to see what he was doing and caught him staring at my bare legs. He waggled his eyebrows at me, and I rolled my eyes.

"Knock that shit off," I said, throwing my pillow at his head. He grinned as he caught it.

"Looking good, B," he said, throwing the pillow back at me. I ducked so it missed me, and I continued to search for my training gear in the piles of clothes in my room. He watched me intently while eating my donut.

"Why bring me a donut if you were just going to eat the stupid thing?" I asked, digging through the pile of clothes that seemed the cleanest. I pulled some pants on and started my search for a bra.

He continued to watch me with his perma-smirk.

"All right, Ink. Spill it or get out and find me a donut that you haven't slobbered on." I turned my back to him for some privacy, half taking off my sleep shirt to put on the bra, then chucking the shirt at Ink's head.

"I was just remembering how you used to let me touch those," he said, nodding toward my breasts.

I sighed. He was in a mood this morning. He probably got laid last night.

"Yeah, that was before I realized that sex was more than 'tab A, slot B.'"

His eyes widened, and if I hadn't known better, I'd have thought I hurt his feelings.

"Besides," I said as I strapped my daggers into my leg sheaths, "we dated for like three seconds when we were teenagers, and you broke it off for some other girl. That lasted all of a night or two."

He faked a pout but at least handed me my sword. I didn't want to rehash our past, especially at this time of the morning, and neither did he. He was trying to get me riled up so I'd get a move on. I just wanted my damn donut and coffee. I put the sword in the sheath I had strapped to my back and reached for the donut, but he held it over my head like every other tall asshole does to short girls. I punched him in the stomach hard enough that he bent at the waist, and I grabbed the half-eaten donut out of his hand, along with the coffee from the table behind him. He laughed as I shoved the rest of the donut into my mouth.

"Wow, someone is feisty this morning."

I finished chewing my half-eaten donut. "First, fuck off. Second, you come in here at an ungodly hour, stare at my tits, and withhold coffee, all the while eating *my* donut, and you expect me to be nice? You really don't know me very well."

We made our way from our building to the Quad. Most of the Team members lived in our building, which had been classrooms at one point but were now studio apartments with private bathrooms. They weren't much, but they were better than the communal living of the dorms. It was one of the perks of being a Team member, even if the building itself was held together with duct tape and willpower.

The sun was slowly starting to peek above the horizon when we made it to the Quad, and my bare arms had goose bumps as the cool spring breeze swept past. It was going to be a beautiful day, and now that I had some coffee in my system, I could appreciate it.

The Captain's tradition was to train every morning. Trainees were assigned days to train with the Captain, and the offer was open to any Team member who chose to join. Ink was in charge of training and assigned Team members who were experts in each field to teach the trainees more thoroughly throughout the week. But having special training time with the Captain was something all trainees looked forward to.

The trainees were standing off to one side of the Quad, whispering among themselves. There were only a handful of them, and I recognized a couple of the girls from yesterday. There was a nervous energy about them that I remembered having myself when I first learned to train. By the look on all of the trainees' faces, they hadn't known that we were making a guest appearance at this training session—and that seemed to ratchet up their edginess.

A couple of areas had already been set up. We were going to be working with daggers and swords. A few other Team members drifted here and there, talking to us as they passed. Styx came running up to me. She gave me a huge hug, then punched me in the arm hard enough that I yelped.

"What the fuck, Styx?"

"Don't you *ever* scare me like that again, B! You turned off your communication device. You know that's against protocol—don't give me that look! You know what would have happened if you were caught? That bitch would have—"

The Captain cut her off with a sharp look, and shook her head slightly. "We are all glad that Blu is alive and well," she said, "but we are here for training, not rehashing yesterday."

We went through our training, teaching the trainees different techniques and helping where we could. One trainee was being a total jackass, so I bashed him in the face with the pummel of my sword and sent him to the infirmary. I had the feeling it was going to be a good day.

After training, Styx, Ink, Jack, and I went to the Captain's office and took our usual seats around the big table in the center of the room.

The Captain was at the head of the table, Ink to her right, slouching in his chair, ankle propped up on one knee. Jackrabbit was next to him, sitting with an unnatural stillness that I had never been able to duplicate. His brown hair hung over his forehead as he looked at me, and while Ink carried a perma-smirk, if Jack smiled at all, it was always just a little sad.

I sat at the Captain's left hand, with Styx next to me, adjusting the bright pink headband that held back her Afro. Apparently, Ink had yanked on it before he sat down, and Styx was reading him the riot act about touching her hair. The Captain took a quick look around the table, gave a long-suffering sigh, and called our meeting to order. The others were quickly brought up to speed on yesterday's shitshow.

Then the Captain explained the plan to grab the blueprints at the Governor's masquerade ball.

"Can't we just pay one of our sources who is already attending the party to take pictures for us?" Styx asked.

"I wish it was that simple, but since we don't know where the leak is coming from, we can't risk it," the Captain answered.

We debated the best method of getting those blueprints while the Captain listened and answered questions when asked. The information the Captain had received indicated that the blueprints were on their way to the mansion today, and on the night of the party, they would be moved to a display in an alcove next to the ballroom. They were supposed to be part of a larger collection of Jurisdiction propaganda, showing Jurisdiction's helpful history or some other bullshit.

We studied the mansion's blueprints (which Jackrabbit, our head spymaster, had acquired), looking for any possible way to break in from the outside. The alcoves had no windows and no outside access. The ballroom had few windows, but there was no way to sneak in through them without being detected, as there would be hundreds of guests there. Every door that led to the outside would have massive security, and the windows of the other areas of the mansion were locked and barred. It seemed that the High Governor, or at least his predecessor, was a tad paranoid. The only way to get them was from the inside.

Once we realized that one of us would have to infiltrate the party as a guest, we sat quietly, knowing that whoever chose this mission would be walking into the lion's den, with a good probability of being caught.

"I'll do it," I said.

Everyone but the Captain said no. Jerks.

"Listen, it's a masquerade ball. If I get a wig, mask, and gown, no one will even recognize me. Styx and Ink are too recognizable even in masks, and I can blend in as long as I don't open my mouth. If I can get in, one of you can cause a distraction of some sort. I grab the blueprints, someone gets me out of there, and we're home free. Piece of cake."

"You know that these sorts of plans sound great on paper but always fall to shit, right? Anyway, the price on your head is double any of ours," Jack said, eyebrow raised.

I rolled my eyes. "I burn down *one* summer cottage . . ." I said in mock exasperation. "She wasn't even *there!*"

It took an hour to convince the Team that this plan would work, and another two hours to finalize the details, but by the end, we had a plan, more or less. We left the Captain's office, each knowing what we had to do between now and then. My role was to memorize the layout of the High Governor's mansion and, at the Captain's suggestion, work on not having such a colorful vocabulary. I laughed when she said it, but she was right. If I was going to fit in with Jurisdiction's elite, I had to speak and act like one of them.

I was heading toward the mess hall to scrounge some coffee and food when I heard Ink's footsteps behind me. He grabbed my elbow and pulled me from the path into a cluster of trees, out of sight from the rest of the Compound. We used to sneak off to these woods when we were teenagers—it was a prime make-out spot. I smiled at the memory and looked up at Ink. His face was solemn, and his green eyes searched my face, concern turning them darker. He ran his hand through his dark hair.

"I don't like this, B," he said. "You're walking straight into a likely trap, with no backup and no weapons other than the palmbox. Jyston himself is going to be there. If he catches you, or if Dagna is there . . ." He stopped and shook his head.

I was going to make a wise-ass comment, but he was being sincere. He was afraid for me, and I understood all too well.

These missions were what we had trained for our whole lives, but that didn't mean it was easy on any of us. The Team was my family, and while I knew our missions came before personal safety, it was still hard to send family into danger, or deal with the consequences of a mission gone wrong.

"I know," I said. "It's not ideal, but I'm not new to this, Ink. You, more than anyone, should know that I can get this done, and I wouldn't attempt it if there was any other way. We have to figure out what Jurisdiction is building and why the Second Counselor is personally overseeing it. It's not just about the blueprints; it's about stopping Jurisdiction at every turn. And if this works, we are hitting them in the heart of their power— and sending a message."

I took his callused hands in mine. "More people are dying every day, and I have to do something about it while I can. I will get the blueprints and get out. I promise no burning the place down."

Ink smiled at that and rubbed the shaved side of my head because he knew it pissed me off. His sword had lopped off one of my pigtails during training; his idea of a joke.

"OK, then. Let's take these assholes down."

7 FARA

"Agent Hanlon, what did you find? If it affects me, then I deserve to know."

I crossed my arms and waited.

"Get in," he said.

I didn't move. He seemed to deflate right in front of me.

"Please. I'm asking that you get into my car. There are two men in a blue sedan about thirty feet from us who have been paying very close attention to our movements, and I have a feeling they are looking for the same thing that I am. I have to assume they are not with the US government. I also have to assume they are dangerous. And so, I ask you again, please. Get. In. The. Car."

I turned to look at the blue sedan, but Agent Hanlon caught my chin before I could and gently turned my head to look at him.

"Don't look at them," he said through clenched teeth. "We need to act as if we don't see them. Smile at me. OK, that's a grimace, but we'll work with it." He chuckled.

My heart pounded. His voice was soft and measured, like he was talking to a rabid dog, or possibly a twenty-one-year-old woman about to freak the fuck out. Whatever the reason, I did as he said and tried to smile again.

"That's good," he said, smiling back. My heart gave a little flutter—this man was painfully good-looking, even if I was about to pee a little from fear. "Now please get in the car."

Now was not the time for me to prove a point, so I slid into the car and he shut the door.

"You could have said something like 'Hey, Fara, there are two creepers out here, so please get in the car,' instead of being Bossy McBosserson."

I was really on a roll today—I was never, *ever* this forceful with someone. Life-threatening situations must bring out the badass in me.

He looked in the rearview mirror and swore.

"What is it?"

"They're following us."

"Not good?"

"No, it's not good."

All illusions of badassery left me as my stomach dropped, and I started to feel nauseated. What was I going to do? This was so far outside of anything I had experienced. I had no point of reference.

"You'll be safe at work—at least, safer than anywhere else right now. I'll take you directly there so I don't lead them to your car or your gym, just in case they don't know to look for you there. I'll make sure that they don't come into the restaurant. Then I need to head back to the office to see if I can find out who they are."

"Agent Hanlon, what did your scan show?"

He didn't answer.

"Did you find something at my apartment and take it? Is that why they're following us?"

"I wish that was the case, Miss Bayne. But my scan came back inconclusive. That's another reason I need to go back to the office, so I can try to make some sense of what I found."

We drove the rest of the way in silence. The fact that the scan was inconclusive meant that I was going to see him again, which made me happier than it should, especially since my life was in danger from whatever nonsense was happening. I stole a glance at him out of the corner of my eye, and noticed that he was paying as much attention to the rearview mirror as he was the road. I hoped that was one of the things that they taught in government do-gooder school: how to drive forward while looking behind you.

He pulled in to The Grill's parking lot and turned to look at me. "Listen, I know that this entire situation is frightening because you have no information. I can't tell you anything more than I already have. Not yet. I know you are scared, and you have every right to be. You don't know what I'm after, you don't know what they're after, and all you have is me telling you what to do. I just need you to trust me for a little bit longer, until I can get more information. Please."

I was surprised at his candor and appreciated that he finally acknowledged that the situation sucked. Maybe more was going on in his head than I was giving him credit for.

"What do I do now?"

"You'll be safe at work, so stay there until the end of your shift. Can you get a ride to your car?"

I nodded. Calum was working the second shift, so I could bum a ride with him if I had to.

"Have someone follow you home and wait with you until your boyfriend gets there. I'll be in touch as soon as I know something, hopefully tomorrow."

"Tomorrow is my day off. Should I just stay home? I'm way out of my league, Agent Hanlon."

"Stay home tomorrow, but make sure someone is with you." He looked nervous.

"Those guys are here, aren't they?"

"They're parked at the back of the lot, so I'm going to wait for them to leave. If they come in the restaurant, I'll be right behind them. Call me if you see them again, or if anything else seems off. Trust your instincts."

I grabbed a pen from my purse, then searched for something to write on—an old coffee house receipt would do. I scribbled down my cell phone number and handed it to him.

"Stay out of trouble," he said, with a forced smile. He was trying to make me feel better. Failing miserably, but trying.

I ran to the restaurant door. No one followed me inside, so either Agent Hanlon intercepted them, or they were waiting to come in. Either way, I needed to find Adora so I could take over my shift, then talk to Calum about a possible ride to my car. Plus, there was this little matter of waiting tables that I still had to do. Bills didn't care that I'd somehow gotten caught up in a spy novel.

I walked through the dining room to the kitchen, Adora came running up to me and gave me a huge hug.

"You OK?" she whispered into my ear.

"I'm not sure. Some seriously weird shit is going down. I don't even know where to begin."

I saw Douche and Hewitt making their way toward us, so I let Adora go, whispering, "I'll fill you in tomorrow. Thanks for covering for me."

"Yeah, girl. I'll call you tomorrow after my shift and maybe I can come over and we can binge watch bad TV while drinking fruity drinks."

"That sounds like heaven."

Adora stared Hewitt down. "What are you even *doing* here, Hewitt? Your shift doesn't even start for another hour! More time to suck up?"

"Clocking in early to make the Benjamins."

"You'll be lucky to make the nickels with your shitty service."

He kept walking, brushing up against me. "Looking delicious as always, Fara."

I ignored him. I was not in the mood . . . not that I was ever in the mood for him.

"Fara, I need to speak with you," Douche said. I sighed and tried not to roll my eyes. From the look on Douche's face, I'd failed.

"You are not supposed to switch shifts without my prior approval. I will allow the shift switch between you and Adora today, but consider this your warning. If it happens again, I will have to find your replacement."

Adora opened her mouth to say something, but Douche cut her off. "I am not speaking to you, Adora. You are free to go." She glared at him for a second, blew me a kiss, then went to the back to get her stuff.

"The second thing," Douche continued, "is that I am not your personal messaging service. If someone wants to get in touch with you, they should call you on your free time." He handed over a business card that said:

Barrington Park
President/CEO
Specter COMS, Inc.

It had a business phone number and email address. I turned the card over, and written on the back in neat handwriting was a mobile number, and *Please call me at your earliest convenience.*

I looked blankly at Douche. "Are you sure this is for me?"

"He specifically asked for me, then told me to give this to Fara Bayne. Why would the most powerful businessman in the Midwest want to speak to you?"

I shrugged. He most definitely had the wrong person—unless it was connected to whatever Agent Hanlon and those two blue sedan guys were after. But that was just me being paranoid.

"Don't let it happen again."

As if I let it happen the first time? I nodded. What was the point of arguing with him?

Calum was in the back room, putting on his apron. I looked at him for a moment, his chin-length dark hair tucked behind his ears, his green eyes not really seeing in front of him—deep in thought. When I thought of Calum, this was the picture that came up in my mind. A dark, beautiful, brooding artist. Apparently, I had been staring at him awhile because he turned his attention to me.

"You OK?"

I thought about it. Although I had been feeling feisty with Agent Hanlon, now that the adrenaline had worn off, I was afraid. I needed to talk to someone, and Calum was the person I trusted the most in the world.

"No, I'm not." Tears stung my eyes, but I wiped them away. I hadn't realized how scared I was. "We don't have time now, but I really need to talk, and I need a ride back to Voldemort after work. Do you mind? I can get an Uber if I need to . . ."

He closed the distance between us in a single step and wrapped his arms around me. I breathed in his familiar scent, releasing some of the tension that I hadn't known I was hanging on to. He stood there for a second, letting me rest my head on his chest, my arms circling his waist.

"Whatever you need," he said in my ear. "Anything, Fara. You know that." I nodded into his chest, then heard a snicker from behind me.

"So sorry—was I interrupting a moment? It looked really sweet and all, but what would Fara's boyfriend say, Calum, if he knew you were making the moves on his girl?"

Calum released me and took a step toward Hewitt. This was going to get really ugly. I stepped between them, my back to Hewitt.

"Calum, we'll talk later, OK? He's not worth it. I don't care about him, but I care about you getting in trouble because he's an asshat." Calum broke his stare with Hewitt, looked down at me, and nodded. He gave me a quick hug, and we made our way out of the locker room. Hewitt let Calum go but blocked my path.

"You know, Fara, if you needed a man's touch so badly, you didn't have to stoop to Calum. I would've been happy to oblige." He ran his hand up my arm, and I pulled it away as fast as I could. Just his touch made me feel dirty.

I saw Calum tense, so I made myself laugh and brushed past Hewitt. He grabbed my arm, and I forced myself to look him in the eye.

"You know, I was hanging out with Agent Hanlon today. You remember him, right? He was wondering how you were doing."

He released my arm, and I kept walking. I hated having to use Agent Hanlon as the boogeyman. I wanted to be the kind of woman who didn't need anyone to stand up for her. I wasn't that woman yet (except, apparently, with Agent Hanlon). Maybe that was a step in the right direction—wanting to be better. Maybe my first real step was to punch Hewitt in the junk. That thought made me smile, as I grabbed Calum's hand and we headed out of the back room. Someday I would wallop him, but today was not that day.

The shifts went by quickly as the restaurant was busy. I made enough tips that I was hopeful I would be able to pay our rent and maybe even buy groceries for the week. Being busy also kept my mind off the fact that there were bad guys of unknown origin looking for me. Here in the restaurant, it seemed like this morning had been a dream. When I finally got back to the back room, Calum was there as well.

"You eat yet?" he asked.

I thought about it. The last thing I had eaten was popcorn over twenty-four hours ago. I shook my head.

"Before I take you back to your car, do you want to stop at Rick's and get some greasy bar food and a beer or three?"

"Let me text Beck quick to let him know." I pulled out my phone and saw that there were a number of unread text messages. The first was from Beck, responding to my earlier text telling him I was at work. It just read "K. Going out with boys. Don't wait up." I told him I was going out for drinks and would see him at home. He wouldn't respond, but that didn't mean I shouldn't let him know. How could I get righteously indignant about his lack of communication if I fell into the same bad habit?

The second text was from Adora, just checking in to make sure I was OK and if I still wanted girl time tomorrow. I responded affirmative to both, smiling.

The last text was from a number I didn't know. I opened it:

Two men left immediately. Still trying to find answers. Will call tomorrow. Stay safe. Hanlon

I programmed his number into my phone as the panic started to trickle back. Calum watched me with concern in his eyes.

"Ready?"

I followed him out to his car. I needed to talk to someone, and a drink. Not necessarily in that order.

8 BLU

Ink laughed so hard he snorted.

I threw a french fry at him, which caused him to laugh even harder.

"You're an asshole, you know that?"

"Ah, there it is! The word you've been trying not to say for a full minute."

"You know I have a good vocabulary, right? But why the hell would I ever incorporate pompous words into a conversation just to sound smart? I mean, how many times can I fit the word 'lugubrious' into a sentence?"

Jack patted me on the shoulder. "At this party? More than you probably want. Anyway, you've been to enough of these to know a thing or two."

"Yeah, but I'm usually hiding and stealing things—not trying to fit in."

"If you do this right, B, then you won't be saying *lugubrious* or any other ridiculous word to anyone." Ink stood to stretch, the eyes of half of the girls in the mess following the movement. "Besides, all you need to do if someone talks to you is giggle and open your eyes wide."

"I'm afraid to ask how you even know that."

"Jack isn't the only one who has dealings with the elite women."

"Ugh! Please don't elaborate." I stood too since Styx was waiting at the tech building to hand over my palmbox.

Ink tossed Jack some coin. "Ten minutes is my bet."

Jack pocketed it with a grin. "That's generous; Styx bet five."

"What the hell are you guys betting on?"

"How long you can make it without cussing at some shithead elite at the party."

Assholes, the lot of them.

I met Styx at the tech building to pick up my palmbox. She had placed as many lock-breaking abilities as she could think of on it, along with stunners and other defensive programs. There was not enough on there to alert security at the High Governor's estate, but enough that if I got caught, I had a small probability of stunning someone enough to get away.

Jack created the identity I would use to get into the party, and Ink did as much reconnaissance of the estate as he could without risking detection. The Captain called upon god only knows what resources and gathered as much information as she could about the attendees of the party, along with getting my new identity on the list. If I didn't have an invitation, I wouldn't get in. If I couldn't get in, none of our preparations would do us any good.

Three hours before the party, the five of us met once again in the Captain's office to make the final adjustments to our mission. If I could steal the blueprints without raising an alarm, I was to do so. But it was more than likely that I would take a couple of photographs of them with my palmbox, leave, and signal Ink for an extraction.

"If you don't signal Ink within ninety minutes, then Jack will create a diversion."

"What kind of diversion?"

"The kind that I'd rather not make if I can avoid it."

"You won't need it, Jack. I'll be fine."

Ink met my eyes over the table. "After Hastings, B, we can't take any chances."

The plan of the High Governor's estate was laid out on the table, and I was memorizing the entrances, exits, and guard posts that Ink had marked. Jack handed a packet across the table.

"Who am I this time?"

"You are the Lady Raven, from the southern region. You have just moved into town for a job and met a low-level aide of the High Governor while at the market, who was so taken with your beauty, he had to invite you to the party."

I raised my eyebrows at that. Not that I was unattractive, but I wasn't attractive enough that something like that would ever happen to me (which I was fine with). Thinking about some random Jurisdiction employee flirting with me over the market's grapes seemed pretty ridiculous. Did that sort of thing actually happen outside of the Compound?

The Captain picked up on my skepticism. "The aide is a friend of mine. If asked, he will say that he invited a blonde girl to the party but forgot her name already."

"I take it that I'm going in as a blonde?"

"Nope," Styx interjected. "I've got better plans for you." By the grin she had on her face, I knew I was in for trouble with my wardrobe.

Back in my room, I was staring at my reflection in the mirror. "Abso-fucking-lutely not! Styx, this dress barely covers my lady bits. How the hell am I going to fight in it if things go bad?"

The dress Styx had picked out for me was less a cocktail dress and more of a sparkly tube sock. The first layer was black and made of the same material as my combat pants— stretchy but with some sort of compression in it. It started mid-thigh, hugged every curve I had and every morsel of food I'd ever eaten. Then, at the top of my rib cage, the dress split into two strips of fabric that barely covered my breasts, and tied behind my neck. The second layer of the dress was a royal blue gauze that was embedded with tiny crystals. It followed the same basic shape as the tube-sock dress but hung more loosely and gathered under my breasts to form an ankle-length train in the back. My purple hair was tucked up under a straight black wig that hit just below my chin, with bangs right at my eyebrows. Since I was going to be wearing a black mask, the only makeup I wore was a bit of lipstick.

"You look fucking hot," Styx said as she surveyed her work. "I'd give a limb to have an ass like yours."

"Styx, you are beautiful just as you are."

"Oh girl, you know I'm happy with myself. I just want your ass."

I looked at myself in the mirror and realized that she had done her job even if I hated it: I looked nothing like myself, except for my eyes, which still looked fierce and tired. I practiced schooling my face into softness, the kind of look that I'd seen on women who didn't have to fight to live. It had been a long time since I saw women like that, and I had to remember that the reason I was dressing up—the reason I was going to the enemy—was that the ability to live without fighting was something worth fighting for.

"I will never disparage another woman for her choice of footwear, but damn if these heels aren't a bitch."

"I hear you. This handbag is just big enough for your palmbox and lipstick. We've already gone over all the programs I've loaded on your palmbox, but most importantly, it will act as a camera." I slipped the pamlbox into my handbag. "You're going in there without backup, B. I won't be able to send in the calvary if things go sideways, so keep your butt out of trouble. You can do this. Keep your eyes open and your mouth shut. I'll see you in a few hours."

There was a knock on my door. Styx looked through the peephole, then opened the door to Ink, Jack, and the Captain. Jack was dressed in a suit, looking very much like a driver to the elite, which was the point. Ink was in combat gear and armed to the teeth. He had his game face on.

"You look good," Jack said. "You'll fit in perfectly at the High Governor's party. Do you have your identification card and invitation?"

I nodded. "You look good too, Jack. I love a man in a suit."

The Captain stopped me.

"Get in. Get the information. Get out. No heroics this time, Blu. If it looks like the mission is a bust, abort, get out of there, and live to fight another day. Styx and I will stay here to make sure that the mole doesn't suspect anything."

I nodded to her and put on my mask. With this final touch, all you could see of my face were my eyes and mouth. We snuck out of the building.

Jack and I made our way to the black town car that he would be driving. Ink would take a different route to avoid suspicion. I double-checked my handbag to make sure I had everything, which wasn't much. I felt almost naked. Not only was the dress struggling to stay put, but I didn't even have so much as a dagger on me.

"Stop fidgeting. You look lovely," Jack said as he opened the car door for me—already getting into character. It was game time.

FARA 9

Rick's was the type of dive bar that normal people avoided. From the outside, it looked like the floor would be sticky and the meat would be mystery. Neither of those things were true, but the owner kept up that façade; he liked keeping regulars as his clientele, people who worked in the service industry, like me and Calum. Rick knew that we would never turn him in for serving beer after hours. In turn, he made the best bar food in town for cheap, and always had drink specials geared toward our service industry incomes.

The bar itself was fairly small, with dartboards, a couple of pool tables, and booths lining three of the walls. It was already packed by the time we got there. Calum grabbed my hand and led me through the crowd, nodding to people we recognized as we walked by. A booth in the back corner opened up, and we slid in. Calum ordered an energy drink, since he was driving, and he ordered me a beer. When I started to protest, he just said, "I'll take you to Voldemort at some point. Or Adora can. Or Beck can. You need a drink."

The waitress looked at me expectantly, and I nodded. We also ordered greasy bar food, which made my heart sing just a little. Honestly, there's not a lot that tater tots can't cure.

Sitting across from Calum, I realized just how much I needed to talk to someone. Adora knew some of the craziness, but I could tell Calum everything and know that he wouldn't judge me; he would help. How many people in the world were lucky enough to have someone like that in their lives? We had been friends for over fifteen years, and he had been through every first with me—first kiss, first breakup, all of it. He knew me better than anyone, and in turn I knew him better than anyone too: I knew that even though he'd had a terrible childhood, it had not made him bitter. He remained kind.

His mom was an alcoholic, and he'd spent so much time at my house that he had called my parents Mom and Dad. They loved him, and they let him stay in our guest room when his mom was too violent, even for him. When they died, he let me crash at his place for weeks, fixing me meals and quietly helping me put the fragments of my life back together. He was the person I trusted more than anyone in the world, and the most selfless person I knew.

"We haven't done this in so long."

"Not since Beck moved in with you. Maybe longer."

Somehow my life had morphed into Beck's life. "I miss hanging out with you like this," I said.

"It's hard to negotiate relationships," Calum said as our drinks arrived. A whiskey shot came with the beer, on the house. I drank it down in one go, relishing the burn.

"I know, but how can I have a relationship and not lose myself? Beck doesn't seem to have this problem, so why do I?" The familiar loneliness and hurt started to creep up. I tried to push them down.

"Do you want my honest opinion?" Calum asked.

I ordered another shot.

"It's because you give everything of yourself to make others happy. You need to make yourself happy too."

"I don't have time to make myself happy," I replied, swigging the second shot.

"You don't *take* the time to make yourself happy," Calum gently corrected. "I know Adora doesn't hold back her hate for Beck, and I know you don't need another friend telling you that he's an idiot. But he takes advantage of your kindness, Fara. You are working double shifts to cover his expenses, but he hasn't made a move to get another job. He will continue to allow you to work yourself into the ground, because it serves him well. He's not malicious; it's just that it doesn't occur to him that maybe he needs to step up. I will never tell you that you need to get rid of him, but if you need someone to boot his ass out of your apartment, I am volunteering."

I laughed at that and wiped my eyes. He had said his piece and would drop the topic now, I hoped. Someday I might take him up on his offer to kick Beck out, but I had bigger problems right now.

My head was fuzzy from the whiskey, but it was giving me the courage to tell him everything, from when Agent Hanlon approached me at the gym, to his text. When I was finished, Calum didn't speak for a long time, his green eyes on his Reuben, but not really seeing it. I drank my beer and picked at my tater tots.

Finally, he said, "Do you trust Agent Hanlon?"

"I think so? I don't know. Everything is so fucked up right now that I'm not sure who to trust."

"You can trust me."

"That's not what I mean. My gut is telling me that I can trust Agent Hanlon. My gut is also telling me that he is not being a hundred percent upfront. Whether he can't tell me or he won't tell me, something spooked him at my apartment, and he doesn't seem to be the kind of guy who's easily rattled."

"Adora told me that you put him in his place earlier."

"It's weird. It's like I'm not scared of him. Irritated and angry, but not scared. He kept bossing me around and I told him to knock it off, is all."

Calum looked skeptically at me over the rim of his energy drink. "She also said you were flirting."

"Adora has a big, fat mouth. You know me. I'm way too awkward to flirt."

Calum shrugged. "Right. Anyway, I don't like it. Any of it."

"Me either. I'm scared, Calum. They know where I live. I'm afraid to go home."

"Stay with me then. You've crashed with me before."

"What about Beck?"

"He probably won't even notice you're gone." Ouch. "Sorry. I didn't mean that."

But Calum was right, and that scared me more than the guys in the sedan.

"You meant it, and that's OK. You're just telling me something I already know. I need to do some soul searching, but with everything else that's going on, the thought of having to deal with him too makes me so tired. And sad. I thought he was the one, you know? I'm tired of being lonely, Calum. What if we break up and I don't find someone else? What if I end up being an old cat lady? There aren't exactly suitors lined up at my door."

Calum moved to my side of the booth so fast it startled me, then slid his arms around me and rested his chin on the top of my head.

"I need you to listen to me. I know your parents were way better than my mom, and I loved them. But they did you a disservice by telling you that your greatest superpower was to make yourself small, to not make waves, to blend in, to not stand up for yourself. You are worth a thousand times more than someone like Beck. You are beautiful and smart and kind. And you will not end up alone, unless you decide that is what *you* want to do. You need to ask yourself, is being unhappy with someone better than being alone? We're still young. Don't settle for the sake of settling."

I hugged him back and breathed him in. "Have you ever looked around and thought, how did I get here? Like, life has so many possibilities, but each time I make a decision, one path is closed off to me forever, and the older I get, the narrower my paths become. What could I have been if my circumstances were different? If my parents had raised me differently? Could I have been a rockstar? An archeologist? An actor? A spy? Was it just circumstances that led me to be a broke waitress with a mediocre boyfriend? Or am I meant for something else?"

I could feel Calum smile into my hair. "You can't sing, you burn to a crisp in the sun, you hate being on stage, and you're a terrible liar." I laughed. "What you are asking is the age-old question: free will versus fate. Nature versus nurture. If you were born to a different set of circumstances, would you be the queen of a kingdom or a ninja? If you were trained as a warrior, would your genetics allow you to *be* a warrior? Can you choose your own path, regardless of who your ancestors were? Regardless of how you were raised? But I think the real question you are asking is, are you allowed to change your path at the ripe old age of twenty-one?"

Calum pulled back to look at me. "Fara, I believe that you are capable of doing anything you put your mind to. If you decided to be an actor, you'd figure out a way to get over stage fright, and you'd be great at it. You could buy stock in sunscreen if you became an archeologist, and you would be great at that too. Although, I really hope you don't become a spy—being a terrible liar is a good thing. You are not a passenger in your life. You drive your destiny. The biggest obstacle you face is low self-confidence. You don't think you deserve better, so you don't try for better. Believe that you deserve whatever it is that you want, and go for it."

He seemed so sure. "Why is it so hard for me to see?"

"I have the benefit of looking at you from the outside, which you don't have." He smiled. "If only you could see yourself through my eyes, you might have a different opinion of yourself."

"I'm sort of hoping I never meet another version of me. I'm afraid I wouldn't like myself."

"You would. I do. Adora does. You're pretty likable. Anyway," he continued, "you don't need to figure it all out right this second either. Right now, we just need to decide what you are going to do about this thing that Agent Hanlon and the goons are looking for."

"Calum, have I told you lately that you're my favorite human? It's too bad that we can't get married. Life would be way easier."

Calum stiffened, squeezed me once more, then let me go and moved back to his side of the booth. "Yeah, it is too bad. It would suck for you being with a guy who could actually make you happy." He winked, and I threw my napkin at him.

"So, what am I going to do about all this?"

"Life, the Universe, and Everything? The answer is 42."

I laughed. "No, about Agent Hanlon and the two sedan guys."

"Let's go to your place, get some stuff, sleep on it, and figure it out tomorrow."

I finished my drink and Calum finished my tater tots in comfortable silence. When we were done, Calum paid the tab, and as we were starting to leave, I noticed two guys in suits sitting in a booth near the door, sipping sodas and looking solemn. They were terribly out of place among the drunk twenty-somethings. I grabbed Calum's arm and motioned toward the booth as subtly as I could. His eyes widened, and he grabbed my hand, and we walked as quickly as we could toward the door.

We all but ran to his car, and as we drove away, I noticed the two men leave Rick's and look around the parking lot. When we pulled out of the lot, I looked behind us to see if they were following, but I couldn't see them. My heart was beating so fast that I thought it would burst out of my chest.

"How did they find you?" Calum asked, maneuvering us through some dark alleys onto a side street. The city was quiet at this time of night, the usual pedestrian bustle nowhere to be seen. As the road opened up, Calum drove faster, and the city streaked by, towering over us on all sides. The image of rats in a maze came to mind, and I shuddered.

"They must have followed me from The Grill. Damnit! Calum, I am so sorry for dragging you into this mess."

Calum glared at me from the corner of his eye. "Are you fucking kidding me right now? Do *not* apologize for letting me help you. Don't blame yourself for these assholes chasing you. You have done nothing wrong—and as your friend, I *want* to help you."

When we pulled into my building's parking lot, I noticed that my windows were dark, which was odd. I always left the bathroom light on so that I didn't have to walk into a completely dark apartment. Beck said I'd watched too many *CSI* reruns. He was probably right, but the darkness still made me nervous. He must have shut the light off on his way out.

"Mind coming up with me, quick?"

"I insist."

I got my keys out as we made our way up the stairs and down the hall. I went to put the key in my door and noticed that it was unlocked. Beck had apparently forgot to lock it, which didn't surprise me. Why was it so hard to just do something right? I pushed it open, but Calum pulled me back.

"Something's off." He stepped inside and flipped on the light.

My entire apartment was ripped apart, from top to bottom.

Everything had been destroyed, like a tornado had landed just on my place. The futon's cushions were sliced open, stuffing flung everywhere. The cupboard doors in the kitchen were hanging by their hinges, their contents scattered on the counters and the floor. The boxes of cereal had been dumped on the ground. Books from the bookcase were ripped apart, their covers torn off. Not one thing was left untouched.

Calum pulled me back into the hallway. "We need to call the police."

I nodded, in shock. I called 911 and they told me they would have a squad car out in a couple of minutes. My brain was in overdrive. I looked at Calum helplessly.

He gave me a squeeze.

"I'll call Beck and tell him what happened and that you're staying with me. Call Agent Hanlon. I'm sure this is something he would want to know about. And maybe this might be enough to get him to tell you what the hell is going on."

Agent Hanlon's phone rang for so long that I thought I'd get his voicemail, but he finally answered.

"Hanlon." He sounded muffled, like he was answering the phone in bed.

And I felt myself fall apart, like someone destroying my apartment was the tug on the final thread that had been holding everything together. The words burst out of me like a tidal wave cresting over the last wall of sanity. I knew I was all over the place, incoherent, as I explained what happened, but I couldn't stop or I would succumb to a full-blown panic attack. Tears ran freely down my face, and I tried to push down the panic, to put it in a box. It wasn't working.

Agent Hanlon waited for me to finish rambling. "Miss Bayne, is there somewhere I can meet you? You said you were staying at a friend's place. Text me the address when you're done with the police."

"I can do that."

"I cannot ask you to lie to the police, but the less they know, the better. You have to trust me on that."

"You keep saying to trust you, but since I've met you, I've been chased, bossed around, accused of hiding a weapon of doom, and now everything that I own in the world has been destroyed. You haven't given me any reason to trust you!" I was yelling now, but I didn't care. Everything that I had worked so hard to get had been destroyed, and it was all because someone thought that I had something I didn't. How was I going to recover? I had no savings, no insurance, and I was barely making ends meet as it was. I was sure Agent Hanlon was going to yell right back at me. That's how Beck would have handled an outburst like this. I took a deep breath, waiting for the retribution.

Instead, he sounded sorry. "That's fair," Agent Hanlon said. "You have no reason to trust me. But I'm trying to keep you safe from whoever trashed your place. You can tell the police whatever you want, but you don't know for sure if it is those two guys who broke in. It's up to you if you mention them, or me, to the police."

"OK."

"You'll text me your friend's address?"

"Sure. Bye."

I looked over at Calum, who was hanging up the phone at the same time.

"Is Beck OK?"

"Yeah—he's fine. He was worried about his guitar. I told him we'd claim it in the police report if we couldn't find it in the rubble, and let him know either way. He's going to stay with a friend for a while."

"That's good, right? Right? Hey, what is it? Why are you upset?"

"It's nothing. We can talk about it later."

I was going to push the matter, but the police pulled up. They went through my apartment and asked me about my whereabouts, who else lived there, if I could tell if there was anything missing, did I keep large quantities of cash in my apartment—I didn't even have small quantities of cash—or did I know anyone who might have had a vendetta against me. That last one gave me pause. I thought about what Agent Hanlon had said. Did I really want another government agency involved in this?

"No—no one that I can think of. I'm a waitress. I don't get out much."

"All right," the officer said, "but if you think of anyone, please let us know. As a courtesy, we will contact your landlord to let him know this happened."

I nodded, numb.

"After we process the scene, you will need to come back here to clean it up. At that point you can file a report of anything that is missing. It appears from the state of your apartment that the perpetrators were looking for something."

The officer didn't know how right he was.

"If you think of anything else, contact us."

It was close to two in the morning when I finally sent Agent Hanlon Calum's address, and we headed out, but not before I found the bottle of Jameson whiskey still in one piece above my fridge. I brought it, along with the only clothes that I could find in the mess. Leggings and a faded T-shirt seemed like a good uniform for the disaster my life had become. Even if it wasn't, it was all that I had left.

Calum and I drove in silence to his apartment. We were both processing what had happened, although Calum seemed more upset by the conversation he'd had with Beck. I'd pester him about it later, but right now I was trying not to fall apart. My home hadn't been much, but it had been mine, and now it was all gone. I know you can replace things—and I was grateful that nothing more serious had happened—but I felt violated and tired. I needed answers and I was going to press Agent Hanlon for information until I got what I needed to arm myself. I'd beat it out of him with a flip-flop if I had to. This wasn't over, and I needed to know what was going on before I got myself hurt.

10 BLU

It was dusk when Jack and I pulled into the High Governor's estate. We sat in silence, the tension mounting. I knew what was riding on this mission, and how much danger I was willingly putting myself in. I exhaled slowly. Jack was looking at me in the rearview mirror.

"Nervous?"

"Yeah."

"Remember who you are, B. You have an uncanny ability to read situations and to get out of trouble. You'll be fine. And if it isn't fine, I'll wreak some havoc."

I smiled tightly at him as we rounded the bend. The main house came into view, sitting majestically atop a well-manicured lawn. The mansion itself was a huge white monstrosity with columns and a circular drive, but the gardens were beautiful, and sitting in front of the house was the largest working fountain I had ever seen. There were half-destroyed fountains around the city center, but I had never seen one working. I had a fleeting thought of jumping in and splashing around.

On the circular drive, other guests were getting out of their cars with an ease that came only with years of wearing this attire. The women clutched their handbags while looking around, impatient to see and be seen. Servants scurried without notice amongst them in an attempt to make every second of their arrival flawless.

Once I got an idea of how the women behaved, I turned my attention to the layout of the grounds. While Ink had managed some reconnaissance, he had been unable to get close enough to the house to get a firsthand view, and I needed that information just in case there was a delay between my running for my life and his coming to my rescue. I studied the length of the drive, how many stairs to the front door, hiding spots on the front porch, and if the windows were open (they weren't). I spotted security cameras every few feet pointing directly at the house and out at the lawn. The entire estate was lit up both by outside and inside lights. Hiding here would be nearly impossible.

"Any last words of advice, Jack?"

"Don't get caught, and keep track of time. I'd rather not provide a huge distraction if you're just flirting with some guest."

I glared at him. "How often have you ever seen me flirt?"

"Never, but now is not the time to start."

"Thanks for the vote of confidence. See you soon."

"Be careful, B. Jurisdiction has plans within plans, and backup plans for those. Nothing is ever as simple as it seems. Trust your instincts."

I took a deep breath and got into character as Jack helped me out of the car, then handed me and my invitation over to one of the High Governor's servants.

"The Lady Raven," Jack said in a bored tone.

The servant placed my proffered hand lightly on his forearm and walked me up the steps to the main door of the mansion, which was held open by flanking servants. The servant then handed my invitation to a giant of a man—the High Governor's security.

"The Lady Raven."

The security man looked at my invitation and then at me. I avoided looking at him and kept my eyes wandering like I was impatient to see who was here, as the other women had done earlier. The seconds ticked by, and I looked up at him through my mask, adding what I hoped was a flirtatious smile.

"I've never seen you before. I would remember you," he said.

"You haven't, but I hope it is not the last time you do," I said with a coy smile and started walking into the party, trusting that he wouldn't make a scene to usher me back outside. I couldn't feel him following me, so I peered over my shoulder at him and caught him looking at my ass with a lecherous smile on his face. I forced myself to smile at him again, as if that sort of attention was something I invited, instead of something I would punch him in the nuts for. Maybe someday I would teach him a lesson about a woman's right to walk around without having to deal with that sort of idiocy, but today was not that day.

Getting my bearings, I saw that I had walked into the main foyer of the mansion, which was flanked by two curved staircases leading up to the mezzanine and ballroom, where the festivities were being held. The first order of business was to get upstairs without drawing attention to myself and get into the alcoves, where the blueprints were.

I grabbed a drink off a nearby tray, plastered a bland smile on my face, and followed a group of guests slowly up the stairs. When I finally reached the top, I had to stop and take in what I was seeing. I had never seen anything like it. The stairs led to the mezzanine, and set below it was the ballroom, where hundreds of people were already gathered in small groups, talking and drinking. I caught myself gaping at all the guests and closed my mouth with a snap. While I had known this was going to be an extravagant party, seeing it for myself was something else. The women wore gowns of rich fabrics in all colors and styles; jewels glittered from ears, necks, and fingers—some of which were as big as birds' eggs. Their masks were truly magnificent, hand painted and adorned with feathers and glitter. The men wore tuxedos of varying shades, although black seemed the most prevalent. The men's masks were more reserved, although some were in the likeness of animals.

The ballroom glowed with the diffused light of dozens of crystal chandeliers. The ceiling was painted in a light blue with patches of white to mirror a summer's day. At the end of the ballroom, musicians played softly on a stage. The whole effect was magnificent . . . and appalling. The amount of wealth in that room alone was unimaginable—and all of it gained by Jurisdiction's rule on the backs of the territory's citizens.

These people, with their clothes and jewels, laughing while servants offered them hors d'oeuvres and sparkling wine, didn't know or didn't care that children and their parents were dying at the hands of their benefactors. They didn't care that I'd been tortured when I was little by the very people who gave them power. Their complacency, or their willful ignorance, created as much of the devastation of our world as Jurisdiction's leadership. As long as it wasn't their children who were suffering, as long as they continued to live in luxury, they would never lift a finger to help those most in need. Beneath the glitter and wealth was a festering disease that I needed to rid the world of. But for now, I needed them to believe I was one of them. Then I would take down Jurisdiction brick by brick, and all of them with it.

I followed the leisurely moving line toward the ballroom floor, then slowly made my way to the alcoves as nonchalantly as I could, hoping I could find the blueprints immediately and get the hell out of here. My feet were already killing me.

The first thing I noticed was that each of the alcoves was connected by an inner archway, allowing the guests to walk through and look at Jurisdiction's artifacts and memorabilia without having to exit into the throng of the mezzanine. High tables had been strategically placed throughout the alcoves to provide space for the guests to eat food and partake in clandestine meetings—at least, that's what I would have done if given the opportunity. I could already see two tables occupied: one by two men having a heated discussion, and the other by a man and a woman, nose to nose, more than likely trying to decide if there was a cozy corner they could escape to for a little drunken sex. I smiled slightly—even in the upper echelons of society, people still thought with their naughty bits.

I turned to survey the rest of the alcove, which was about twice the size of my studio apartment. There was no sign of blueprints in this one, but it had a very nice suit of armor equipped with a sword that still looked sharp. I couldn't think of a time in the territory's history that armor like that was worn, which made the display seem out of place. I read the placard:

On loan from Second Counselor Jyston's Personal Collection

Ah, that made more sense—even though the collection was supposed to be Midwest territory-centric, if Jyston himself had offered the armor for display, then the High Governor could hardly refuse. Did the Second Counselor have the armor lying around his house and wanted to show it off? What a weird thing to have just hanging in a closet. Then again, from all the accounts I had heard of Jyston, he was a warrior through and through, battling his way through the ranks of Jurisdiction to be the second in command of the whole world. He probably wore armor in the bath just to prove he was tough. The mental picture of Jyston bathing in armor made me snort out loud, and the guests around me looked startled at my sudden outburst. I ducked my head and moved through the archway to the next alcove, sweeping my eyes to see if there was any sign of the blueprints, but there wasn't.

The walls of the next alcove were lined with pictures of all shapes and sizes. Pictures of people building skyscrapers, smiling and waving at the camera; pictures of people on ships; pictures of people building machines. They each had placards describing how Jurisdiction was altruistically bringing our world forward for a better future through building and other sundry things. Propaganda at its finest—and complete bullshit. Nowhere did it show the torture chambers, mass graves, or fields where nothing grows anymore because of the weapons Jurisdiction had unleashed on its people. I kept my face neutral as I continued through, but my anger was starting to rise. I needed to find the blueprints and get out of here before I burned this place down just for spite. The Captain would be angry with me if I did that—again—so I kept my face as vapid as I dared and forced myself to carry on with the mission without lighting the place on fire.

As I walked through the next archway, I noticed the musicians had stopped playing, and heard a smattering of applause from the crowd. I poked my head out into the ballroom to see the High Governor walk onto the stage, followed by the Second Counselor and Dagna. Shit, shit, shit. Knowing that they were here in theory and being in the same room as the two of them was a whole different thing.

I would recognize Dagna anywhere. She was a striking woman, tall and slender with white-blonde hair that hung just to her shoulders. Her dress was a deep red satin with a slit up to her hip on one side, and a neckline that plunged to her navel, almost revealing everything she had to offer. I would have to ask Styx how someone would keep a dress like that attached to one's body. I'd be afraid of losing the whole thing with a sneeze. She wore a matching mask and was smiling into the crowd like a cat who ate a canary. My blood froze.

I turned my attention to the Second Counselor, appreciating how imposing he was. I had never been this close to him. Dressed in a black tuxedo, he was at least a foot and a half taller than I was. His dark blond hair was tied in a band at the nape of his neck, and even through his tuxedo, I could tell that he had the build of a warrior. His solid muscles were straining the seams of his jacket. He wore a simple black mask that accentuated his eyes. They were such a startling gray that I could see them from where I was, and they were sweeping the crowd with a gaze that was equal parts predator and annoyance. I wondered what he was looking for, or if he was just used to looking for threats, like I was. My breath caught as his eyes met mine and held my gaze. I was frozen in place, every muscle in my body tensed and ready to run. He nodded slightly toward me and I blinked. Did he recognize me? How could he? He knew generally who I was, but could he see through this disguise? I had to find the blueprints and get out of there.

The High Governor—who looked remarkably like a penguin—continued to speak about progress, cooperation with Jurisdiction, and some other bullshit. I ducked back into the alcoves and continued my hunt.

I was starting to think that the Captain's sources might not have given us accurate information when I entered another alcove and breathed in relief. Hanging on the wall between pictures of more happy-faced construction workers and engineers were the blueprints. They were encased in a glass frame. Above the frame was a sign that said: *Jurisdiction Builds for the Future*, and underneath it was a placard that read:

Jurisdiction Plans School and Dormitory for Orphans of the War

I almost laughed out loud. That couldn't be right— Jurisdiction would never willingly build anything helpful for anyone but themselves. This had to be more propaganda.

I studied the blueprints in earnest; maybe they were actually a code for something else? Or maybe the real blueprints were hidden behind these? I took a picture of them and then started to inspect how the large glass case was mounted on the wall. It didn't appear that there were any security measures attached to it at all; and why would there be? They were only showing a new school and nothing nefarious like the Team had originally thought. Were we wrong? Was all this planning for nothing? Why would Jyston be overseeing something so . . . normal?

I considered whether it was worth trying to take them back to the Compound. Shoving them in my dress seemed like it would be an act of futility.

"You aren't planning on stealing those, are you? The High Governor would be very put out if you did."

I whipped around to see the Second Counselor leaning against the archway, a slow smile spreading across his face.

11 FARA

Agent Hanlon was leaning against his car in front of Calum's apartment by the time we parked. He was dressed casually in track pants and a T-shirt. But even "casual" Agent Hanlon looked put together, like a Calvin Klein ad. Maybe when you were used to this bad-guys-running-around thing, you stopped looking like the disheveled mess that I was. Or, maybe he was just blessed with better genetics than us mere mortals.

I made the introductions, and Calum led the way around the back of the house to a door set below the sidewalk by some steps. He rented the garden level of this mid-city fourplex, and it was small, lovely, and completely hidden from the street.

Calum held the door open for us, and we walked into the apartment. I turned on the lights, and a warm glow filled the area. I smiled as I looked around the small space: at the David Bowie poster on the living room wall, the art supplies lying haphazardly on the coffee table, the dusty television that he never turned on. The apartment even had a tiny nook that managed to have good natural light in spite of its semi-subterranean location. Calum used it as an art studio. This area was beautiful and expensive because of the architectural details and location, but Calum rented the space for cheap because he knew a guy who knew a guy who knew the landlord. Lucky.

Calum grabbed the bottle of Jameson out of my hands and headed for the kitchen. I heard him open the cupboard and then the clink of glasses—I was going to need a big drink for the conversation that was about to happen. Actually, I needed a big drink after what had just happened.

"Just so you know, I told Calum everything. He's the closest thing to family that I have, so anything you have to tell me, you can tell him too."

"I want you to think about what you are saying," Agent Hanlon said quietly. "The information I am about to tell you is classified. Once you know this, you will be in danger."

"What would you call being chased by two dudes and having my apartment trashed? I don't mean to be rude, Agent Hanlon, but I think the 'I'm in danger' ship has already sailed."

"Those 'two dudes' are only the tip of the iceberg, Miss Bayne. And as sorry as I am about your apartment, it could have been much worse. I'm breaking the rules just being here right now. I've been thinking about how much I can tell you—"

"You can tell her everything," Calum interrupted. He reached over to offer Agent Hanlon his drink.

The two men stared at each other for what seemed like an eternity. Finally, Agent Hanlon looked away, taking the drink.

"Miss Bayne, what I'm about to tell you could get you killed."

"Not knowing could get us killed," I countered.

Agent Hanlon let out a long breath through his nose, then pulled out the item that I had assumed was an ancient BlackBerry and placed it on the coffee table in front of me.

"We believe a device like this is in your apartment, Miss Bayne."

"I don't know what that is," I said, but something in my brain was buzzing—a memory that refused to surface.

Calum studied it. "It looks like an old-school PalmPilot."

Agent Hanlon shook his head. "If only it were. The agent who originally retrieved it thought that it was some sort of new weapon, but once the department started running tests on it, we realized we had no idea what this thing did."

He took a long sip of his drink.

"When my department couldn't figure it out, we turned it over to some people at the university to see if they'd have better luck. They passed it around, and it stumped everyone who studied it."

"It seems like a huge fuss over something so little," I said.

"You have to understand, the government was convinced it was some sort of new weapon. If we couldn't figure it out, then we couldn't be prepared for what it might do."

"Why didn't they just take it apart?" Calum asked.

"Well, they might not be able to put it back together—and then we'd be screwed. Or, even worse, it could blow up the entire country." He stopped, staring at the drink in his hands. The seconds stretched on, and I was afraid he was reconsidering telling us the whole story.

"Agent Hanlon, what happened next?"

"Miss Bayne, this is your last chance to back out. Once I tell you—"

"I want to know."

He took a gulp of his drink. "One of the scientists at the university was a theoretical physicist, and she was the one to finally figure it out." He looked me in the eye. "She claimed that the device came from a different universe."

"Another . . . universe?"

"You know what I'm talking about, right, Miss Bayne? The theoretical physics theory of parallel universes?"

"Why would I know anything about that?"

Agent Hanlon shook his head. "Sorry—I just thought you would know what I was talking about since the scientist was your mother."

And the world dropped out from under my feet.

"Is that why everyone seems to think that I'm involved?"

Agent Hanlon nodded. "That's part of it."

Calum handed me his half-finished Jameson, and I drank it down in one gulp. I wasn't normally a heavy drinker, but tonight seemed like a reasonable time to make an exception.

"What's the other part of it?"

"I'll get to that. But obviously her discovery created an entirely new question: How did it get here? We soon realized the only person who possibly knew the answer was the original owner of this device, who was dead. The government poured money into your mother's research. She figured it out. She was able to create a portal between universes."

"How?"

"We don't know. She hid or destroyed all her notes."

"Why would she do that?" Calum asked.

"My guess is that she didn't trust them," I answered. "You knew my mom. She was a peace-loving hippie. Something must have happened to make her think that the government wasn't going to use this power to sing songs and build campfires."

Agent Hanlon nodded. "We don't know how long she hid her findings. She continued the ruse of performing tests, and eventually the department lost interest. That is, until one of her assistants exposed what she had found to the department. The head of my division confronted your mother and demanded that she turn over her research."

Of course my mother refused, and they told her assistant to confiscate everything. But she had been clever. Agent Hanlon described how she had hidden her notes. "And before we could find them," he continued, "your mother and father were killed in a car crash. Up until a few nights ago, we believed whatever discoveries she made had died with her."

"Then how did you get the device? Or is that even the one that she had?"

Agent Hanlon studied his drink. "It is. An agent retrieved it from the crash site."

The weight of his words sunk in. As I was getting the phone call that would irrevocably change my life, the government was stealing the device out of the wreckage.

He looked at me, his gray eyes tired and a bit sad. "Miss Bayne, I'm here because I'm trying to do the right thing."

I held his gaze and forced myself to take a deep breath. Losing my shit before I got all of the information wasn't going to do me any good, even if I wanted to scream that those assholes had no right rummaging through the wreckage. I motioned for him to continue, not trusting myself to speak.

"Without your mother's notes, we couldn't replicate her work, and thought that the assistant might have been making the whole thing up. That is, until a few nights ago, when the device started beeping and pointing right at your apartment. From there, it wasn't a big leap to assume that your mother had left you another device somehow, and that you had activated it for the first time—"

"But she *didn't* leave me anything," I interrupted.

Agent Hanlon held up his hand. "Miss Bayne, I believe you. I'm not accusing you of anything, OK?"

I sat back and folded my arms.

"At your apartment," he continued, "I thought that there was something wrong with the device. I was able to turn it on, but the only time it picked up anything was when it was pointed directly at you."

"This is nuts."

"I saw it myself. Believe me, I wish I knew why this was happening. Somehow, you are the key to all of this."

I didn't know what to think—Agent Hanlon's words swam around my head, making it impossible to form a cohesive thought.

"What do I do now, Agent Hanlon?"

He was quiet for a minute, like he was formulating a plan on the spot. I was getting the impression that Agent Hanlon was always a man with a plan, and this—whatever this was—was making him uncomfortable.

"I think our best bet is to go through your apartment after the police are done processing the scene tomorrow to see if we can find anything. I need to go back to the office and follow up on some leads."

"What leads?"

"I can't tell you that."

"Bullshit! You mean you *won't* tell me that!"

He sighed, which somehow managed to be condescending. "Miss Bayne, I have told you everything that I can right now. I have questions of my own. I will tell you what I find out, if it amounts to anything. I will pick you up tomorrow morning."

"Fine." I was bone weary with too much information already swimming through my head. I honestly just needed Agent Hanlon to leave so I could get good and drunk and forget everything for a minute.

Calum walked him to the door. No lengthy goodbyes between us, apparently. Then, Calum poured us each another tall drink, and I snuggled up next to him on the couch, my head on his shoulder. Calum absently rubbed my arm. We were quiet for a minute, processing.

"Do you believe him?" Calum asked.

"What part?"

"All of it."

"To be honest, it's a lot to take in. Last week I was just trying to figure out how to get Voldemort's nose back on, and now I'm in the middle of a government conspiracy. What is the multiverse anyway? Are there other versions of Agent Hanlon out there bringing in bad guys and wearing T-shirts that are two sizes too small?"

Calum chuckled. "Yeah—there could be another Fara out there running amok and breaking hearts."

"Fat chance. No hearts would be breaking; I'd just be broke, and frumpy, in all universes."

Calum stopped rubbing my arm. "Is that what you really think of yourself?"

"It's no secret that I'm broke, Calum. It's also not a secret that guys fall all over themselves to fawn over Adora or ask me for her number. In a world that worships glamazons, I obviously don't measure up."

Calum started rubbing my arm again, laying his cheek on the top of my head. "In no universe would I ever describe you as 'frumpy.'" I snorted, but he continued, "But you didn't answer my question—do you believe Agent Hanlon?"

I thought about it, and somehow knew deep down that Agent Hanlon was telling the truth—even if he wasn't telling me all of the truth.

"I do. I think hiding her findings because she didn't trust the government with this power was exactly something my mom would do. But if it's true, then I'm fucking freaked out. What if they don't believe that I have nothing to do with any of this? What if Agent Hanlon hauls me in for questioning?"

"You are my family, Fara, and whatever happens, I'll keep you safe. We'll figure this out together, OK? Even if we have to battle governments to stop them from traveling to parallel universes or whatever. I'm here for you." He kissed the top of my head.

I nodded, grateful to have him in my life, and we both sat quietly, thinking our private thoughts. I must have passed out because when I woke, I was lying on the couch with a pillow and blanket, and the bedroom door was shut. I didn't think I had been asleep for long, the unholy trinity of booze, bar food, and running for my life causing me to toss and turn.

I lay there in the dark, trying to piece together what Agent Hanlon had told me. Why did he think I knew more? I considered what I did know, which wasn't much. My mom used to take me to her lab when I was little—but I didn't remember much of it. I would play or color, and she would run her experiments—that was the gist of my memories. I tried to remember what her lab looked like, or anything that she might have told me that was even related to her experiments—but I came up empty. But I had one vivid memory of my parents fighting about my mother taking me with her, and my father refusing to let me go anymore. I had been about seven or so. My mild-mannered father, who had never yelled or said no to my mother, had been so scared that he told her that if she insisted on taking me back to the lab, he would leave her and take me with him. I remember cowering in my bedroom during that fight. I never went back to the lab.

As I lay there thinking of my parents, the familiar ache of grief made it hard to breathe. Remembering my mom, in her lab coat, smiling at me as she left for work, and my dad, in his painter's smock, grinning at a poem I wrote, made my heart hurt. At that moment, in the dark of Calum's apartment, the weight of it all seemed too much to bear. Tears streamed down my face. My parents were dead, and they weren't coming back. My mother wasn't here to help me with what she had started. She'd never help me with anything ever again. They had left me nothing, not realizing that they would be gone so soon, and now I was in a situation that I couldn't see my way out of.

Calum must have heard his bedroom door open, because without a word he lifted the covers and moved over to make room. I slid in next to him, breathing him in as he wrapped me in his arms.

"Shhhh. It's OK," he mumbled. "We'll figure it out tomorrow." I took a shuddering breath and thought, *What if we don't?*

BLU 12

Fuck. Jyston was staring at me with a predatory smile. He'd been standing there for a while. I put my hand to my chest to show that he had startled me (which he had), hoping that the action was a distraction from putting my palmbox back into the bag.

I had hoped not to have to use what I had practiced with Ink, but I preferred having to be the Lady Raven to being dead.

"Oh my goodness!" I pitched my voice a bit higher and added some breathy emphasis. "You snuck up on me! I didn't even hear you come in. How did you do that?"

The Second Counselor chuckled. "Years of practice. I'm sorry for startling you." He inclined his head toward me, pushed himself off the arch, and took a few steps closer. He was even more terrifying up close, each move precise, no wasted energy or nervous tics; his stillness reminded me of a tiger ready to pounce.

He stopped about ten feet away, and I quickly realized that he was not coming in for an attack. I didn't see any visible weapons, and he made no move to apprehend me. Either he didn't know who I was, or if he did, he wasn't acting on that information . . . yet. Either way, I needed to get the hell out of there as fast as I could without raising suspicion. I remembered to relax my face and straighten my legs from a fighting stance, reminding myself that the Lady Raven wouldn't know how to fight. I dropped my hands and clasped them before me, willing myself to breathe and smile—sweetly, I hoped.

"Oh gosh! No need to apologize. I'm just easily startled, especially in this city where everything is so new. I feel a bit like a fish out of water."

"Well, my apologies anyway. You're new to town? How long have you been here?" He took another step closer. I tried to even out my breathing. I needed to get out of here before I blew my cover, or he delivered the grand reveal that he knew who I was.

I took a step back. "Not long at all. I only just arrived."

He advanced. "Are you staying long?"

I retreated. "I hope so! I really like it so far, although it's very different from where I'm from."

"Where are you from?"

These alcoves weren't that big; I was running out of room. I planted my feet and stuck out my hand.

"Oh gracious—where are my manners? I am so sorry! My name is Raven. May I ask who you are? I know this is a masquerade ball and all, and we're supposed to be mysterious, but I would feel better if I knew your name." I pasted what I hoped was a demure smile on my face.

I had to give him a bit of credit; he didn't even flinch that Raven didn't recognize the second most powerful person in the world. He put his hand in mine. It was huge and callused— the hand of a warrior, or a horrible tyrant. Or both.

"Jyston. It's a pleasure to meet you, Lady Raven."

"Oh wow—I am so sorry! I should have recognized you, even with the mask! I feel so dumb now. I certainly am making a terrible impression! It is an honor to meet you, sir. I thought I saw you on stage. What are you doing away from the party?"

"I could ask you the same thing. And please, it's just Jyston." He stared into my eyes like he was looking for something. I hoped he wouldn't find what he was looking for—especially if what he was looking for was me.

He shook his head slightly, then smiled at me. Whatever moment he was having was gone.

"Lady Raven, is it? I wonder if your mother knew that you would be as beautiful as your namesake?"

I blushed at that. Why was he putting on the charm? His behavior didn't make sense, but at this point I had a mission to do, and to do it I had to escape this conversation alive.

"Thank you, that's very kind. I'm sure you say that to all the girls you startle while admiring blueprints, and who don't recognize you."

He laughed at that, a deep, rumbling sound. It might have been quite pleasant if I hadn't been afraid he was going to skin me alive.

"Don't worry about recognizing me—I honestly prefer that you didn't. It isn't very often that I can talk to someone who hasn't already made their mind up about me. Besides, isn't that the allure of a masquerade ball?" he said. "That we can pretend to be something different than we are, if only for one night?" He gave me a wink.

I tipped my head to him in acknowledgment. Did he know how close to the truth he was?

He stepped even closer to me, and grinned. "So, Lady Raven, why are you hiding with the pictures and blueprints? Wouldn't you rather be finding a young man to dance with?"

No, what I would rather be doing is stealing this blueprint and running for my life, but I didn't say that.

"I prefer the quiet, honestly. And besides, I don't know anyone, and the crowd is a bit overwhelming. I decided to come explore and learn about my adopted home."

I leaned against a display case that held notes of some sort. He had effectively backed me as far away from the exit as possible. Great. I had to keep him talking while I figured out a way to leave. Maybe in the process I could get a bit of information? It was a long shot, but if he could play this game, so could I.

"I answered your question, but now, if I may be so bold, it's my turn: Why are *you* 'hiding with the pictures and blueprints'? Wouldn't you rather be on stage with the High Governor? Or dancing with a pretty girl?"

He closed the distance between us and leaned against the display case next to me, so close I could almost hear him breathing. I was alone with the second most dangerous man in the world, he was not actively trying to kill me, and we were talking about parties and dancing. What the actual fuck?

"Not too bold at all—I'm rather enjoying our conversation, Lady Raven. There are a couple of reasons why I'm no longer on stage, if you'll allow me. The first reason is that the High Governor loves to hear himself talk, but I have found that I am not particularly fond of his talking, so I got bored and left."

I thought about the penguin—and the look of annoyance on Jyston's face as he scanned the crowd while up on stage—and I didn't even need to force the laugh that came out of my mouth.

"But the second reason is a secret," he continued. "Can you keep it?"

I widened my eyes and nodded conspiratorially.

"When I saw this beautiful woman in the crowd, I had to come find her—and apparently startle her and introduce myself."

The blush on my cheeks was not an affectation, and I was struggling to keep my bearings. This man was nothing like I had expected, and I was having a very hard time reconciling the rumors of his tyranny with his humor and, quite frankly, his charm. Maybe it was just an act, and maybe I was more susceptible to flattery than I'd imagined, but Jyston did not come off as a cold-blooded killer. But, then again, most truly diabolical people don't.

"I am humbled by your attention," I said, forcing myself to look into his gray eyes. "And I'm really glad you found me, but I should probably be going."

"So soon? I was hoping to talk to you about the blueprint that you were admiring—it is a special project of mine."

Where was this going?

"Oh—well, I do love architecture, although I don't know anything about it. I suppose I can stay for a moment to hear about this project of yours."

He was so close that my shoulder was touching his arm. He towered over me; if I were to look at him, I would have to look straight up. I inhaled deeply to steady my heartbeat, and realized that he didn't have that cold, metallic smell every other agent of Jurisdiction had. He actually smelled good, which was a weird thing to think about at this moment.

"Sorry," I said, lowering my eyes. "I'm a bit nervous around new people. Especially rulers of the universe."

Jyston was so close that his laugh rumbled in my chest.

"Lady Raven, I am nowhere near ruler of the universe, but if I was, I would still come find you in a crowd, introduce myself, and talk to you about blueprints."

Just then, I heard applause and Jyston's head whipped around, like he'd heard something. He turned to me and grabbed my hand, pulling it up to his lips for a gentle kiss.

"I must take my leave—and I implore you to do so as well." His eyes were staring into mine; then he looked back over his shoulder again. At the same time, I got that familiar *tug*. Things were about to go to shit.

When I turned to leave, he held me back for a second. "You know, the only reason the High Governor has these blueprints on display is to appease me. It's not even the most notable project Jurisdiction is working on this moment. The more interesting blueprints are in the lower level. You might want to peruse them if you have the chance. I hope to see you again soon, Lady Raven."

He gave a small bow, released my hand, and strode away. I stood there for a minute, trying to process what he had just said. Reading between the lines, this blueprint was a decoy. But *why?* Had he figured out who I was? Did I dare risk a trap to see if it was true? I only had fifteen minutes before Jack did whatever he was going to do.

As I stood there, I heard a woman's voice, and I froze.

"Ah, there you are, Jyston," Dagna purred. "I was wondering where you'd run off to."

"I was nodding off during the High Governor's lengthy speech, so I excused myself for a nice walkabout."

I stuck my head out of the alcove. Dagna had her back to me and was standing about as close to Jyston as she could without wearing his tuxedo with him. His face was blank, although he removed the hand she had placed on his chest. As I peeked out, he looked over Dagna's shoulder directly at me, grabbed her by the elbow, and steered her in the opposite direction. If I didn't know any better, he was leading her away from me. Maybe he thought she was enough of a psychopath that he would keep anyone away from her, enemy or otherwise. His reasons and whether I figured into them, whatever they were, didn't matter at this point. I was getting the hell out of here.

I quickly left the alcove and walked toward the double stairway, hoping not to draw any attention to myself. I paused before I headed downstairs. As I saw it, I had two options. The first was to consider this a completed mission and leave. I had photographs of the blueprints I'd come to retrieve; that was the extent of the mission. This was the most reasonable option, and one I was sure the Team would agree with.

However, if I was to believe Jyston, then the photographs I'd taken of the decoy blueprints were worthless. We probably wouldn't have this opportunity again. I thought about all the possible pitfalls of staying longer, and then I saw an unmarked door right before the stairs. I had to take this chance.

The door was unlocked, so I slipped in, shutting it quietly behind me. The stairwell was lit by wall sconces that were more subdued than the rest of the mansion. Apparently only servants used this stairway, so why bother making it look ostentatious? I looked down the stairs, holding my breath to listen for any sounds coming from below. I could hear the musicians from beyond the door, and people talking and laughing, but nothing from the stairwell. I still had just over ten minutes to send my signal to Ink. Hopefully, that was plenty of time to get down these stairs, take a quick look around, then get back up and out.

The thought of running downstairs in heels made me want to poke myself in the eye with the shoe itself, so I kicked them off and left them by the door. Best-case scenario, I'd find the blueprints and would need my hands free; worst-case, I'd have to run for my life.

I took the stairs two at a time just to be safe. I couldn't afford to be caught in this stairwell, and every second counted. Somehow my dress was still hanging in there despite how fast I was going. I would have to make sure to thank Styx for whatever magic she worked to keep everything in place.

The stairs ended in another plain, unlocked white door. I opened it slowly, into a back hallway. After a heartbeat, I slipped out into a dim hallway. The only light came from a single lightbulb hanging from the ceiling. To the left, a dozen doors lined the hallway on each side, and it ended in a dead end. On the right, it made a sharp turn, and although I couldn't see where it led, I could hear the clinking of dishes. The kitchens. To the left it was.

I walked as quietly as I could and tried the first two doors. They opened into storage rooms full of desks and beds, lamps and stools. The last door I came to was locked. I looked at my palmbox—I had less than ten minutes left.

I placed the palmbox up to the handle of the door, and it unlocked. "I will hug you for this, Styx."

The room was huge, at least twice the size of the storage rooms. Files and file cabinets covered most of the available space, and papers lay in huge stacks on desks along the walls. Bookcases full of more files were lined up in rows. It appeared that this was document storage—for who or what I wasn't sure. I shut the door behind me and walked in the room. If only I had time to go through all these papers, but I didn't. I needed to focus. Maybe someday I'd lead a Team to come search through this stuff. Just not today.

I walked farther into the room, casually reading the titles of the folders on the bookshelves, but nothing looked damning enough to stop. As I rounded the last of the filing cabinets, I came up short. There stood a huge worktable, and on it were blueprints. Jyston had been telling the truth, although I had no idea why he would help me—unless it was a trap. I had to get this back to the Team right away, preferably without getting caught.

I had just taken out my palmbox to take a photo of the blueprint when the lights went out and my palmbox died. It just died. There was that *tug* again. I shoved the now useless palmbox back into my bag, fumbled in the dark, grabbed the blueprint, rolled it up as small as it would go, and headed in the direction of the door, bumping into things along the way.

I finally found the door, opened it, and looked around the corner; I could hear voices coming from one of the storage areas—a man and a woman. I shoved the blueprint down the back of my dress, hoping that the train would cover it up just enough that it wouldn't be conspicuous. Creeping by the door with the voices, I realized that talking had turned into moans and some other noises that sounded suspiciously like sex. I briefly wondered if the couple from earlier had made their way down here, and laughed to myself. Serves me right that I get caught by two drunk, horny socialites.

The groaning of the lovebirds barely covered the sound of additional voices coming down the stairs. I rushed into the other storage area, cracked the door, and stood very still.

The lights came back on. "Are you sure you saw someone come down here?" Dagna asked.

Shit, shit, shit.

"Yes, ma'am. Our cameras picked up a young woman down here a few minutes ago."

I heard the click of high heels as Dagna walked toward the blueprint room. She paused in front of the storage room I was hiding in, and I held my breath and backed up into the dark. I didn't want to fight my way out of here, but I would if I had to. She started to open it, and then by some miracle the woman in the other storage room let out an exceptionally loud and well-timed moan that caught her attention. I had to go. Now.

Hoping that the couple's sloppy noises were enough to cover up my escape, I slowly opened the door, looked both ways, then sprinted to the bottom of the staircase, taking the stairs two at a time to the second floor. I heard a shout from below as I grabbed my shoes, slipped them on, and cracked open the door to see a security guard standing to the right. Shit, shit, shit. How was I going to get out of this? Whatever I decided to do, I had to do it now or I'd be caught.

An idea popped into my head, and I said a little prayer to the universe that my luck would hold. I had two minutes to get outside and signal Ink. I smeared my lipstick and took one of my shoes off. I flung open the door, stumbled, and grabbed the security guard's arm.

"Did you see my boyfriend?" I slurred, looking up at him through my eyelashes.

"What?"

"My boyfriend, he said he'd be right back, but then I saw him head in this door with another girl!" I made my eyes start to water. "I went after him, but now—I can't find him. That slut!"

At first, the guard looked annoyed that this drunken socialite was interrupting his post. Then, as his eyes met mine, recognition flitted across his face.

"Hey! Don't I know you?" he said, as he grabbed my arm.

"No! Let me go!"

The security guard's face melted into a sneer, and his eyes ran up and down my body. "I don't think I will. I think Dagna will reward me for turning you in to her . . . Blu."

Oh fuck! I couldn't have just escaped Jyston and Dagna to let this idiot sound the alarm. Thinking quickly, I grabbed my palmbox out of my bag with my free hand as discreetly as I could, letting the bag fall to the ground. I sent another little prayer into the universe as I powered it on, hoping that whatever weird glitch made it stop working downstairs had run its course. People were starting to stare at the guard roughly holding a socialite, so whatever I was going to do, I needed to make it quick. I turned to face the guard, wrapping my free arm around his neck, and kissed him. His eyes widened when I jammed the palmbox into the back of his neck, sending the disabling power through him. He let go of my arm and fell. The small crowd gasped.

"Oh my goodness! What just happened? I kissed him and he . . . fainted? I'm so embarrassed! Can someone please help him?"

People started to excitedly whisper as I took off my other shoe and hurried down the stairs, avoiding other security that came rushing toward the commotion. I dodged and hid behind a large potted plant until the coast was relatively clear; then I ran out of the mansion and onto the drive. Flashing my palmbox's light twice in the air—the sign for Ink to come get me—I started to walk down the drive, hoping that he could get to me soon.

I heard a screeching of wheels. Ink opened the car door, his eyes wide.

"Get in! Get the fuck in!"

Whatever he was seeing behind was freaking him out, so I sprinted the last few feet to his car and jumped in as he pulled away. I looked over my shoulder to see Dagna staring at our car as we drove away. That was way too close.

"Glad to see you made it." Ink grinned, then looked at my dress. It had hiked up my legs. "Nice dress."

I was too tired to even give him shit back. We had to get the blueprints back to the Captain. If what I understood they meant was true, it was worse than we thought. Though they definitely wanted the public to believe it was a school, it wasn't; it was a work camp and prison. For kids.

13 FARA

My hangover clung to my skull. It seemed unfairly disproportionate to the amount of alcohol I had consumed. I lay in bed listening to the sounds of Calum taking a shower and tried not to move. The pang of guilt I felt regarding last night was a nice complement to my hangover. I wished them both away. Calum thought of me like family—like a sister—and sleeping in his bed meant no more to him than if I were actually related to him. I had crashed with him countless times after my parents died, not wanting to be alone, chasing away the sadness and fear. Nothing had ever happened—not that I hadn't thought about it once or twice. But that had been before Beck, before being in a serious relationship. Did that change things? If Beck was supposed to be the love of my life, why wasn't he the one I was sharing this frightening and unbelievable set of circumstances with? Wasn't he supposed to hold me and tell me we'd figure it out?

I forced myself to get up. I needed ibuprofen, coffee, and a donut. I started the coffee, dug around in Calum's kitchen until I found something that passed as donuts, and popped a couple of ibuprofen while I checked my phone.

I had a voicemail from a number I didn't recognize and a couple of texts, but nothing from Beck. As I crafted yet another message to my unresponsive boyfriend, I got a message from Agent Hanlon. He'd be here in an hour.

Calum came out of his bedroom dressed for work, hair wet and smelling of soap and cologne. I pressed a mug of coffee into his hand. He stole a donut from my plate.

"I see you found my secret stash," he said, shoving my donut in his mouth.

"Hiding donuts from me is futile. I will assimilate them."

Calum laughed. "Fair enough. You are the Borg of the donuts. Thanks for making coffee."

I sighed. "It's the least I can do."

He cocked an eyebrow at me over his coffee mug.

"It's just—I'm so sorry. About last night. About dragging you into this mess. About—"

He waved me off. "We're not having this conversation this early in the morning, OK? Or ever, really. There's no need to apologize. Just like there is no need to thank me. Stop making it awkward and give me another donut." He smiled and I laughed as I ran away from his donut-grabbing hands.

After he left for work, I realized that I had nothing to change into—no makeup, not even a brush to detangle the rat's nest of my hair. I knew Calum kept extra toothbrushes in the bathroom and other feminine hygiene type items for when he brought girls home, so I used those. It made me smile to think that even when he was being a player, he was considerate. How he ended up being such a good guy despite having such a shitty mom was beyond me.

After I washed my face and put my hair up into an unintentionally messy bun, I grabbed my phone and waited for Agent Hanlon. The beginning of panic was starting to settle into my stomach. With Calum here and coffee and donuts in my system, last night had settled into a dream-like memory, the edges smoothed enough that it wasn't real. But the reality of facing my trashed apartment, facing Agent Hanlon, facing the knowledge that there were threatening people after me and that there were parallel universes—I wasn't ready. I tried to give myself a pep talk, but all I managed to do was freak myself out more. I wasn't good at crisis situations. That was where Adora and Calum came in—they helped in any minor crisis that I experienced. And this certainly wasn't minor. I wasn't sure what that said about me, that I allowed other people to handle my shit. I ignored the thought, not willing to worry about my lack of badassary yet.

Just when I thought I was going to lose what little of my mind I had left, I heard a knock at the door and looked through the peephole to see Agent Hanlon standing there, arms crossed across his athletic-cut, polo-adorned chest. He already looked irritated for some reason: an auspicious start.

I opened the door and was greeted with "Ready?"

"Good morning to you too! Would you like some coffee and a donut?"

"This isn't a social call, Miss Bayne. Do you need to get dressed?"

I was mad at him for even asking—like he didn't remember why he was here in the first place.

"I would love to change *if I had clothes.* But all my clothes are at my trashed apartment, so you're stuck with this. Not everyone has an unlimited supply of polo shirts stashed in their cars."

His face was unreadable as we headed up the stairs and out to his car, and his irritation continued while we drove to my apartment. I waited for him to say something—anything. But he glared out into the spring rain like the weather had intentionally wronged him.

"Did you find out anything?"

He gave no indication that he'd heard me.

"I said, did you find out any—"

"I did, although nothing useful for you right now."

"Then what are we doing this morning?"

"We need to comb over your apartment to see if there is anything missing, or if the perpetrators left anything behind. I doubt we will find either, but it's a start."

Agent Hanlon had brought along garbage bags.

"How do you want to go about this? What am I looking for?" I asked.

"You need to determine if anything was stolen. Also, see if anything doesn't belong to you or your boyfriend. Let's start in the living room."

As he carefully stepped inside, I took a deep breath and started the process of reassembling my life. We started slowly, creating piles of my things. At first the piles were in distinct categories, not that I had much to begin with. Eventually we ended up with only two piles: "trash" and "keep." The trash pile kept getting bigger, while the keep pile was depressingly small. We worked silently, Agent Hanlon taking the destroyed furniture out to the dumpster, along with the bags of broken dishes, spoiled food, and other unidentifiable items. I sifted through the other things, realizing that even before my apartment was trashed, I didn't own much.

I was in the kitchen, sweeping up cereal, when I noticed Agent Hanlon looking at the torn cookbook on the counter, a faint smile on his lips.

"That was my dad's," I said. "He was an amazing cook. It's one of the only things I have left of him." I wasn't sure why I was telling Agent Hanlon that, except that it was the first time I had seen anything other than a glare on his face all morning.

He looked up and gently put the cookbook in the "keep" pile. "I have the same one," he said.

"You like to cook?"

"Why do you sound so surprised?"

"Because you are so serious all the time! The thought of you doing something so normal, like cooking, just seems out of place in my head."

One side of his mouth quirked up in an almost-smile.

After a few minutes he said, "Italian."

I put the tongs I was holding into the "keep" pile and looked up. "What?"

"My favorite kind of food to cook is Italian."

I couldn't quite place it, but there was something almost tentative in the way he'd said it. Like he was worried about showing me he was an actual human being, instead of Agent-No-Fun. If I hadn't been worried that he might whisk me away to a black site to interrogate me, I would have found it sweet.

"My dad used to make the best penne and meatballs with red sauce," I said, looking at the cookbook like it could bring him back. "He'd cook the sauce all day, and the whole house would smell of garlic. I never learned his recipe, and my attempts haven't been successful—it never tastes like his."

"Maybe you should try to make it taste like yours. You never know, it might be better."

He had picked up another cookbook and put it on the pile, but his eyes were on me.

I looked away, his gaze too intense to meet for long. We sat in silence again, and I realized that he had been trying to make conversation. He must be as quiet as I was, if he was struggling. Somehow that made him a bit more endearing.

"What else do you like to cook?" I asked.

He thought for a moment. "I'm honestly not home enough to cook very often, but I'm trying to work my way through the half of a cow that I have frozen."

"You bought half a cow? Like, the cow's ass is in your freezer?"

He actually laughed at that. "No, you can buy cows at auction, or half cows, and the farmers take the cow to the butcher to have it turned into various cuts of meat. I'm saving the good cuts for summer when I can grill, so right now I'm working with the ground beef and other tougher cuts. There's only so much you can do with hamburger."

I laughed, remembering the horrible ground beef and cream of mushroom casserole my mom made on her nights to cook, and I told him about that and her other casserole disasters. He told me a few stories about his cooking triumphs and explained the whole buying-a-cow process, letting some humor sneak out in the retelling. He wasn't an amazing storyteller, or the funniest person I had met, but he had this kind of solid relatability that I found myself enjoying in spite of myself.

We finally made it to my bedroom, which was an even bigger disaster than the rest of the apartment. My clothes were all over, the mattress sliced open down the middle, the box spring in no better shape. My tiny closet had been emptied of its contents, as had the dresser drawers. Beck's stuff was mixed in with mine. His guitar was broken and had been shoved under the dresser. I reached for my phone, noticing that Beck hadn't responded to my earlier text.

"Who are you texting?"

"Why?"

"Because you can't tell people what we're doing."

"I'm not—I'm just texting my boyfriend to tell him I found his guitar and it's not in one piece."

"He's a guitar player?"

"He wanted to be. He wants to be a singer/songwriter someday."

"Is he any good?"

He probably would be great at it if he put some effort into it, but like everything else, he just sort of expected it to happen.

I shrugged—I wasn't going to get into that whole thing with Agent Hanlon.

"So, I can text him?"

Agent Hanlon nodded as he picked up a pair of my underwear, then dropped them once he realized what they were. The look of mortification on his face made me laugh.

"You've never seen women's underwear before?"

He actually rolled his eyes at me, which was a first. "Miss Bayne—I just find it inappropriate to be handling your underthings."

"My . . . underthings? What are you, ten years old? You can call it what it is, you know. We're all adults here."

"I couldn't tell," he said with a smirk as he held up my Hello Kitty pajamas. I snatched them out of his hand. The thought that he had been teasing me made blush.

We organized everything left in my apartment. What was in my "keep" pile was woefully small and mostly clothes. Without all the trash and destroyed furniture, my apartment looked sad and empty. I wasn't sure where I was going to go next. I needed to talk to Beck to see if we'd stay here or if we'd find another place. Would he still want to live together? Did I still want to live with him? That thought made me sad, but I couldn't dwell on it now.

Agent Hanlon was studying me intently. "Now what?" I asked.

"Did you find anything that was out of place, or anything that was missing?"

I thought about it, cataloging everything that we saw against my measly possessions, and realized that one thing was gone: my journal.

"Did your journal contain anything important?"

"Of course it contained important things—it contained my deepest secrets!"

He sighed. "What I meant was, anything that pertains to the device, your mom. We all have secrets, Miss Bayne. I'm sure yours are not as terrible as you think."

I snorted. "How do I know that it won't end up on the Internet?"

"Because while you might find your love of Justin Bieber embarrassing, I'm sure no one else cares."

Agent Hanlon wasn't exactly smiling, but his eyes sparkled. He was trying to make me feel better in his own, awkward way.

"Fine. I only started keeping a journal after my parents died as a part of my self-therapy—so it isn't anything more than a place to vent, and express my undying love for boy bands."

"If *NSYNC is a matter of national security, we'll worry about it then."

"*NSYNC? How old *are* you?"

We finished putting stuff in piles, and I grabbed whatever clothes I could and shoved them into a leftover garbage bag, along with what remained of my bathroom items and makeup. I didn't know how long I was going to be at Calum's, and I couldn't keep using his secret stash of girl stuff.

My stomach audibly growled as we got into his car. "Zip it—you're fine," I said.

"You name your car, and you talk to your stomach?"

"Sorry—old habit and all. That's what Adora and I say when we're too broke to eat."

"How often is that? I mean, that you're too broke to eat?"

"On and off since my parents died. Recently it's been a bit more since I'm covering the expenses for two people now."

He was quiet for a second, then seemed to make up his mind about something. "Want to get lunch?"

The question surprised me, but what surprised me more was that I did want to get lunch with him. Unfortunately, I couldn't afford it. I hesitated.

"This one is on me," he said. "Do you like Asian food?"

"Who doesn't like Asian food? At this point, I'm so hungry I'd eat paste."

"I know a place. It's in a gas station, but it has the best spring rolls in the city. Trust me."

That was the issue, wasn't it? So far, he had done exactly what he said he would, and hadn't spirited me away. I had to start trusting him at some point, didn't I? He was the only one who knew what was going on and could help me. Without overthinking it, I nodded.

We pulled up to a gas station that I had driven by hundreds of times. He parked out back and held the door open for me.

As soon as we walked in, my mouth started to water from the amazing smells that were wafting from the kitchen. The place was tiny with only a few tables and a counter to order. No one in there was speaking English, and the menu was not in English either. He pointed to a table, and I sat while he walked up to the counter and started a conversation with the guy working there. It took me a second to realize that they both were speaking in another language. When he sat back down, the look on my face must have said what my mouth didn't.

"I know a couple of different languages. Mandarin is one of them."

"What? How?"

"It's a long story. I hope you don't mind that I ordered for us? I like to let the owner choose what's best today, always with spring rolls."

I looked at Agent Hanlon, really *looked* at him for the first time, and realized that while he certainly was Agent-No-Fun, there was something beneath that. Someone who spoke Mandarin and liked adventurous food. Someone who joked about boy bands to make me feel less freaked out about goons trashing my place and stealing my journal. Someone who I wouldn't mind getting to know a little better. After I figured out what was going on with Beck, of course.

We waited in not quite uncomfortable silence for our food and checked our phones. Calum had responded to let me know he'd be home around dinnertime, and he'd bring us back something from The Grill. There was another voicemail from an unknown number, but nothing from Beck. I needed to figure out what was going on with him. Hopefully, he was OK.

The food came and it was everything Agent Hanlon had promised. He put a plate in front of me and started loading it up with a little of everything, including the best spring rolls I had ever eaten. He explained what everything was while I sampled it, and told me the story of how he knew the owner and how long this place had been around. After a while, we just ate in comfortable silence.

"Thank you for lunch," I said. "That was more fun than I thought."

"Because I'm Agent-No-Fun?"

I chuckled. "Something like that."

"Miss Bayne, you realize that this is my job? When I'm on the clock, I am a federal agent with a professional responsibility, but I'm really not a bad guy."

I nodded, unsure of how to respond. Did I think he was a bad guy? No. Did it matter to him what I thought? Probably not.

We pulled into the gym parking lot, and I saw Voldemort staring at me in noseless contempt. As we parked, I turned to thank Agent Hanlon again, but before I could open my door, he grabbed my arm. I noticed that his hands were giant, almost as large as my entire forearm.

"The two gentlemen in the sedan are here. We need to go. You can get your car later."

At the back of the parking lot, the blue sedan was partially hidden by the spring downpour we were experiencing. Agent Hanlon started to drive away, checking to see if we were being followed. We weren't.

Once we got a safe distance away from my car, I swore. Obviously, they knew about the gym; I had written about it in my journal. That meant that they also knew that I had misgivings about Beck's sexual prowess—but now was not the time to dwell on that.

"Well, they know where you work, where you live, and where you work out. Hopefully, you never mentioned Calum in that journal, or they might find his address too."

I shook my head, still in shock.

We drove in silence until we finally pulled onto Calum's street, and Agent Hanlon gave one last look around.

"I don't like that they are still following you, even after they didn't find anything in your apartment. Do you have to work tomorrow?"

I shook my head. Douche had given my shift to Hewitt to punish me for swapping with Adora, so I had another day of not making money.

"OK—stay here until I contact you tomorrow. Understand?"

I sighed. "You know, I was starting to think you're a normal human until you bark orders at me like that. You've turned back into Bossy McBosserson. Haven't we already covered this? How about 'Fara, your life is in danger and it would probably be wise if you stayed at Calum's until we know more'? Or 'Fara, I can assume you aren't an idiot, so please don't go frolicking around the city advertising your whereabouts on social media,' or, my personal favorite, 'Fara, I'd prefer you not to die since it would cause me mountains of paperwork, so can you please keep your ass at home?'"

There was a noticeable tic in his clenched jaw.

"Miss Bayne, it would make my life a lot easier if you stayed inside tomorrow so that I can do some investigating without worrying about you getting killed. Would you mind?"

I patted his arm. "Was that so hard? No problem, Agent Hanlon. I'll stay put until I hear from you."

I thought I saw him smile as I got out of the car.

14 BLU

Ink pulled the car into the Compound, parked, and got out as I grappled with my shoes, the blueprints, my handbag, and my dress. He stood there, practically tapping his foot, waiting for me; seriously, men have no idea what it is like to be responsible for a million things other than themselves. I sighed, opened the door, and looked at him.

"A hand?"

He came over and took the blueprints out of my hands and started walking toward the Captain's office. I hurried behind him, barefoot. I looked at the shoes I was carrying and tossed them onto the grass with a feeling of relief. I would retrieve the shoes tomorrow—although I would pay to see the groundskeepers' faces when they came across black stilettos lying willy-nilly on the lawn.

Jack, Styx, and the Captain were all in the Captain's office when we arrived. Styx looked me up and down.

"Lose your shoes?" she asked with a perfect eyebrow raised.

"They ran away." I collapsed in my usual spot at the table. Everyone else filed in and looked at me expectantly. Ink spread out the blueprints on the table, and while they studied them, I recounted everything that had happened. As I spoke, I realized that I was almost positive Jyston knew who I was, which made his behavior even stranger than I'd originally thought.

Ink was the first to speak.

"How did Jyston know it was you? Could the mole have gotten that information to them? If we were the only five people who knew of our plans, and none of us told him, then how did he figure it out?"

The Captain steepled her fingers, thinking.

"What is confusing me," I interjected, "is how he acted, especially if he knew who I was. He was anything but a psychopath. He was . . . almost charming. He didn't blow my cover, even though he had every opportunity to, and he even led Dagna away from me so that I could go downstairs—"

"Which could have been a trap," Ink said.

"But why set an elaborate trap when he could have just captured me in front of everyone and made an example out of me? The price on my head is enough that all he had to do was tip off a guard. Why tell me about the real blueprints, and not just let me come back here and tell you about the school? I don't know what to think of it, but nothing that he did aligns with what we think we know about him. Jyston even smells different—" Even I wasn't quite sure what I meant by that.

"He *smells* better? And since when are you on first-name terms with the Second Counselor?" Ink glared at me. I wasn't sure why he was angry, but he was. I'd have it out with him later. Now, we needed to focus on what to do with the information.

The Captain had been studying the blueprints. She stood up, and we all looked at her expectantly.

"I trust Blu's instincts as it pertains to the Second Counselor." Ink rolled his eyes, but her tone was final. "It appears that he might be more than he seems. However, until we can verify that he is not the warmongering psychopath that he's said to be, we need proof that this building really is what he says it is. We need to set up a reconnaissance mission— probably multiple missions—to see if Jurisdiction has broken ground on this building, where it is located, whether it's guarded—the usual information."

The Captain dismissed us with orders to come back tomorrow after training to start the plan. She asked Jack to stay, and Ink left without a word. Styx and I followed slowly and carefully since I no longer had shoes.

"What's with him?" I asked Styx, tilting my head at Ink, who stomped ahead of us.

She looked at me like I had just asked the dumbest question in the world. "Did you drink too much at the party, or are you really that blind?"

"What are you talking about?"

"Ink! He didn't like the way you were talking about Jyston. It made him jealous."

"That's ridiculous."

She stopped mid-step and stood in front of me. "Look, I don't get into your business. We're all grown-ups here, mostly. But Ink has loved you since you were little, and it broke his heart when you broke up."

"He's the one who ended it with me! I think you're reading into things that aren't there."

"Believe me, I wish I was, but he still holds a candle for you and would die of happiness if you got back together."

"That is so dumb! He broke it off with me because we are way better as friends and almost killed each other as a couple. He has a different girl in his room almost every night. He's not hurting for attention. Any one of those girls would gnaw off their own arm if it meant he'd seriously date them—which he wouldn't, because he's a total player. Which was reason 12,093 that he broke it off."

Styx just shook her head. "Think what you want, B, but the way you talked about Jyston set him on edge."

"What do you mean 'the way I talked about Jyston'?"

She laughed outright at that. "Girl, for being smart, you are pretty dumb. Your eyes lit up and you blushed when you talked about the Second Counselor. Blushed! He made quite the impression on you, and not the hideous he-tortures-children sort of way we were expecting. Ink noticed and didn't like it."

I thought about it and knew, deep down, she was right. Jyston had been charming, funny, and self-depreciating—and I would have thought it was all the act of a sociopath if he hadn't warned me of Dagna's approach, led her away from me, and given me the tip about the blueprints. But what to do with that information? My personal feelings, whatever they might turn out to be, couldn't interfere with the missions. I'd ignore it for now. I sighed.

"I'll talk to Ink and explain that I'm not going to run off and join Jurisdiction so I can get into the Second Counselor's pants."

Styx let out a belly laugh. "Let me tell you, B, if you can get into Jyston's pants without getting killed, I'll do your laundry for a year."

As I made my way to my apartment, I saw Ink unlocking his door and I called out to him.

"Hey—are you going to tell me why you're being an ass, or are you going to make me guess?"

He made a rude gesture and went inside. I followed him and shut the door.

"OK, grumpy—spill it. Why are you mad?"

He flopped down on his bed and glared at me.

"B, after all these years, you don't get it, do you?"

"Get what? That you're being a complete ass?"

"What the fuck is up with you and the Second Counselor? I mean, how can you even think for one second he's not a horrible sadist?"

"Ink, you weren't there. It was weird—"

"Weird? My parents are dead because he did nothing to help them! He sat by while Dagna tortured and killed them because they were providing supplies to the Compound, Blu! And yet here you are, talking about him like you respect the guy and might even like him."

"That's not what I'm saying! I just think that we might want to consider—"

"Consider what? The only thing I want to consider is how to kill him! He is what we have been fighting against since we could walk! What he represents—Jurisdiction—is everything that we are against. Have you forgotten why we have trained for years? So that we can take Jurisdiction—him—down."

"Of course I haven't forgotten! My parents were killed too, Ink. You're not the only one that's gone through horrible shit because of Jurisdiction."

"Which makes your reaction to him even more fucked up. It's like he's gotten into your head or something. He is the enemy, B! No matter what you think, he is the enemy. You can't just trust him because he seemed like a normal person for all of an hour and smelled good!"

"I don't trust him!"

"He could have killed you! He could still kill you, and I couldn't live with that."

He took a ragged breath and wiped his eyes with the back of his hand. I crossed the room and sat next to him on his bed.

"But he didn't kill me, Ink. I'm still here, and that's the point. He could've killed me and didn't. He could have turned me in, but he didn't." I wrapped my arms around him. "Regardless, I don't trust him. I'm smarter than that—and I know you know that. We have worked so long and given up so much to take these assholes down, and I'll keep doing that until my very last breath—or theirs. One encounter with the Second Counselor doesn't change that. But the Captain is always telling me to listen to my instincts, and they're telling me that the Second Counselor is not what we thought he was."

I rose, standing between Ink's knees so I could look into his eyes. I cupped his face, forcing him to look at me.

"But right now, that really doesn't matter, and I would never put anyone, including myself, in that kind of danger because of a hunch. Never. You guys are my family—I've already lost one; I can't lose another. OK?"

He held my gaze, then finally nodded. "Fine. Whatever you say. But it's hard to take you seriously looking like that. You're a fucking mess."

I laughed because he was right, I was a fucking mess.

I kissed him on the forehead. "You're a pain in my ass, Ink, but I wouldn't have you any other way. I'll see you in the morning—and bring a full donut this time." I left him chuckling to himself, whatever anger he had toward me gone. I was glad that he wasn't still feeling betrayed. He was the only family I had left.

15 FARA

I had showered, changed into one of my few surviving outfits, and read part of a book by the time Calum came home from work smelling like grease and a touch of perfume. When I teased him about his fruity new scent, he rolled his eyes and shoved a Styrofoam container into my hands.

"I took care of her."

"Like in the storage room?"

He playfully punched my arm, trying to look outraged and failing.

"Ugh—no! I told Carrie that if she didn't stop trying to lick my face, I'd tell Hewitt she had a thing for him."

"You didn't!"

He smiled, kicking his shoes off. "She has a thing for everyone."

"They all have the hots for you, you know, but she's the worst. I think that she would stab me in my sleep if she thought she could get you in bed."

"Don't they realize that you're irreplaceable?"

I shrugged. "Just be careful with that one. She is seriously looney tunes."

I put the container in the refrigerator and brought Calum up to speed about what happened in my apartment, along with my missing journal. We went over everything again, and we both realized that we knew just as much as we did yesterday, which wasn't much at all. At that, Calum brought out the Jameson.

"And we still don't know how the device works, or why it's been pointing to your apartment?" he asked, taking a sip from his large pour.

"Agent Hanlon thinks that maybe someone is purposely misdirecting the device to me—or at least to my apartment—but he's trying to dig up more information."

"What exactly did he say about the device alarm again? That the alarm went off around 3 a.m., and the screen showed your address or a map or some shit? Did anything weird happen at 3 a.m. either of those two nights? Like the smoke detector going off, or your microwave behaving strangely or anything?"

I thought about it and was about to dismiss his question outright, but then it occurred to me that something weird had happened around 3 a.m. the second night; that was the night that creepy window ghost thing appeared. It probably was nothing, but I mentioned it to Calum anyway.

"I'm still not quite convinced I wasn't dreaming the whole thing."

"It can't just be a coincidence."

I shrugged. With everything else that had happened, I had forgotten about it. It was too tenuous to be a real connection—I needed more information. But how?

Neither of us could come up with anything useful, and eventually Calum poured us another Jameson. He put on a movie and we snuggled in on the couch. I hadn't realized how tired I was, or how emotional it had been to go through my busted apartment. How hanging out with Agent Hanlon had been surprisingly pleasant. How worried I was that Beck hadn't responded. How grateful I was for a friend like Calum.

I dozed off mid-movie and started to dream. I was walking up a tree-lined path with someone else, and I was hurrying because I had to tell someone something important. It was dark, but I wasn't afraid of the dark—I was afraid of what had just happened. I had to hurry.

"Fara! Wake up!"

Someone was gently shaking me. I opened my eyes, disoriented, and it took me a second to remember where I was. That dream had been so real—I could still smell the cologne of the person I was with, but I looked around and I was on the couch at Calum's place, and my head had somehow landed in his lap. I looked up at Calum's face to see why he was waking me up, but he wasn't looking at me; he was looking directly ahead, his eyes wide.

"What is that?" he whispered.

I turned my head, and about a foot in front of us was another window—but this one was twice the size. I could feel the breeze through my hair again, and smell the cologne.

"You can see that?" I asked. Calum just nodded. "Are we dreaming?"

"I don't think so," he said. "What is it? Are those trees?"

I sat up slowly so I could get closer to it. Through the window I could see trees straight ahead, and they looked like the same ones from two nights before. When I looked down through the window, there was a brick path, and it was as if I was standing on the path looking through the trees. What I was seeing was not possible. It was the same path as the one I had been dreaming about just moments before—I was sure of it. I sprang to my feet and peered through the window at all angles, trying to see if I could recognize anything else. Calum reached out his hand, and I was going to tell him to stop, but the words froze in my mouth. As he reached for the window, my phone started to ring. I ignored it, but then it rang again. I found it in the couch cushions—why was Agent Hanlon calling? I turned back around to see Calum reach through the window.

"Fara, what the hell is happening? The device is going crazy! Are you OK?"

I turned back to Calum. He had pulled his hand back out of the window and was looking with shock and wonder at the handful of leaves in it, his hair blowing in the breeze.

And as if my subconscious had been working overtime putting together everything that happened, pieces of the puzzle snapped into place. I knew why the device had been pointing to me. I didn't understand *how*, but I knew *why*. The window snapped shut and Calum looked at me, still holding out the leaves.

"Agent Hanlon, I found the answer to your question. I know why the device is pointing to me. The device doesn't open portals to other universes. I do."

16 BLU

Clutching my coffee like the life-giving extract it was, I made it out of my apartment and to the Captain's office right on time. As we took our seats, four trainees walked into the office. They clustered uncomfortably at the door, and the four of us exchanged glances. What the hell was the Captain up to?

"Come in, come in," she said, gesturing for them to sit down at the table. Jack nodded to a small girl named Willow who I had trained once or twice, and she made a beeline for the seat next to him. A giggling girl from training the other morning pulled a chair as close to Ink as she could without sitting in his lap, and I rolled my eyes. The douche trainee I'd bashed in the face sat as far away from me as possible, and the last guy stood there like he had no idea what to do.

"Dev," Captain said to him, "come sit next to Styx—you'll be working with her today."

Styx looked at the Captain questioningly but pulled up a chair for Dev anyway.

The Captain continued, addressing the trainees. "The Team did not know that you were joining us today, which is why they look surprised. Under better circumstances, we would go about this differently, but since Jurisdiction seems to be accelerating their plans, we need to accelerate your training. It goes without saying that what we are about to discuss is top secret; only those in this room need to know. The Team works on trust, and violating that trust means expulsion from the

Compound. You four have shown aptitude in your training. So here you are."

She looked each trainee in the eye, waiting for them to verbally acknowledge that they understood. This somewhat archaic practice kept anyone from the age-old "I didn't know" excuse. When it came to secrecy, the Captain and the Team didn't fuck around, which made the mole situation so much more horrible.

The Captain continued, "Team, I'm sorry to spring this on you, but unfortunately my contacts do not have any indication of where the new Jurisdiction facility is supposed to be built, or even if its construction has begun. All we know is what Blu was able to retrieve—that the building will be in the High Governor's territory. At least that narrows the area, somewhat. Unfortunately, the territory is still too much ground for the four of you to cover. We are short on options and time. Therefore, and to give the trainees some real-world experience, I'm pairing you up for a reconnaissance mission. Then the eight of you will split up for your own missions. This is only until we can gather more information. Trainees, this is your time to show the Team what you can do and how well you can listen."

I was about to object. These kids had barely any training. Other training groups had more experience, even if they were younger. More importantly, the other trainees didn't include a douche canoe who I'd had to bash in the face and a girl who looked like she wanted nothing more than to crawl into Ink's lap. Ink caught my eye and shook his head subtly. There was something else going on here; I kept my mouth shut.

The Captain gave us our assignments, pairing Dev with Styx, Willow with Jack on the east side of the city, douche Bullfrog with Ink on the west side, and the giggling girl, Silver, with me.

Silver made the mistake of interrupting the Captain. "Wouldn't it make more sense if Ink and I—"

"Missions are not the time to play footsie, Silver. The faster you learn that this is not a singles mingle, the better."

I stifled a laugh. Silver at least had the sense to look chagrinned. Ink kept his face blank, although his eyes betrayed his embarrassment. I was going to give him monstrous amounts of shit for this.

"Trainees, go get geared up and meet back at the Quad in an hour. Team, stick around for a minute, if you would."

The trainees left, looking shell-shocked. I was dying to tease Ink, but the Captain looked more serious than usual. Styx was the first to ask.

"Captain, I'm not one to complain about getting some help, but there are fully trained Team members out there who we can lean on for this mission. Why the newbies?"

"And especially why *those* newbies?" I added. "I mean, the recon will be hard enough without having to watch my back from getting stabbed by some poor girl who has her priorities out of whack."

"You mean she'll get you killed because she's not paying attention?" Jack asked.

"No, she'll stab me in the back so she can get into Ink's tighty-whities."

"You can get into my tighty-whities anytime, B," Ink said with a smirk and a wink.

Styx threw up her arms in irritation. "Ugh! Can you not stop thinking with your man jewels for just one second?"

"Nope."

"Enough." The Captain didn't have to yell to get our attention, and we all stopped talking immediately. Although we were used to the Captain allowing us some good-natured taunting during our meetings, she was not having it today. We mumbled our apologies.

"I understand that using these trainees is not ideal, and I understand two of these particular trainees are a bit . . . problematic. Unfortunately, I'm running out of options. The information that is leaking from the Compound is top secret, which means that the mole must be a member of the Team. Expanding this mission to more members of the Team risks the information getting out, and we can't take that risk, which means that we cannot use other Team members. Regardless of their personal idiosyncrasies, these trainees have shown the most aptitude for this type of mission. All of you are the best we have here at the Compound, and so these newbies will be well trained."

She looked around the room, meeting each of us in the eye to cement her point. Our personal feelings regarding these trainees didn't matter. The Captain thought that they would be good assets, and so we would oblige—especially since she normally didn't press matters like this.

"Remember," she said, "the goal is to find out where the building is to be located and survey the area. Do not engage with Jurisdiction minions if you see them. Stay out of sight. We find the location quickly, then reconvene for next steps. No heroics. Do I make myself understood?" She looked directly at me. I nodded. You burn down one summer cottage . . .

After a few minutes of discussing some of the specifics of the mission, and a special conversation regarding what Silver and I would be doing, we were dismissed. Styx ran back to the tech building to get ear comms for all of us, and to program our palmboxes with recon tech, and the rest of us headed back toward our apartments to gear up.

When we reached our building, Ink caught my eye and motioned that I should go to his room. Once inside, I noticed he looked troubled.

"Look," I started, "I was just giving you shit about Silver. She's a nice enough girl—"

"I don't care about her," he said with a shake of his head. "This whole thing with the newbies doesn't feel right. The Captain would never pair us up with trainees for this sort of mission. It just doesn't make sense. We could cover more ground without them slowing us down. And something else . . . She said that the mole had to be someone on the Team, but she made it seem like she knew who it was."

"You think she knows?"

Ink nodded. "I think she has her suspicions. And that's why I think the trainees are coming with us. If she suspects someone, but needs proof, what would be the best way to get it?"

"By having someone catch the spy in the act."

"And the only way that she could catch someone on the Team—"

"—would be to pair them up with someone who would rat them out to get ahead. Someone who has no personal attachment to us."

"Bingo."

I thought about what he was saying, and it made sense. The Team was a tight-knit group, and the Captain knew that. If one of us was the mole, she couldn't be sure that the rest of us wouldn't try to cover for them or take care of it ourselves. However, the trainees didn't have that sort of loyalty to us— not yet anyway. Case in point: two of the trainees hated me already, so if they thought I was the mole, they'd turn me in to the Captain in a heartbeat.

"But why do you think she suspects it's one of us?"

Ink ran his hand through his hair, making his bed head even more pronounced. "Only the five of us knew you were infiltrating the party, but somehow the Second Counselor knew you were there and that you would be in disguise."

"That's assuming he knows who I am—and that's a pretty big assumption." Ink shrugged, and I continued, "But I know I'm not the spy, and I'm pretty sure you're not the spy. You can't lie to save your life."

"Yes, I can!"

"No, you can't. You can't even lie about which girl you bring home—you get busted every single time."

Ink looked like he was going to argue; I held up a hand to stop him.

"But that's beside the point. You were ready to kill someone when my original blueprints mission was compromised, so I can safely rule you out. That leaves Styx or Jack, and there's no way they are spies. I can't accept that.

"So, assuming that the four of us aren't the spies, then you're right. Something isn't adding up with the trainees. Maybe she thinks that one of *them* is a mole?"

"If one of these kids is the spy, then that puts us all in danger," Ink replied. "Regardless, there is some weird shit happening right now, so watch your back, B."

"You too, my friend. And I'll try not to kill your girlfriend in the process."

He grinned and ruffled what was left of my hair. Jerk.

"She means well, B. She's just young and misguided. I can't help being such a sexy beast."

"Yes, yes you can."

We met at the Quad an hour later, wearing our combat gear. Although it was already midmorning and the sun was shining, my arms were chilled by the spring breeze. My chosen gear—black leggings, boots, and black tank top—was meant for stealth and not necessarily for warmth. I rubbed my arms to get the circulation going and tried find a patch of sunlight to stand in. Ink saw me shivering and mouthed "wuss." I thought about throwing one of my daggers at him. Eventually I decided against it; re-strapping them to my thighs was more trouble than he was worth.

Styx was handing out palmboxes, each loaded with as much surveillance tech as she and Dev could think of to help in our search for the building. For their mission, they would attempt to hack into the Jurisdiction system, which would allow them to scan thousands of cameras in the area and possibly point Ink or Jack in the right direction. If they couldn't hack in, then they would be our ears if things went to shit and we needed an extraction or backup. And things always went to shit.

Silver and I had a different sort of reconnaissance mission. While the others were searching areas, we were going to be talking to people. It had been bothering me since my mission at the Jurisdiction satellite office that vagrants were living that far out from the city center. I was hoping that their presence meant something, and paying them some coin might convince them to talk to us. Not the most methodical plan, but it was a start.

It was time to get this show on the road. "You ready to go?"

Silver didn't respond; she just buckled her seat belt. My car was small and black, and I'd built it (with Ink's help) from the frame up, using parts that we had salvaged and saved for years. I didn't love many material items, but I loved my car, especially since it was such a rare commodity. After the war, cars were hard to come by. There were only a handful of manufacturers left in the whole world, and they catered to the Jurisdiction elite. If you didn't have tons of coin, you had to walk or build one yourself. I didn't mind so much; it rattled and wheezed, but it was mine.

The Compound was lucky in that a lot of the Team had their own cars, and there were a variety of vehicles for Compound use. We needed them for most missions, since the

Compound was so far from the city center, and we rotated them out as best as we could so that they weren't recognizable. Besides, they didn't last too long—the territory's roads were a disaster. At any given moment, a road could end in a crater or swallow the front end of your car in a giant pothole. The roads in the city center were better than some, but still littered with giant slabs of concrete and potholes. Out here there were more fallen branches than bricks, and I steered carefully around them.

I always wondered why the territory's roads were such shit. The Captain told me that one of Jurisdiction's first acts of war was to destroy all the roads, including the highways connecting the cities within the territories. Without roads or cars, people were stuck where they were. They had effectively isolated the populations, which helped Jurisdiction control them. It made sense, and it pissed me off. Thanks to Jurisdiction's assholery, getting supplies between cities was nearly impossible, and people were starving. Jurisdiction didn't care about that; they had fleets of cars, as well as a couple of flying machines. They used them to travel between territories and continents, keeping an eye on their handpicked local rulers. Right now, I really wanted a flying machine as we hit another pothole. I cursed under my breath. Maybe I could convince the Captain to let me steal one.

17 FARA

Calum and I sat on the couch, staring at the leaves he had reverently laid on the coffee table. It was still dark in the living room, the only light coming from the purple lava lamp lazily bubbling in the corner.

Figuring we weren't going back to sleep anytime soon, I broke our reverie to make us a pot of coffee. When I got back, I asked Calum what had happened before he had woken me up. He told me that he had turned off the movie and fallen asleep after me on the couch. He wasn't sure how long he was out, but he woke up because he thought I was talking to him. Then he noticed a shimmer of light in front of my face. He thought he might still be dreaming, but the shimmer of light began to grow, and he felt a breeze and smelled cologne—just as I'd told him earlier. The shimmer kept getting bigger, turning into the window, and he noticed a faint thread of light connecting the window to me.

"That's when I woke you up. I was freaking out. When you described what you experienced earlier, it never occurred to me that I'd be able to see it. I don't know what I expected . . . but not that."

I shook my head, still not quite believing what we had just seen. "At least now I know I'm not hallucinating."

"So, those leaves are from a parallel universe?"

I picked up the leaves carefully, turning them over in my hand. They didn't look or smell any different from the leaves outside. They weren't purple with yellow dots or anything like that. I handed them to Calum, and he studied them as well.

"How do we know that you didn't just open a window to Vermont? Or California?" He looked at the leaves like they were going to get up and walk away.

"Even if it's just a window to the park across the street, it's still really weird."

"True."

"Anyway, I don't know how to explain it, but I think I've been doing this for a long time."

"What do you mean? If it's been going on for a while, why did Agent Hanlon just show up now?"

I had been thinking about that since I woke up, remembering things, and I had a theory.

"Do you remember my nightmares? The ones I had when I was a kid?"

Calum nodded. He'd often crashed at my place growing up, and he had heard about them at more than one breakfast.

I told him I could never remember the specifics of them when I woke up, but they always had this certain *feel* to them. They were different to my other dreams, but I can't describe how. They started when I was about seven years old. According to Agent Hanlon's timeline, that would have been right around the time my mom got the device, or right after it.

I took a sip of my coffee and realized that it needed more sugar.

"Whenever I had one of those 'special' dreams, my mom would come into my room and stay with me for the rest of the night. But I think that she never came in for any other bad dream I would have, just the ones that felt different. Even if I didn't cry out, she came into my room like she knew. I figured it was mother's intuition." My eyes rimmed with tears. "Even later, when I was a teen, and I hated that she came in, she just said she 'needed to check on her special girl.' And I yelled at her."

I shook my head and hoped wherever she was, she forgave me for being an asshole of a teenager.

The words came faster now. "I always thought she was just being overprotective, but maybe it was something more? Maybe the device was alerting her, like it is now, and that's how she knew. Maybe the first time it happened, she came in and saw a window like we did, and that's why she came in every time after that. She would have known that being able to open portals put me in danger, if she could do it too. She needed to keep it secret, or the government would take me and probably never let me go."

Calum looked skeptical. "But once she died and the government took the device back, why didn't they come get you? If the dreams are causing the portals somehow, and the device picks up on them, why did they leave you alone for years? Why is this happening now?"

"I wish I knew. It's like I'm grasping at anything that makes sense. I don't know *how* this is happening or why it has started again now after four years. But somehow, deep down, I'm causing this."

I knew I sounded crazy. While I felt certain that everything was connected somehow, the connection was tenuous, at best. Calum was quiet as we both stared at the tree leaves. They looked so ordinary.

"I believe you," he said finally. "It sounds fucking insane, but I believe you."

My shoulders drooped. I hadn't realized how badly I needed him to believe me. I threw my arms around his neck, burying my head in his shoulder. He hugged me back, then pulled away with a concerned look.

"Is Agent Hanlon coming over?"

"He said he was."

"OK, then I need to say this before he gets here. If you're right about this, then I'm terrified about what comes next. In every book or movie or TV show about people having crazy abilities, when the government gets their hands on them, it doesn't end well. *Firestarter, ET*—even the Avengers had to deal with the government using them. Agent Hanlon seems like he's less of a shithead than most, but I don't trust him not to snatch you up and run tests on you."

"He won't."

"How can you say that? You can't trust anyone!"

"I don't trust him a hundred percent, but I also don't think he's going to experiment on me."

"He might not, but he reports to people who might want to. If you're really opening up portals to other universes, then you're capable of things that people have only imagined. You literally have universes at your fingertips. Once that gets out, no one who wants that power will let you live in peace."

"They know where I work and where I live—well, used to live. What do you want me to do? I don't even have an apartment to hide out in!"

Calum grabbed my hands in his, his green eyes burning into mine. "I need you to promise me that if you think things are going to shit, even for just one second, you'll run to where they will never find you. Promise me that right now."

"And what? Leave you all behind?"

"Say it out loud, Fara. Swear that you will run away, without looking back, not to me or Adora or Beck. That you will disappear and never come back. I need to keep you safe. Promise me, right now. If anyone finds out that you are the one creating portals, there will be a war to control you that you will have no say in. At best, whoever gets you will lock you up so that you have to do what they say."

"I'm not an idiot, Calum. I won't just do what they want because they ask nicely."

"Fara, all they would have to do is threaten to hurt me, or Adora, or Beck, and you would help them however you could. Not because you'd be afraid for yourself, but because you'd be afraid for us. I can't live with that on my conscience."

"But I can't do it on command! I don't even know how this works! I mean—we just figured out what this was, like, three seconds ago!"

"They could keep you asleep for *the rest of your life*, Fara, and you would let them if it meant keeping us safe. Promise me that you'll run at the first sign of trouble."

He was right, and I knew he was right, but did he really understand what he was asking? He knew that if it meant hurting myself to keep the people I loved safe, I wouldn't even think twice. He also knew that I didn't take promises lightly, and that was why he was making me promise.

I took a deep breath. "I promise you that I will run away if it looks like I'm in danger."

Calum visibly relaxed. "OK, then, what's the plan?"

There was a knock on the door, and Calum answered it. Agent Hanlon walked in, once again looking like some sort of athletic wear advertisement in track pants, and a T-shirt that was so tight, it looked like it was going to shred itself at any moment. Did they not make shirts his size? His muscles were nice and all, but it was a bit ridiculous.

Calum got him a cup of coffee, and he took a seat in the chair, took a deep breath, and said, "Tell me everything." And so I did.

When I was done, Agent Hanlon sat quietly, and I started to worry—caught between needing him to believe me and freaking the fuck out that somehow I was creating portals to parallel universes. If anyone found out it was me . . . I didn't want to think about it.

"Well, that makes this situation more complicated. Have you been able to replicate it?"

My brain short-circuited for a second. He hadn't even flinched.

"You believe me? You have to admit it's pretty out there."

"It is no more 'out there' than that I am currently in possession of a device from a parallel universe, or that your mother was able to travel between universes. It actually means the readings I took at your apartment make more sense now."

"So, now that you know, are you going to run experiments on me like some kind of alien at Area 51?"

Although I was trying to make light of the situation, Agent Hanlon didn't laugh, and that worried me. It must mean that I was close to the truth. And Calum had been right.

"Agent Hanlon, are you going to bring me in?"

"Those are my orders."

Calum immediately put himself between me and Agent Hanlon, his fists in balls at his sides, but Agent Hanlon held up his hands in a placating manner.

"Mr. Ames, I'm not going to bring her in, so if you would let me finish before you do something really stupid, I would appreciate it."

Calum waited a couple of heartbeats before sitting back down, his body still tense—and I sent a little prayer to the universe that whatever Agent Hanlon was about to say would help calm this potentially ugly situation.

"I'm not going to bring you in for questioning," he said, "although this new information does complicate things. As you know, I brought the results from your apartment scan to the assistant to see if she could make heads or tails of it. She immediately took the information to my department head and convinced him that the only way they were going to get any answers was to bring you in for questioning. I was less than pleased with how they want to handle your 'interrogation.' The assistant insisted that she would be able to get you to confess to hiding a device, and my superior agreed with her. They asked me to bring you in today. But I would rather have more information on what it is that you can do before turning you over to her."

Calum looked tense, but at least he didn't look like he was going to start a fight with Agent Hanlon. "How much does she know?" he asked.

Agent Hanlon paused. I gave him a little nudge.

"Agent Hanlon, if she is going to dissect me like a frog, I would like to know what I'm up against."

He looked genuinely startled at that analogy—the first time I had seen anything other than a calm, albeit tired demeanor.

"The assistant only knows of the first time the device alarm went off, and that the reading at your apartment pointed to you. Since I have the device with me, she doesn't know that the alarm has gone off the other two times."

"Because you don't trust her," Calum said.

Agent Hanlon nodded.

"Can you just tell her that the device was malfunctioning and that I have nothing to do with this?"

"I can keep the device for a bit longer. I'll stall the assistant and my superiors, although I'm not sure how long that will work. I'll have to give the device back to them eventually, and as soon as you open another portal, they'll bring you in—with or without me."

"It sounds like I need to figure out how to stop myself from creating the portals in my sleep, or at least control it so that I don't make the device go off anymore. Not to mention the two goons in the sedan. Did you find out anything about them?"

"I do have a lead. Ever heard of Barrington Park? The man who owns that global technology company, Specter COMS?"

Where had I heard that name before? I ran to find my purse, and after digging around, I pulled out the business card Douche had given me during my last shift. In all the chaos I had forgotten about it. I handed the card to Agent Hanlon, and he didn't seem pleased.

"Where did you get this?"

"Douche gave it to me during my last shift. Said this guy gave it to him and asked that it be passed on to me, specifically. Do you think the goons work for him?"

"I'm almost positive. Who's Douche?"

"My boss at The Grill. He deserves the name."

"He deserves worse," added Calum, "but Douche is what stuck."

The corner of Agent Hanlon's mouth went up, but as soon as the shadow of a smile started, it stopped. A piece of me was disappointed. He had the nicest mouth—and I could not believe I just thought that. My world was crumbling, I might be kidnapped by a guy with a name that sounded like a suburban subdivision, but I was thinking about Agent Hanlon's mouth. I needed to get my priorities straight.

Agent Hanlon flipped the card over, reading the handwritten note. "My department has been keeping an eye on him for years, and his company has been a personal project of mine since I started."

"Why?" I asked. "I know he's like a bazillionaire, but I thought he only manufactured communication stuff. Why would the government be interested in him?"

"Mr. Park's business is almost impenetrable, which raises my suspicions that he doesn't necessarily play by the same rules as everyone else. He has a lot of contacts at the Department of Defense, and he is a major contributor to many senators' campaigns. He golfs with the governor at least every couple of months. Anytime we try to get information about his business, we are met with an army of lawyers and a request from a senator or three to back off. We know that his technology—his real technology—is not communications but weapons. But no one can get close enough to find out the specifics."

"That's all great," Calum said, "but how would this Barrington Park know about Fara? The only way you figured out she had something to do with it was from the device."

"I don't know for sure, but I'm going to try to find out today. In the meantime, Miss Bayne, you need to stay here."

"OK, Bossy McBosserson."

The muscle in his jaw twitched and he slumped a bit. "If you would be so kind, Miss Bayne," he tried again, "I would appreciate you staying in the apartment today while I get some more information. It would also be most beneficial if you could work on this ability you seem to possess. Would that be amenable to you?"

I rolled my eyes. "Whatever. It's fine. I'll work on that today—I have the day off. Calum, do you have to work?"

"Yeah, but I can call in sick."

"No, I'll be OK. I won't leave here, and I'll work on replicating opening the portal when I'm awake. If I can, maybe I can figure out how it works and stop it when I'm sleeping. It's a long shot, but I don't have any better ideas."

Agent Hanlon stood. "I'll grab your mother's file. Maybe there is something in it that will help you figure out this ability of yours. I'll also review a list of the original scientists who tested the device and see if I can get any leads regarding the goons in the sedan, or Mr. Park. I would like to stay here while Calum is gone, if you don't mind, to make sure that you don't have any surprises."

Calum and I exchanged looks. Did I really trust Agent Hanlon not to drag me in to the government once Calum left for work? He had already passed up multiple opportunities to haul me in, and hadn't. He also told me he wouldn't—and I believed him. Anyway, he was all we had.

"OK, Agent Hanlon. I mostly trust that you aren't going to sell me out. Yet."

● ● ●

Once Agent Hanlon left, Calum asked if I needed to go back to sleep, but I was afraid to. What if I opened another portal and it sent the Barrington Park guys our way? Plus, my mind was racing too much—it would be a miracle to fall asleep now. I asked him to put on another giant pot of coffee, and I told him that I was going to text Beck.

"Has he texted you since your apartment was trashed?" he asked.

"No. Why?"

"Then I wouldn't bother."

I knew Calum didn't like Beck, but something else was going on, and Calum was keeping it from me.

"What's your deal? You've been pissed at him since that night my apartment was trashed. What happened?"

"Do you really want the truth?"

"Of course I want the truth! He's my boyfriend, damnit!"

Calum looked at me, pity in his eyes. "No, he isn't. Not really."

I stopped dead in my tracks, my heart plummeting. I had a feeling I knew what Calum was about to say, and I didn't want to hear it—even though I needed to.

"What are you talking about?"

Calum paused, seeming to choose his words very carefully. "When I told Beck what had happened to your apartment, he asked about his guitar and his stuff."

"Yeah. So?"

151

"He didn't ask about you. At all. He didn't ask if you were hurt, or if you were there when they ransacked your place. He didn't ask where you were going to stay, or if you had called the police. Nothing. And when I finally told him that you were OK and staying with me, his only response was 'Well, you finally got what you wanted.' And then he told me to tell you not to bother texting him. I'm so, so sorry, Fara."

I put my coffee down on the table. My brain could not process what was happening. Did Beck just break up with me *through Calum*? I looked at my phone—I had a voicemail from an unknown number, but nothing from Beck. Were we over and I didn't know it? Was this why he hadn't responded to anything I had sent the past couple of days? Was he ghosting me?

"When were you going to tell me?"

"I was hoping I wouldn't have to. I hoped he would man up and call you. Or that he'd respond to your texts eventually."

I didn't say anything. I couldn't say anything. Calum went to hug me, but I dodged him, grabbed my coffee, and headed to the bathroom so that I could sob in peace. I didn't have it in me to hear Calum say "I told you so" because I knew he would be right—and I was an idiot.

I filled up the bathtub with water as hot as I could take it, stripped down, and submerged myself. I leaned my head back, reveling in the heat and steam, and waited for the tears.

But they didn't come.

I waited to be sad, heartbroken, but all I felt was this pinprick of anger. It started in my stomach and worked its way up until it was a throbbing in my head. Then, when the pressure was almost unbearable, it exploded, and for the first time in as long as I could remember, I was so enraged I felt like my body would ignite.

My boyfriend, the one who I had financially supported and taken care of without ever asking for anything in return, the one who I worked double shifts for and didn't fix my car so that he could go out drinking with his friends. The one who couldn't remember to text me when he went out, who abused my kindness and allowed me to doubt myself. The one who was nothing more than a parasite. That boyfriend? I had given up almost a year of my life to him—and now he didn't have the fucking decency to have an adult conversation with me? He thought that I was going to fuck Calum, like I was a prize to be passed around. No way. It was easier to let the rage fill me up than accept the reality that I had let myself be taken advantage of yet again. When I got out of the bathtub, I was going to call him, and I was going to tell him *exactly* what I felt. I was going to burn him down.

I jumped as Calum banged on the door. "Fara, are you OK? Agent Hanlon is on the phone. He says the device is going nuts again."

I opened my eyes to see another window in front of my face.

"Holy shit! Calum, I opened another portal!"

He came running into the bathroom, and we both stared at the window that was hovering right around my face.

"How?" he whispered.

"I don't know! I was thinking about Beck and I got really mad, like burn his place down mad—as if he had a place to burn down—and then you banged on the door."

We looked at the window, and then he went to the opposite end of the tub, looking puzzled.

"I can't see it from this direction. I can only see you. Agent Hanlon? It's another portal. Yeah, OK. I'll tell her."

I sat straight up and looked through the window, expecting to see the tree-lined path again, but that wasn't what I was looking at. Instead, I saw two white buildings flanking an open green space, like a park. There were people standing in the green space in groups, although I couldn't make out anything specific about them.

Calum came back to my side of the tub and started to reach his hand into the window when, all of a sudden, it closed. I hadn't meant for it to close, just like I hadn't meant for it to open, and I wondered how either of those things had happened. At the same time, I realized that I was naked. Very, very naked.

"Uh . . . sorry. Excuse me," I said as I stood up and grabbed a towel. Calum started to leave the bathroom, an unspoken understanding that we would talk about what just happened about the portal but only after I found my underthings (as Agent Hanlon called them). He reached the doorway and stopped.

"This would have been a dream come true in high school."

"What?"

"I would have cut off an appendage to see you naked then."

"Glad it didn't come to that, and that you still have all your appendages."

He smiled at me as I tried to wrap his pitiful towel around myself.

"You know you're beautiful, right?"

I waved him off. "You probably say that to all the girls who can open portals to other universes while naked in your bathroom."

He chuckled softly and walked out. I scrambled to get dressed. I needed to see if Calum had seen what I did, and if I could recreate it again—but with clothes on, this time.

I walked out of the bathroom, clothed, with my cold coffee in hand. Calum already had the pot waiting and switched mugs with me, handing me a hot one.

"What did Agent Hanlon say?"

"He said he was in his car, so no one else heard the device go off. And he wanted to let you know that he saw the two goons sitting on the street outside of my apartment, and not to leave under any circumstances until he got here."

"Did you call him Bossy McBosserson?"

Calum cocked an eyebrow at me but didn't respond. I shrugged. I wasn't planning on leaving anyway—it just irritated me that Agent Hanlon was so bossy. Was my irritation rational? No. Was it probably misplaced anger from the lack of control in my life currently? Probably. Did I care? Not so much. But how had those two goons known where to find me? They must have a device or something—unless they had been questioning people. The only two people who knew where I was were Adora and Beck. Ugh—Beck. I didn't want to think about him right now.

I collapsed onto the couch. "OK—so that was weird, right?"

"What part?"

"The opening the portal in the bathroom part! We assumed that I've been opening up the portals by dreaming, but I definitely wasn't dreaming in the bathtub. So—what did you see when you looked in the window?"

He thought about it, his artist's mind painting a picture for him to describe. "I saw an open green space, and two buildings in the distance. They were white and dirty—concrete and stone, I think? They were old and almost falling apart. And I saw some people standing around in the open space. There were probably a dozen of them or so."

"Did you get a good look at the people?"

"I couldn't make out any specifics—it was like they were blurry."

"I thought that too. OK. Did you smell the cologne?"

"Not this time."

"Me either. Did you see a path or trees or anything?"

He thought about it. "I didn't—although the perspective was the same. Like the eye-level of someone standing."

"That's a good point. It's not like looking up, or down from the sky. The perspective is, well, people height. Huh. So, since it was different scenery, do you think it was the same universe? Or did I accidentally open a portal to a different universe where people are blurry and all buildings are dirty?"

Calum laughed. "I don't know. The only other window I saw was last night, and the lighting was different. Like it was nighttime and the path was lit by artificial lights of some sort. This window looked like the lighting was around dawn—but I could be guessing. Do other universes have the same twenty-four-hour cycle we do? I'd assume, because of scientific universal truths, they would have to. Is it weird to say that this window 'felt' like the other one? I don't know how else to describe it."

We were having the weirdest conversation in the most normal way: like you would talk about going to the grocery store or what songs were on the radio, we were talking about the day-night cycle of a parallel universe. Is this how humans coped with extreme things? To try to normalize them?

Calum interrupted my train of thought. "How do you feel? I mean—does it hurt to open the portals?"

"No. I mean, I feel tired, but that's because we only got a couple of hours of sleep. I really don't feel any different."

"That's good to know. It's not like one of those superpowers that drains you, and you'll need a restorative sleep or anything. I guess that makes sense because it comes from sleep—or sometimes comes from sleep."

"I'm not part of the Justice League, Calum. I'm not sure what I do is considered a superpower."

He grinned. "But you have to admit, it's pretty fucking cool."

I grinned back at him. He always looked at the bright side of everything, and I loved that about him. And it would have been pretty cool if I wasn't being hunted for possible government experiments.

"So . . . want to talk about the Beck thing? Or do you think it will make you open another portal?"

"I *want* to open another portal, but on purpose. I might as well talk about it. But I honestly don't know what to say. That you and Adora were right? That I'm not as sad as I should be, but I'm angry as hell that I let my insecurities dictate my choice in boyfriend? That I'm tired of allowing myself to be shit on—by Hewitt, by Douche, by Beck? I'm tired of allowing others to fight my battles for me, and this one time where I could have stood up for myself and broken up with him—I didn't. I worked my butt off to give him everything, all because I wanted him to love me. I'm so mad at myself for feeling grateful that he would even choose me. How could I have been so stupid?" I punched a pillow for emphasis. It didn't open a portal, but Calum was looking at me with a hint of a smile.

"What? I'm pouring my heart out and you're smiling at me? Don't be a dick, Calum!"

He held up his hands and laughed. "This is the first time I've seen you feeling anything other than defeated in forever. I'm enjoying it."

I threw the pillow at him. "Why are you being such an asshole?"

"I'm not! I mean—I'm not happy that you're hurt or that you feel that way, but I'm relieved that you are finally *feeling* something. You spend so much time making sure that others are happy that you don't ever express how *you* are feeling. It's nice to see you're human." He ruffled my hair, and I smacked his hand away.

"And about Beck," he continued, "you weren't stupid—you were kind and he took advantage of that. That's on him, not you, OK? And I really am sorry that he turned out to be such a selfish bastard. You deserve better. Remember that."

I looked around again—no portal. Calum noticed too.

"It didn't work. No portal."

I slouched down into the couch. After almost immediate success in opening a portal, I was hoping it was going to be that easy every time. Apparently not. We talked about Beck some more, but nothing. I was back to feeling numb; disappointed in myself and tired. Really, really tired.

BLU 18

We pulled up a block away from Jurisdiction's satellite office and parked between an old dumpster and some building rubble. Before getting out of the car, Silver scanned the surrounding areas to see if there were any immediate dangers. Good.

"See anything?" I asked her.

"There are two cameras on either side of that abandoned restaurant," she said. "One is facing Jurisdiction's office and the other is facing that wreck of a building."

"Can we get where we need to go without the cameras spotting us?"

She studied our surroundings; then she nodded. As we picked our way through the piles of concrete and brick toward the alley, rats scattered away through the trash. As I'd noticed during my first mission to retrieve the blueprints, this part of the city was still in ruins. Why were vagrants here? And why had Jurisdiction set up an office here?

We stopped just outside of the alley, and I could hear low voices coming from it. I checked my ear comm.

"Styx—you there?"

"Yep! What's up, B?"

"We're heading into the alley. Do you have eyes on the area?"

"We are still trying to break in. Those asshats changed the code again, so it's taking longer than we thought."

"We're pretty hidden back here, so we'll go in. Squawk if you see anything—I don't want to be running for my life again. Three times in as many days is too much."

"OK, ladies. Be careful and happy hunting."

I spoke to Silver in a low voice. "Why do you think that the vagrants are here?"

"I'm not sure."

"Doesn't it strike you as odd? Considering how far away from the city center we are, and how there is no discernable food source around here. Other than a couple of office buildings and the Jurisdiction building, there isn't anything out this way—so why are they here?"

She studied her surroundings like the building debris would give her the answer.

"It's weird."

"That's why we're here, because it is weird. So we need to be careful in how we interact with them. Most of these folks have been displaced by Jurisdiction in some way or another, but that doesn't mean that they can't be bribed or tortured into telling them about our whereabouts. We need to find out why they are here, but we also need to find out if they have seen or heard anything coming out of that office."

Silver looked doubtful. It was a long shot.

According to the information Jack had been able to gather, neither Dagna nor Jyston was at the satellite office this morning, leaving only the Jurisdiction grunts performing their bureaucratic evil: sinister paper-filing, that sort of thing. With the real baddies gone, Silver and I had a couple of hours to ask questions and scout around a bit. Time to go to work.

I entered the alley to see a homeless shanty town where there hadn't been just a few days ago. Cardboard boxes and other debris were stacked up against the walls of the narrow alley, creating makeshift homes. Seeing them living like this, after the

High Governor's masquerade ball, stoked my anger, although if I was honest, there was probably a homeless population before the war. It's just easier to have an enemy that is tangible than to chalk up people's misfortune to societal apathy.

The group of about fifteen people stopped talking as soon as Silver and I walked into the alley. They eyed us warily, reaching into their tattered clothes for improvised weapons— sharpened pieces of metal or pipes. I held up my hands to show them that we meant no harm and nudged Silver to do the same thing. If I had to, I could kill each one of them and get out of here alive, with my bare hands—but that didn't mean I wanted it to go down that way.

"Easy. We're just here to talk."

"We don't want to fucking talk to you," said the woman closest to us. She was wearing three different sweaters and had a giant bruise on her cheek.

"I have coin attached to my belt, and I'm going to reach for it now. You can have it if you answer some questions. If the answers are helpful, I have more."

A particularly wild-eyed man looked me up and down, track marks on his arm indicating that he had more than blood running through his veins.

"What makes you think we won't just take it from you, after we have our way with you and your pretty friend?"

"Because she's from the Compound, you idiot," someone behind him said, "and could flay you alive before you realized you were in trouble." The crowd parted to let the person through. The first thing I noticed was his eye-patch, along with a mess of red hair and a matted beard that hung to his chest. He was a full head shorter than the wild-eyed guy, but everyone gave him a wide berth.

He continued, "The question you really should be asking is, why would the Captain send her principal Team member to talk to our lot? And what will they give us for not telling Jurisdiction that they're here?"

"We'll let you live," Silver said with deadly calm.

"She's right, if not a little less diplomatic than I'd hoped," I added. "And like I said, we also have coin for you."

"Well then, step into my office."

We followed him through the crowd to a three-sided lean-to. As he ducked inside, Silver stood lookout at the doorway. Smart; she was starting to grow on me. I followed the guy inside.

The guy who resembled a pirate looked at me expectantly, and I threw the coins onto the pallet in the center of the lean-to. He picked them up quickly and tied them to his belt.

"What do you want to know?"

"Why are you here? At this location? It's so far from the city center."

"If you hadn't noticed, there's a homeless problem. There's more space here."

I closed the distance between us so that I was standing directly in his personal space.

"Stop lying to me, I'm not stupid. You can't get food easily here, or really anything else. This is a horrible location for scavenging, and you know it—so *why* are you here?"

He studied me for a minute, then shrugged and slumped onto an upturned crate. "We were asked to be."

"By whom?"

"Ah ah ah! I know how to play this game. An answer for an answer. What is so important that the Captain sent her principal Team member to interview a bunch of homeless folks?"

This was the second time he'd mentioned the Captain— how did he know her? I tried to answer carefully.

"We both felt that your presence this far out of the city center was an anomaly, and it's the Team's job to make sure that anomalies don't become catastrophes, if you get my meaning."

He nodded, thoughtful. "That earned you one answer. Jurisdiction moved us here. They offered us the abandoned restaurant over there, but we like the alley better because it's easier to monitor people coming and going."

"Who at Jurisdiction asked you to come?"

He shook his head. "You first. Does the Captain still run the Team?"

"Yes. Now, who asked you to move?"

"Dagna."

That made me pause. Why would Dagna move a bunch of homeless people to squat outside of Jurisdiction's satellite office? That wasn't her style.

"Did she give you any orders? Is she paying you?"

"Patience, girlie. My turn. What is the Team working on right now that has the Compound so paranoid?"

How did he know that the Compound was "paranoid"? How did he know anything about the Compound at all? Or the Team for that matter? Was our leak bigger than we thought? And to answer his question; should I tell the truth or lie? I decided that telling the truth, while risky, was the only path I could see to find out if he knew anything about the new Jurisdiction building, even if it meant that he might report it back to Dagna.

"We learned that Jurisdiction is going to build some kind of work camp for children. Obviously, we want to stop that. You wouldn't know where it's going to be, would you?"

His eyes got wide; it was the first sign of emotion he had shown. Something about the kids was bothering him, above just the sheer atrocity of a prison for kids.

"She promised to not kill us slowly if we did what she asked. No, I have no information about that work camp. If

I did, I'd give it to you for free." He looked at me. His eyes were a clear light blue and full of intelligence. How did he end up here? I had so many questions, but I knew my time was limited.

"One last question. What were Dagna's orders?"

I heard a rustle of clothes, a muffled scream, and a deep voice that drawled:

"To spy on me, I suppose."

Jyston, his hair loose and dressed in black combat gear, was holding Silver by the hair with a dagger to her throat. My daggers were in my hands before I realized it.

"Second Counselor, what a . . . surprise. I can't say I expected to see you here."

He looked over my shoulder. "You probably don't want to do that." I heard metal hit the ground. Whether the pirate guy had been planning to stab Jyston or me, I didn't know or really care. I needed to get Silver and get out of here.

She started to struggle but I caught her eye and shook my head. She was no match for Jyston yet, and the more she fought, the more likely he would kill her.

"I'd love to talk, but I'm having a hard time focusing when there's a dagger to my friend's throat."

"Ah yes, that might cause a bit of anxiety. How about this: you drop your daggers and I'll drop mine, and then we can have a nice little chat?"

I dropped the daggers to the ground, and he gently shoved Silver to me. As she stumbled toward me, I grabbed her and tugged her behind my back. She was rubbing her neck, but otherwise looked uninjured.

Jyston smiled at me, and the overall look of it was frightening. "Now since that unpleasant business is over, let's chat."

I nodded, wondering what was coming next. Was he stalling so that someone could come capture us? We could try to make a break past him to escape, but my gut was telling me that there was more to Jyston than the Team originally thought. Unfortunately, that didn't mean that he wouldn't kill us all right here and now.

"My apologies to your lovely friend. I don't like to meet under such circumstances, but I couldn't have you stabbing me either." He sketched a bow, with a smirk on his face. "I don't plan on killing either of you today, so you can relax. It's hard to talk if someone thinks they're going to die." He made a show of sheathing his daggers and leaned against the flimsy doorway.

"There, that's better. So, where were we? Oh yes—you were trying to figure out why I'm here, and why he's here, and why Dagna's involved, and why I'm not trying to kill you. I don't have much time, so let me sum up. Dagna wants to be Second Counselor, but there is only one way for that to happen: I need to die. She has tried to kill me in various ways, and I won't bore you with the details." He actually rolled his eyes at that, as if it was a nuisance.

"She realized that I'm harder to kill than she originally planned, so she was forced to get creative."

He tilted his head toward the pirate guy. "I came down here to visit, and here you are, the infamous Blu, off guard and with just the gentleman I wanted to see." I heard the pirate's sharp intake of breath behind me. "And there we have it. You're all caught up."

"What do you want from me?" Pirate asked.

Jyston shrugged, seemingly relaxed in this very volatile and strange tableau. "To find out why Dagna sent you here. Blu wasn't the only one who noticed you were out of place. Now, why don't you go ahead and answer the lady's question.

What were Dagna's orders to you? And you might want to be quick about it. Her minions are about two minutes away, and I'd hate for them to catch any of you."

"She'll kill me for telling you," Pirate ground out.

"And I'll kill you for not telling me. The choice is yours."

Jyston casually reached for his daggers. I squeezed Silver's hand. Just when I was about to make a break for it, Pirate decided to answer.

"Dagna asked that we spy on you, to report directly to her when you come, when you go, who you meet with. All of it. She threatened to kill us all if we didn't do it. I believed her."

"As you should. She's a bloodthirsty one, that's for sure." He ran a hand through his hair. "So where does that leave us? I can't have you spying on me anymore, and she will kill you if you stop. If you had somewhere else to disappear to, I might recommend it."

He stepped away from the door. "Blu, they're about a minute away. You and your friend might want to consider running, especially with that price on your head. How much is it up to now?"

"Why are you letting us go?" This had to be some sort of trap.

He shrugged. "Dagna hates you almost as much as she hates me. The enemy of my enemy is my friend, or something like that. Anyway, the fact that you keep eluding her is driving her mad, which is delighting me to no end. One day the price on your head might be enough to capture you myself, but not today."

I headed for the door, and he made no move to stop me. I paused; now would be a perfect opportunity to slit his throat as I left. We could be rid of one Jurisdiction pestilence for good. If I was going to do it, I needed to do it now, while his guard was down.

But I hesitated.

Even though I thought my gut was insane, it was telling me that Jyston wasn't the homicidal maniac I had thought. He raised one perfect eyebrow at me, like he could read my mind.

"You are a lively one, aren't you?" He chuckled.

As Silver and I stepped through the door, Jyston leaned in toward me, his lips grazing my ear and his hair tickling my cheek. He smelled of sweat and sandalwood; my breath caught in my throat. He stood perfectly still for a moment, breathing in my ear, and whispered: "I like the purple hair better than the black. It suits you."

And he pulled away, winking at me as we headed down the alley.

I stumbled, and Silver grabbed my elbow to steady me. We sprinted for the car, and I yelled into my ear comm, "You got eyes yet, Styx?"

"Holy shit, B! What's happening?"

"Long story. I need eyes to get us out of here to my car. Jyston found us."

"What! You saw your boyfriend?"

I barked out a laugh. "If he's my boyfriend, then my love life is more fucked up than I thought."

"Did he look sexy?"

"Styx? Currently running for our lives here. Can you hurry it up? We need eyes!"

"Hang on—just give me a second."

"We don't have a second, my friend. We are up shit creek and our paddles have been destroyed."

"OK, OK, keep your panties on, I've almost got it. Oh my god, you weren't kidding! There are a dozen minions about a block in the other direction. If you turn left now, you have a clear shot to your car." My lungs burned, my legs shook, and I reminded myself one more time why I shouldn't skip training. Silver was keeping up with a determined look on her face.

We jumped into my car and sped away.

FARA 19

Agent Hanlon, carrying various file folders that were as thick as a novel, a giant thermos that smelled like coffee, and a box of donuts, still managed to look completely in control of the situation. I squealed at the donuts, then was immediately embarrassed.

"Apparently I chose the right breakfast."

"She would marry a donut, if she could," Calum called from the bedroom.

"Quiet from the peanut gallery," I called back. I took the box of donuts out of Agent Hanlon's hand, grabbing one and putting the rest in the kitchen.

"The two guys who were sitting outside left as soon as I walked in," Agent Hanlon said. He set the thermos and files on the table. He was in yet another pair of track pants and an exercise T-shirt that was stretched to an almost indecent state. Did he just keep buying the same size shirts he wore in middle school, not realizing that he had grown up? I wasn't going to complain, again, because he really was in ridiculously good shape. He rubbed at the light stubble on his chin, catching me staring again. Awkward.

"So, you opened another portal?" he asked. "Was it on purpose?"

"Yes—and no. I have no idea how I did it."

"Explain."

I raised my eyebrows at him. Bossy. I described how the window had appeared above the bath.

"Was this one different in any way?"

"The scenery was different."

"How?"

I described what Calum and I had seen. Calum came in from getting ready and added, "I also noticed that I couldn't see the window from the other side—I could only see it from Fara's perspective."

"You saw the portal too?" If Agent Hanlon had any thoughts about Calum in the bathroom with me, he kept them to himself.

"You weren't sleeping or dreaming in the bathtub?"

"No, and another thing: the last two times this has happened, the place I had been dreaming about ended up being what I saw through the window, and both times it was a tree-lined path. It was like it was pulled right out of my head. But this time, I wasn't thinking about the portal stuff at all—it just happened."

"What were you thinking about?"

I shook my head. I wasn't about to get into the Beck fiasco with Agent Babydoll Shirt.

"Calum and I tried to recreate the portal by thinking about . . . it . . . again, and it didn't work."

Agent Hanlon narrowed his eyes but didn't push further. "So, what you are dreaming may be what creates the portal, but it is not necessary."

We sat there eating our donuts and drinking our coffee while Calum got ready to leave. He walked over to me, stooped to give me a hug, and whispered in my ear.

"Remember your promise to me. Even him, OK? I'll be back in a few hours."

"I'll make sure she's safe," Agent Hanlon said.

"Make sure you do." And with that, Calum was gone, and I was alone with Agent Hanlon again.

"What now?" I asked.

"You try to open a portal, and I'll read this file to see if there is anything in it to help us."

That sounded like as good a plan as any, but I had no idea where to begin.

Two hours later, Agent Hanlon was still reading his files, and I had nothing to show for my efforts—not even a light breeze. I had managed to consume a couple of pots of coffee and half a box of donuts. I had tried to meditate, to sleep, to distract myself, and even the *Caddy Shack* "be the ball" technique—except with multiverse portals ("be the portal . . . be the portal").

And nothing.

I might have sighed for the thousandth time when Agent Hanlon looked up.

"I haven't seen a portal, so I'm assuming your attempts have not been successful."

I banged my forehead on the coffee table. "I am a portal loser."

His eyebrows shot up into his hairline. "That seems to be a rather huge reaction to something only one other person has done before."

"Are you calling me a drama queen?"

It was easy for him to say, sitting there reading about my mother when I was the one who was supposed to be able to do this amazing thing and couldn't. Why did I have to be a failure at everything I tried? I couldn't even keep my dumbass, broke, unemployed boyfriend from leaving me. Ugh. Beck.

"What was that look?"

"What look?"

"It's like you are thinking something, then your face goes blank—like you are no longer thinking or feeling anything."

"Oh—it's a coping technique my mom taught me. I had huge emotions as a kid, even though I was shy, and she would have me practice taking those emotions, putting them in a box, then tucking them away in my heart. It would calm me down."

"Every child has huge emotions, Fara. That's what kids are—emotions. It seems like she wasn't letting you work through them. I mean, I'm not an expert on parenthood—or dealing with emotions—but that doesn't seem healthy."

I shrugged. I had been pushing down my emotions for so long that I didn't even think about it anymore. Agent Hanlon looked pensive but went back to reading.

"Do you have kids?" I asked him.

He looked up, surprised. "Why do you ask?"

"Because I'm curious. Because I'm tired of sitting here, failing. Because I'm bored. But mostly because I know nothing about you, and I'm supposed to trust you. It'd be easier if I knew a little bit of something—otherwise my overactive imagination fills in the blanks, and you are now married to a beautiful woman, living in a loft downtown with three gorgeous children and a pet labradoodle, silently waiting for me to go to sleep so you can sneak me away to your secret lair and run horrible experiments on me."

He blinked once, then threw his head back and laughed, a deep, rumbling sound that made my knees shake a bit. When he finally looked at me, he was smiling.

"Fair enough. What do you want to know? I reserve the right to veto any question. Agreed?"

I nodded. "Where are you from? Why did you get into this line of work? Do you like animals? I mean—anything you tell me is going to be more than I knew a few minutes ago."

He shrugged. "OK—the short story is that I was raised by a single mom in Southern California with my younger sister.

My dad died in active duty when my sister was little—Air Force. I wanted to join the military right out of high school, but my mom wouldn't let me. I went to college, got a degree as an engineer, and the Department of Weapons Technology recruited me right out of college, so I went to training and got stationed here. My mom died a couple of years ago, so my sister is my only family left. She married her high school sweetheart, and they have two kids."

"What do you do for fun? Read? Watch TV? Race turtles?"

"Race turtles?"

"I'm trying to give you exotic tastes."

"Are you making up things because you don't think I have hobbies? Do you think I'm a stick in the mud?"

"A what?"

"A humorless, boring person."

"You aren't boring."

"But you think that I have no sense of humor . . ."

"Maybe you do, and I just haven't seen it."

"I wish I could say that was the case. My ex-girlfriend always said that I wasn't fun or funny. That's the reason she gave when she packed up her things, took the dog, and moved out. I was too serious for her party girl ways. I don't begrudge her, but going to the clubs isn't my style."

"I'm so sorry."

"Why? You didn't ask her to leave. It was for the best anyway. Please stop apologizing for things that aren't your fault."

"OK, sorry. How long were you together?"

He sighed and rolled his eyes at me, which looked weird on his face. "A couple of years. She moved out a few months ago."

"So no wife, kids, or labradoodle?"

He laughed. "No. I have a houseplant named Robert—that's about it."

Robert? That actually was funny. I laughed and he smiled at me.

"Enough about me. Let's talk about you."

I groaned.

"Seriously," he said, "I'm pretty boring. I work, I work out, I cook when I have time. That's about it."

"Friends?"

"I hang out with some of the other agents sometimes, but our jobs are so time-consuming that we don't see each other outside of work very often."

"How did you learn to speak Chinese?"

He laughed at that. "It's sort of a long story."

"I obviously have time."

"All right. I was taking martial arts and was the smallest kid in the class. This group of kids would taunt me in Chinese. I knew they were saying terrible things to me, but I didn't know what. I told my mom that I wanted to learn Chinese, she got me a tutor, and I learned it fairly easily—apparently I have a knack for languages. Anyway, once I got the hang of it, the next time the kids bullied me, I was able to understand them—and then respond in their own language. It startled them enough that they left me alone. That, and I grew another two feet."

I laughed. "Why did you join the government?"

"I wanted to serve my country. I come from a long line of men who served in one way or another."

His manner had become so easygoing that it was hard to remember that he was a government agent who may or may not try to take me away. He looked so at home here, his ankle resting on his knee, thermos of coffee in his hand, smile playing on his lips, that I could almost trust him. But not quite. I still had questions.

"This is a serious one. Why are you here, really? Are you here to help me stop randomly opening portals? Or are you here to figure out what I can do so that you can report back to your superiors? Or worse, drag my ass down to the assistant?"

He was quiet for a second, and I started to get nervous. What was I going to do when he suddenly broke it to me that I was under arrest, never to see daylight again?

"I'm here to help you, Fara."

Relief flooded through me, probably more than it should. I really didn't want to end up living my life as a government lab rat. But a small piece of me was relieved because I was starting to like Agent Hanlon. A lot. That might be a problem.

"But why? Why are you disobeying direct orders to bring me in? You don't seem like the 'break the rules' type of guy."

He chuckled at that. "I'm not, normally, but some things have happened in the past few days to make me reconsider my department's position on this whole situation."

"I'm going to pester you until you tell me, so you might as well just get it over with."

He looked as uncomfortable as I had ever seen him.

"After I realized that the assistant couldn't be trusted, and that she had the ear of my superiors, I knew I needed more information. I stole these files."

My eyebrows shot up—he really was living on the edge. I waited for him to continue.

"I don't like what I'm finding in them. According to this, the first thing the department wants to do with the ability to open portals is to find weapons—and before any other government does."

"My mom was right to be paranoid."

"She was. And this is exactly the opposite of why I joined the department in the first place. My job is supposed to be finding weapons so that they can be *destroyed*. By locating and destroying the weapons, I can keep people safe. Bringing in more weapons from other worlds goes against everything

I thought my department stood for. Couple that with how easily my superiors were persuaded to consider illegal means of interrogating you—I decided that I needed to help you however I could, even if it meant going against orders. I came here to see how you opened the portal—not to turn you in, but to help you hide, if at all possible."

I didn't know what to do with that information. Agent Hanlon had essentially switched sides. I wasn't sure I could trust him yet, but if what he said was true, not only was I in bigger trouble than I thought—I had gained an ally.

"Do you think that they will try to take me?"

"If they think that you know anything about the portals, then yes, I do."

Agent Hanlon looked truly shaken. I could only imagine how he felt. His whole career, he had been convinced that he was one of the good guys—following orders and keeping people safe. Now the government that he trusted was betraying those principles.

"Calum made me promise that if I thought I was in danger, I should run away and never come back. Do I need to run now?"

"Not yet, but I'll tell you if you do."

"How can I trust that?"

"Fara, I understand that you have no reason to trust me, but I promise you that I will do whatever I can to make sure that you are safe and that no one takes you against your will, including the people I work for. And if I can't protect you, I'll tell you to run."

"Even if it means you get into trouble?"

"Yes."

We sat, looking at each other in a not quite uncomfortable way. I wasn't sure what he was thinking, but I was thinking that I was in way over my head, and I was thankful for his being here.

"There's something else," he said, taking a sheet of paper from the second file. "This is a list of all the scientists and technology experts who tested the device before it was handed over to your mother. Barrington Park was one of them."

I blinked a couple of times. The coincidence was too much—it couldn't be a coincidence at all. He must have figured out a way to duplicate the device—or at least part of it—and then lied to the government, telling them he didn't know what it was or what it was capable of. He had a device somehow—and since I was making it go off, and he now wanted to know why.

"So, now that he wants to talk to me, or possibly kidnap me, what do I do? He knows where I live and where I work. I've opened another couple of portals. That's probably why his goons were parked out front. Assuming he has a device, or something similar, I can't hide from him unless I get this portal thing under control. He'll be able to find me wherever I go."

"Then we should probably get to work on that," he said. "But first, I answered questions about me—you still owe me a couple of answers about you."

I groaned again. I hated talking about myself, although talking with Agent Hanlon was easier than it was with most people.

"Don't you already have a file on me? Can't you just look there?"

The corner of his mouth tugged up, but he shook his head.

"Not for this sort of stuff. What's your favorite food?"

"Cheeseburgers."

"I should have guessed. How long have you known Calum?"

"Since kindergarten."

"Have the two of you dated?"

Huh—I wondered why he wanted to know that. "Nope—he's never been interested."

Agent Hanlon raised an eyebrow at that.

"For real," I said. "He's never given me any inclination that he's interested—I'm like a little sister to him."

"Fair enough, plus you have a boyfriend. How long have you two been together?"

And just like that, my good mood was gone. Ugh, Beck. Agent Hanlon noticed.

"Close to a year, until apparently two days ago."

"Do you mind my asking what happened?"

"It's fine. I guess someone breaking into my apartment was too much for him. He broke up with me. Through Calum."

"He didn't even tell you to your face?"

I sighed. "No. I guess I wasn't worth that sort of time."

"It's not that you aren't worth the time—he's a coward, is all. How did you meet him in the first place? You guys seemed mismatched for the brief time I met him. Did you meet at work?"

"No, he was a bartender at a place Calum, Adora, and I hang out. It's a long story. Are you sure you want to hear it?"

"I obviously have time."

"It's really not that exciting. I had just turned twenty-one and felt special that he had singled me out and asked for my number. He was really charming. He bought me flowers and talked to me for hours about life, and I fell for it. About a month after our first date, he quit bartending, saying that he had a line on a great gig. That lasted a few weeks, and then every few weeks after that it was the same thing—a new 'opportunity' that was going to be the best thing ever; then he'd quit his job, he'd be unemployed for a bit, lather, rinse, and repeat. I didn't mind picking up the tab since he was trying to get back on his feet—or so he said. And honestly,

I was just so flattered that this popular guy wanted to date me—the shy girl that has two friends—that I ignored a lot of the warning signs."

"Shy?" Agent Hanlon asked, eyebrow arched—again. Too cute.

"Somehow you bring out the worst in me." He laughed, and I continued. "It took me a really long time to realize that it was never about me, you know? That he talked about *his* life, and usually the flowers were after he had stood me up or done something equally stupid. Then a month ago he had this idea about starting a business, and when he got kicked out of his apartment, he asked if he could move in. He'd never wanted to move in with me, so when he suggested it, I jumped at the chance. But as you can probably guess, he never started the business and went out every night with his friends. I started working double shifts to cover our expenses, and I just thought that's how life was supposed to be. I guess I was so desperate to feel like I was part of a relationship that I ignored all the warning signs—including Adora telling me that I was an idiot."

"Not only was he a coward—he was using you."

"Yeah—thanks. Nothing like making a girl feel great by saying the only reason that the guy liked her was because of what she could give him."

Agent Hanlon rubbed his hands over his face. "I'm sorry— that's not what I meant. I'm sure he loved you for what you are. Who wouldn't?"

"Don't be a jerk, Agent Hanlon! Most people—that's who! Me being me isn't enough to get most guys' attention. I'm not pretty enough, thin enough, tall enough, rich enough, funny enough, good enough. I thought I had finally found someone who saw me as enough. But his selfishness overrode any of that. Why am I even telling you this?"

I took a deep breath. It felt so good to talk about this breakup, even though it was painful, and I was embarrassed. Why had I chosen this guy, who I knew nothing about, to pour my heart out to?

"I'm pretty sure you have no problem getting dates. What I meant was, you deserve better."

I threw my arms up in the air in frustration. "Everyone keeps saying that I deserve better, but how do you know? I mean, you've known me for like three seconds! Why do I deserve better? If my boyfriend, who is supposed to love me, didn't think I deserved better, then how can you know? You don't even know me. Maybe I deserve to be alone—especially now that I randomly open up portals to other universes. That's going to be a great first date conversation. 'Hi—what do you do?' Oh—nothing much, just open portals to the multiverse in my sleep, you?' Great relationship starter. Maybe I'm so much of a basket case that I'll end up a crazy cat lady!"

"Do you own cats?"

"That's beside the point!"

"Well, don't let me stop your pity train. You're on a roll now."

"Don't be a jerk! I'm serious!"

"So am I, Fara. The way you talk about yourself is painful. Please listen to me. I might not be good at talking about these things, but I know that the way your boyfriend broke up with you had nothing to do with you, and everything to do with him. He's an asshole and you're not. Now you're rid of him and can start over. It's pretty simple—and it really has nothing to do with cat ownership or living alone. For god's sake, you're, what? Twenty-one? Twenty-two? You have your whole life ahead of you! And who says that being alone is a bad thing? Stop putting yourself down and apologizing for other idiots!"

"Stop being Bossy McBosserson and telling me what to do! And why do you even care? As soon as the department gets what they want, you'll be gone!"

I stopped and immediately felt bad. I knew the anger that was starting to grow in my stomach really wasn't directed at Agent Hanlon, and I knew I was being unfair, but I didn't want to be rational right now. I didn't want to play the game of being grateful for the scraps that others threw my way. I was angry at everything at the moment, and maybe that was OK. I was angry at Beck for being selfish, at Agent Hanlon for being a know-it-all but not knowing me at all and being gorgeous and probably leaving after all this was over. At myself for wondering what it was like to kiss his lips, which were pulled down in an almost-frown at the moment. At my mom for leaving me this weird legacy and not being around to help me. Yeah—I guess Agent Hanlon was right. I was throwing myself the biggest fucking pity party ever, and I was going to revel in it. Right now I wanted to be pissed off at my apartment being trashed, at not having good sex for over a year, for jeans never fitting right, for my parents dying, for not being able to reach the top shelf, for not being able to afford college, for broccoli not tasting like tater tots, for ending up with this life: in someone else's apartment with a stranger who wasn't my friend and was going to leave me like everyone else. I was going to sit here and be mad and feel sorry for myself for a bit. I'd put it in a box in a second. I just needed to *feel*.

"Fara?"

I didn't even look at him, my eyes closed—willing my tears to stay behind my eyelids.

"Fara, you need to see this."

I couldn't face him. I knew I was being ridiculous, but I didn't care.

"Fara? Open your eyes. Please."

He had moved to sit next to me on the couch, and something in his voice made me open my eyes. Maybe it was the way he said "please." I looked at him, but he pointed in front of me.

There was another portal.

We both stared at it. I had done it! I didn't know how, but I had.

I sat up, wiped my eyes, and looked inside. It didn't look like either of the other landscapes I had seen before. It looked like I was inside a room of some sort, but it was hard to tell from this vantage point. I could hear voices, but they were muffled—as if we were listening through water. I got closer to the portal and looked down and noticed that the perspective was the same as the other times this happened, like I was standing. On the floor of the room were piles of—I couldn't tell what they were, but they seemed to be fabric of some sort. I tried to see if I could locate the source of the voices, but I couldn't from where I was. One of the piles of fabric was on the ground, just on the other side of the portal. I took a deep breath, willing myself not to be afraid. I reached through the portal, and it felt like putting my hand through the top of a swimming pool—a bit of resistance, but not much. I bent down and grabbed the first thing my hand touched, pulling my arm back as fast as I could. The portal closed with a slight hiss.

At first, I couldn't determine what I had grasped in my hand—it was black, soft, and not that big. When it didn't eat my fingers or explode, I held it up and immediately knew what it was; I had one just like it. It was a black tank top—and I started to laugh because of all the things in an entire alternate universe I could have possibly grabbed, the sheer ordinariness of it . . . I couldn't put it into words and so I laughed. I had just been in someone's bedroom in a parallel universe. It was so mind-boggling and ordinary at the same time. They had bedrooms too? And tank tops, apparently.

We sat there for a second, looking at the tank top. Finally, Agent Hanlon asked, "How did you do it?"

"Which part?"

"All of it."

"I have no idea how I opened the portal."

"Was it hard to grab that?" he asked, indicating the tank top I was still clinging to.

I thought about that. "Not really—it felt like I was putting my hand through a bubble—or maybe breaking the surface of water. Not painful—just a bit strange."

We sat, not moving or talking, for a while. At some point I noticed how close Agent Hanlon was to me; my entire right side was pressed against him. I became very aware of his breathing and how good he smelled; how his hands were giant and gently clasped between his knees as he rested his forearms on his legs. I wanted to reach out and grab his hand, but I quickly ignored that feeling and got up. I needed to figure out how I had just opened that portal, and I couldn't focus being so near to him.

I paced, thinking. Something in particular was bothering me.

"Calum said he couldn't see the portal from the other side—how did you know?"

He thought about it. "I didn't see it, at first. There was a slight shimmer in the air in front of you, then a very faint silver string that seemed to lead from your head to the . . . shimmer. I moved over here to get a better look, and that's when I saw the window."

"Ah. I see." He had been looking at me when my eyes were closed. That felt too intimate—too personal.

I was still holding the tank top. Would its owner in the other universe notice that the tank top was missing? Could I return it at some point? Did I need to keep it to study it? I had so many questions and no answers.

"Fara—you did it. You opened a portal."

But I didn't feel like I had accomplished anything. I still couldn't control it. I'd opened it by accident, again. "But I didn't mean to . . ."

"It's a step in the right direction." I rolled my eyes. "Now all we need to do is figure out why it opened this time and in the bathtub, but not when you were trying the past two hours. What was the common factor between the two times that worked? It has to be some sort of mental ability. Were you thinking about opening the portal either time?"

I shook my head.

"What were you thinking about?"

The easy answer was Beck. I was thinking about him and how fucked up my life was right now. How hurt I was. But if I was honest, that wasn't all of it. I was so angry both times—wait, that wasn't quite it either. I was *allowing* myself to be angry, which I never did. I never allowed myself to be anything other than steady and reliable and calm. My mom used to say that getting worked up did me no good. Put it in a box, push it down . . .

"Fara?"

That had to be it. I stood there, the pieces falling into place. I didn't know *why* but I knew more about how.

"It's my emotions."

"What?"

"I'm pretty sure that the portals are triggered by my emotions, and my mom must have known that. It's also why it happens when I'm sleeping—it is the only time my mental walls are down enough that I can't control them."

"Take me through your thought process."

"It was something that Calum said earlier—that I was finally allowing myself to *feel* something. My mom always said to put the feelings in a box and put them away. I just thought that I was *too much* as a child, but she must have known that if I got too worked up, I could accidentally open a portal. In the bathtub and just now, I allowed myself to feel anger."

"What were you angry about? Do you think that matters?"

"I don't know, I was mad about everything! At this weirdness that I didn't ask for. At Beck for being a shithead. At you for being perfectly calm through all this like you deal with girls opening portals every day."

"You have been through a lot in the past few days. You do have a bunch to be mad about."

"I shouldn't be allowing myself to feel anything if I risk opening portals. Better to put it in a box."

"I still say that's an unhealthy way to handle things."

"You handle everything without it fazing you! How do you do it?"

"It does faze me—I just don't show it. But on my weird-o-meter, this is probably at the top. This is definitely not everyday for me, Fara." He smiled.

"Weird o-meter?"

He laughed and we sat in silence, staring at the tank top some more. He looked tired and, amazingly, a bit unkempt. His stubble had grown out and his short hair was disheveled. It was like he had taken off his agent costume and was sitting there as himself. This guy sitting across from me, the one who had a plant named Robert and poked fun at himself for not having a sense of humor; who learned Chinese so he could stick up for himself; who joked about boy bands and liked to cook; who was refusing to take me in for questioning because he didn't think it was the right thing to do. I liked this guy. And I was hoping that this guy sort of liked me too. Something occurred to me.

"I know this is a weird time to notice this, but you're calling me by my first name. Why? I thought you could only call me Miss Bayne."

A sad smile flashed across his face. "I'm off duty."

"Ah! You're rogue and feeling wild, so you can call me Fara?"

He laughed. "Nothing quite that dramatic, but something like that."

"What's your first name, then? It seems only fair that I call you something other than Agent Hanlon. I can't exactly call you what Adora calls you."

"What's that? Agent-No-Fun? Or something else?"

"That too. But also Hot Agent Guy." I blushed. He laughed.

"That's a new one. Normally people call me worse things than that." He shook his head, a slight blush reaching his cheeks.

"So?"

"My friends call me Jay, but that's a nickname."

"What's your full name?"

"That's for another time. It's something only my mother called me."

"What is it?"

"Not telling."

"That bad?"

"No—it's just something that's very personal to me."

I had a crap car because it was personal to me. I understood what he was saying.

"Are we friends, then?"

He was quiet for a second, a shadow passing across his face. "Honestly? You're the only friend I have right now."

BLU 20

"Want to talk about it?" I asked Silver. She had been glaring out of the window since we left the alley.

"I'm not sure what there is to talk about. I failed in keeping a lookout, got myself captured, and was useless in getting out of there. I might as well stop trying to be on the Team."

That was not the response I was expecting. She wasn't freaked out; she was pissed, which was a good thing. I told her as much.

"You don't get it—I failed in front of *you*. All I wanted was to be like you, and I screwed it all up."

"First, you didn't screw up, so knock that shit off right now. You didn't die or get anyone else killed. We were able to get information and escape the second most notorious person in the world, so I call that a win. You are smart, quick, and didn't panic when shit went to hell. And believe me, shit *always* goes to hell. We lived to fight another day."

"How do you do it? How do you face this day after day?"

That was a great question—and it was good that she was asking it. Sometimes I forgot that these trainees compared my outsides with their insides. They didn't know that I was scared out of my mind most of the time, or questioned my decisions, or had nightmares about certain missions. They only saw the results. But if she was going to become a Team member, she needed to know the truth.

"I'm not fearless, Silver. And I'm far from perfect. I have screwed up so many missions—including some this week, and the week isn't over yet! I have my moments of panic, of doubt, of despair. We all do. That's what being human is about. You have to find your 'why.' What is the reason you do this day after day? Because this life isn't easy."

"What's yours?"

"My 'why' used to be revenge. Those fuckers killed my parents and countless others. They tortured me when I was little because they thought I knew something that I didn't, and after I escaped, I couldn't sleep for a year without nightmares."

"That's awful. Do you still have them?"

"Sometimes. I wanted revenge—I wanted to see them all dead—and that is what drove me to become what I am today."

I took a breath to steady myself. "But after a time, I realized that revenge was the short game. I could kill them all, but it won't bring my parents back—won't bring my innocence or childhood back. But if I work hard enough, I might be able to save another kid from my fate. If I help destroy Jurisdiction, maybe one day we won't need the Team, and kids can learn art instead of how to kill someone with their bare hands. And that desire, that hope, is what fuels me."

"So what do we do now?"

"We complete the mission or die trying so that no one else has to live through what we have. Having that bigger purpose is what helps keep me going. That, and friends." At that, she gave me a shy smile. I grinned back at her.

Styx chirped in my ear as we pulled into the Compound. "Ink and Jack are heading back in an hour or so. We're supposed to meet with the Captain in ninety minutes."

"Awesome—I'm starving."

Silver and I went to the mess hall. She ordered a salad, and I ordered a cheeseburger with fries and a cup of coffee the size of my head. She raised an eyebrow at my tray as I sat down. I shrugged.

"I like food. I train, I fuel my body right most of the time, but sometimes you just need a cheeseburger."

She laughed. "I think I'm going to like hanging out with you." Then her expression became serious. "A couple of things don't add up."

I nodded, shoving a french fry into my mouth and motioning for her to continue.

"I'm assuming that one of the people from the alley told Dagna that we were there, which is how the minions started chasing us. But that doesn't explain how the Second Counselor beat them there."

"He wasn't supposed to be in the satellite office at all," I added. "So either our information about his whereabouts was wrong or—"

"—or someone tipped him off."

"But why?" I said. "If he had a hunch that Dagna had hired pirate guy to spy on him, it couldn't just be a coincidence that he showed up when we did. And why did he intercept us and then let us go?"

"It was almost like he wanted to warn us. Maybe the enemy of his enemy is his friend." She gave me a pointed look.

"But that can't be all there is to it. He reports to the Counselor, who would flay him alive if he knew his Second was letting us go. They've been trying to capture us for a long time."

We threw out every possible theory we could come up with and still came up blank.

"What did he mean that the purple suited you?" she finally asked.

I tensed, thinking about that last moment with Jyston. How his lips grazed my ear, the low rumble of his voice reverberating through my chest. How he smelled good. How I was less afraid of him than was smart or reasonable. I finally answered Silver.

"He meant that he knew who I was at the masquerade ball."

I heard Jack yelling as we made our way to the Captain's office. I turned to see that he was carrying a nearly unconscious Willow, and blood was covering both of them. I couldn't tell whose blood it was.

"Go get the Captain."

Silver took off at a sprint, and I moved to intercept Jack.

"What happened? Are you hurt?"

His face was ashen, and he was breathing hard. I took Willow's feet from him so that we could carry her together. We walked awkwardly toward the infirmary as fast as we could. I still had my ear comm on.

"Styx—we need medics out here—on our way to the infirmary. One down. Tell Ink and his trainee to get back here now."

"Shit! On it. Who's hurt?"

"Willow, but I think Jack might be too. We need assistance out here!"

We trudged up the path, Jack looking worse and worse as we carried Willow between us.

"Do not pass out on me, Jackrabbit. I can't carry her by myself."

He grunted, but then three medics came running out of the infirmary with a gurney. They gently lifted her onto the gurney and ran with her back through the doors. Jack stumbled after them, but I grabbed his arm—my eyes sweeping over him to make sure he was OK. He had some cuts and the makings of a magnificent black eye. When he moved his arm, I could tell that his wrist was jutting out at an odd angle. It looked gruesome, but I kept my face neutral.

"You need that set."

He tried to push me off, but I held tight. "Styx, Jack is injured too. Let the medics know we have a broken wrist and other unknown injuries coming in."

He glared at me but didn't object when I put my arm around his waist and helped him through the infirmary doors.

"How in the hell did you carry Willow with your wrist like that?"

He shrugged. "Didn't have a choice."

The infirmary was in chaos when we walked in; medics in white coats rushing around barking orders to lesser medics in green coats. The Compound was lucky—it had the only fully operating infirmary in the territory that wasn't controlled by Jurisdiction. We had some of the best medics in the world—those who weren't butchered or forced into Jurisdiction's service. Jurisdiction didn't believe everyone deserved medical help—only the elite.

A white-coated medic noticed us and came rushing over, taking Jack out of my arms and leading him back to the treatment rooms. I said a little prayer into the universe that those two would be alright, and I sat down to wait.

Moments later the Captain and Silver came running through the doors. The Captain nodded to me, then headed toward the room where Jack was being treated. Silver sat down next to me, looking pale.

"Did the Captain know anything?" I asked her.

"Not that she said. Are they going to be OK?"

"I don't know."

Ink and Bullfrog ran in a few minutes later. Ink closed the distance between us with two strides, pulled me out of my chair, and grabbed me by my shoulders, inspecting me for injuries.

"I'm OK. We're fine," I said, my voice hitching a bit.

"The blood?" he asked.

"Willow and Jack."

He pulled me into a fierce hug, and I put my head on his chest, letting his steady heartbeat comfort me. Both of us were thinking about Hastings, feeling that combination of anger, relief, and guilt. Anger that they were able to hurt our people, and guilt at the relief we felt that it wasn't one of us. Survivor's guilt, I guess.

"What happened?"

I stepped out of his embrace. "We don't know. Silver and I were leaving the mess when we saw Jack carrying Willow. Jack has a broken wrist, but Willow has a stomach wound—dagger or sword, probably. How did you guys know to come here?"

"Styx and Dev are on their way."

"When I commed Styx, she didn't know that anyone was hurt. Do you know why Jack didn't contact her?"

"I don't know, but whatever it is, it can't be good. Styx said that your mission was compromised; that the Second Counselor was there."

"That's not the worst of it. He confirmed that he knew I was at the High Governor's house. Someone must have told him who to look for. There's all sorts of weird shit going on." I told Ink all of what had happened.

At the end, he let out a low whistle. "What the fuck, B? What kind of game is Jyston playing?" He ran his hand through his hair.

"How was your mission?" I looked pointedly at douche Bullfrog, who suddenly found his boots very interesting.

"Uneventful."

"Think he's the spy?"

"No—he's an even worse liar than you are."

Styx and Dev came in a little bit later, Styx giving me a hug, then joining the rest of us in our vigil. And we waited. Finally, the Captain came out, looking more tired than I had ever seen her. Lines crisscrossed her face, and dark circles ringed her bright eyes. She smiled grimly at us, as we stood up to greet her.

"Jackrabbit is going to make a full recovery. He has a broken wrist and a few cracked ribs, but otherwise is on the mend. He is with Willow, much to the irritation of the medics." We all sighed with relief.

"Willow just came out of surgery and is recovering, although it is still touch-and-go. She had massive internal bleeding, and some of her organs had been damaged, but the medics think that if she lives through the night, she'll recover. They are asking that we keep visitors to a minimum.

"Go get some dinner, then meet me in my office in an hour. There are many things we need to discuss. In the meantime, please keep the chitchat to a minimum, if you know what I mean."

After a somber dinner, we all headed back to the Captain's office, preparing ourselves for whatever bad news we were about to be told.

"Let's start with the good news. Jackrabbit and Willow found the location of the prison."

We all let out a collective sigh of relief but then noticed that the Captain looked as if she was barely containing her rage. Something was very, very wrong.

"The bad news is that the building is completed, and Jurisdiction is already moving children into the facility."

My heart sank. Burning down a construction site was one thing, but if the prison was already operational? This had just turned into a rescue mission. Shit. Ink looked across the table and our eyes met. He was thinking the same thing.

"What happened to Jack and Willow?" he asked.

"When they found the building, they saw kids being unloaded by the truckload and ushered inside the facility. They got out of the car to get a closer look, but some minions got the jump on them—Willow was stabbed, but before she passed out, she killed one of them. Jackrabbit took care of the rest and got her back here."

"Why didn't he call for help?" Styx asked.

"None of the palmboxes or ear comms worked on the property. Whatever security they have makes our technology useless. And it continues to be useless."

Styx was wide-eyed. That sort of technology was theoretical, but somehow Jurisdiction had figured it out.

The Captain stood up from her seat, a look of determination on her face. "Do not forget for one moment that we are the Team. While this changes our plans, we are adaptable and will do what we've always done. We'll plan a recon mission to get as much information as we can so that we can rescue those kids."

"And then burn it all down to the ground," I added.

The Captain nodded. "And burn them all down. Every last one of them."

FARA 21

Agent Hanlon—Jay—and I tried for another hour to recreate the portal, to no avail. He tried various ways of pissing me off, but nothing worked. I would just end up laughing at his attempts, and then he would get frustrated, and I would laugh harder.

"Are you even *trying* to be angry?"

"Of course! It's just that you're so funny when you're trying to make me mad."

He snorted. "Now you find me funny! Most people find me intimidating."

"I'm obviously not normal people."

"Obviously."

I laughed again.

"Are you not at least a little scared?

"You haven't even really been trying that hard. I mean— short jokes? C'mon. I know I'm short. It just seems to bother others more than it bothers me."

"It doesn't bother me."

Was that a smile tugging at his lips? I shrugged. "Of course it doesn't bother you. You're a giant."

"Only to wee people like you."

"No—to most normal humans. Wait a minute! Did you just call me 'wee people'? For real? I just happen to be weer than most. OK, try something else."

"What makes you angry?"

I thought about it. Beck. Ugh. People taking advantage of me. My inability to stand up for myself. When someone I loved was in trouble. I said as much to Jay.

"I'm not going to take advantage of you, and my other attempts have been met with ridicule. Why is it so easy for the Hulk?"

I laughed. "His secret is that he's always angry."

"And you're not?"

"Honestly, I'm not sure what I am."

"What emotion do you feel the most?"

I thought about it—that seemed like a weird question, but then again, I had been pushing my emotions down for so long, I didn't know the answer. In the past twenty-four hours I had felt anger and fear, but something else; something more. I looked at Jay and let my guard down. What was I feeling? A little bit of anxiety for the unknown, lingering anger from my breakup, sadness from that too, I guess, but I was feeling . . . happy. The past hour had been fun, if not a little peculiar. We had a sort of comfortable camaraderie going on; Jay trying various things to make me mad and me laughing it off. He looked back at me, his gray eyes questioning, and I felt a rush of something. Longing? Butterflies? I sat with it for a minute, allowed the feeling to stay without ignoring it. It felt good. I knew that I needed to get a handle on my emotions so I wasn't randomly opening portals when someone cut me off in traffic, but just for this second, sitting in Calum's house with this man who was giving up his time and possibly putting his career on the line for me, who was trying to make me mad and make me laugh.

"I don't know. Right now, I'm happy."

He looked away, and I had a sinking feeling I had just crossed some sort of invisible line. I pushed the feeling down.

Jay looked back at me. "There! That look. Did you just put your feelings in a box again?"

"Yes."

"Why? What were you thinking this time?"

"Honestly? That I had crossed some invisible line by saying I was happy."

"Do you ever bring the feeling back out? Like, to work through it?"

"No. But do you work through all your emotions?"

He snorted. "I'm a guy, Fara. My emotions are simple compared to yours."

"That's a crap excuse and you know it."

"Not really. I just want basic creature comforts. That's about the extent of my emotional range. But you—you've had to push down your emotions for years, and if you haven't ever dealt with them, that's a lot of pent-up stuff. At some point it's going to explode. And if our theory is right—that your emotions control the portals—that sort of emotional upheaval could be catastrophic. Hulk like."

He was right. I needed to figure out a way to work through my emotions without setting off a thousand portals. Yoga? Meditation? Kickboxing might work to channel some of it. I'd have to go tomorrow, as long as Jay thought it was safe.

I wasn't sure what Jay was thinking, but I was getting tired—this was worse than therapy. I got up to scrounge food in Calum's kitchen. As I walked by the couch, Jay grabbed my arm. I looked at him—we were almost eye-level even with him sitting down.

"You didn't make me uncomfortable just now. What's happening is just . . . complicated." I tried to pull my arm away, but he held on. "I'm happy too," he said.

I didn't know how to respond. My feelings toward Agent Hanlon were complex, and I would have to sort through those after I got some sleep, but he was risking everything to protect me.

"Thank you. For everything." I hoped he understood how much those words meant.

"Am I interrupting something?" I hadn't even heard Calum come in. Jay released my arm.

"Nope—but I'm the Incredible Hulk."

Calum blinked. "Of course you are."

"How was work?" I asked. This was not awkward. Not awkward at all.

"Fine—but that Barrington Park guy came back in asking for you. Hewitt told him you would be in tomorrow, of course. And those guys are still outside."

"I'll take care of them." Jay stood up and stretched, his shirt riding up. I stared at his bare stomach. How did a normal person even begin to get abs like those?

"Are you going to talk to them?" Calum asked. Had he noticed my leering?

"They've been a nuisance long enough," Jay said. "I'll show them my badge and make some bureaucratic stuff up. It won't work for long—people like Barrington Park have armies of attorneys at their disposal—but maybe it'll get them off your case for a bit."

"Should I ignore him until then? What if he comes into The Grill tomorrow?"

"I would tell you not to work tomorrow, but I know you won't listen to that."

"My life can't stop because I'm now Master of the Universes or whatever. That title doesn't pay the bills."

"That title is already taken, so don't get ahead of yourself," Calum quipped.

"Whatever. Dream Warrior? Portal Purveyor? Window Rebel? Regardless, as much as I'd love to just quit my job and hang out with you guys full time, I have to go to work."

We told Calum what had happened with the portal, and then the three of us discussed what the heck I was supposed to do. When we finally parted ways, we had a basic plan in place. It felt like we were grasping at straws, and the more we talked, the more afraid I became. But both Jay and Calum seemed to think that if I could get a handle on how to stop opening portals by accident, then I at least had a chance of avoiding being kidnapped. And that was a start.

Jay turned to me before walking through the door. "I'm going to run interference on my end, but be careful tomorrow."

"I will. Thanks again."

I stood in the doorway, not really wanting to see Jay go. He seemed reluctant to leave too, and lifted his hand toward my face. I stood still, partly afraid that he was going to kiss me in front of Calum—and mostly realizing he would never do something like that, and it was just wishful thinking on my part. After a moment's hesitation, he turned and left.

Calum closed the door after Jay and walked into the kitchen. "Want to tell me what happened between you and Agent Hanlon today? Or should I call him *Jay* like you do?" There was an edge to his voice that hadn't been there this morning.

"I told you what happened. I got pissed again, accidentally opened a portal, and grabbed a tank top." It sounded way weirder, condensed like that.

"And that's it?"

"That's it. What did you think happened?"

"The way you two were looking at each other, I thought that, you know, you guys . . ."

"Calum, nothing happened." I laughed again, trying to lighten the mood. "Not only is he out of my league, but I've been single for all of three seconds, just found out that I can rip the space-time continuum with a temper tantrum, and have been trying to avoid getting killed—so I've been a bit busy." I walked into the kitchen. He was leaning against the counter with his head hanging—black hair in his eyes.

"Just . . . be careful, is all." He looked up at me with wary eyes. "I can't lose you. You're all I have."

"You're all I have too."

"Hungry?" he asked. He unloaded some takeout containers from The Grill. "We need sustenance if we're going to make you Master of the Universe."

I spent the rest of the night trying, without success, to open another portal. Like Jay, Calum's attempts to make me mad only ended in both of us laughing until I couldn't breathe. He repeatedly told me I was nothing like the Hulk, and while that statement was obvious, eventually it got me thinking: anger was not an emotion that I experienced very often. Sadness, loneliness, envy—those were emotions with which I was more acquainted, but if those emotions worked for opening portals, then I would have been doing it right and left my entire life. Maybe those emotions weren't strong enough, or I didn't feel them strongly enough to trigger . . . whatever it was.

I shared my thoughts with Calum. He popped a grape into his mouth. "What emotions do you feel when you have those nightmares? Can you remember?"

If there was a connection between my emotions, portals, and my nightmares, I needed to figure it out so that I could suppress it, go back to living my life, and leave this craziness behind.

"Fear, mostly. I wake up in a panic, like I'm being chased by someone."

"When did your mom start coming into your room? How old were you?"

"About seven, I guess. I do vividly remember that very first dream. It's the only one that I remember that clearly. I had been captured by some bad guys, taken away to what looked like a dungeon cell, and tortured. I woke up when they were torturing me."

"Holy shit, Fara! That's terrible. You were seven?"

I nodded, remembering the feeling of being so helpless in that dream, the fear, the pain, and then my mom waking me up and holding me all night long. Knowing what I knew now, she probably stayed there to make sure I didn't open any more portals that night.

Even with my mother training me to suppress my emotions for years, I still couldn't control it when I slept. And no amount of Xanax in the world could keep me from ever being afraid.

"No scary books or movies for you. No Chinese food before bed. No asshole ex-boyfriends. No driving fast, roller coasters, haunted houses . . ."

I was laughing by the time Calum finished his list, which included Richard Simmons videos and conference calls. We both knew that it was useless—if opening portals really was tied to my emotions, I was going to need a way to work through them without setting off the portal detector. The only hope I saw was that working out seemed to take some of the strength out of the negative emotions. At this point, it was all I had. I still couldn't control this power. I was a terrible superhero.

It was late, and I was exhausted. I started to curl up on the couch with a yawn.

"You can't stay out here by yourself—what if you open another portal?"

"Then I'll grab a pair of leggings to match the tank top."

He rolled his eyes. "Seriously. We need to keep an eye on it, and you can't do that if you are sleeping. At least this way, I might catch you, wake you up, and stop Jay from panicking." Calum pulled me to my feet and led me to his room.

"It's just like every other time you crash here—except with the new excitement of inter-universe shopping," he said. That made me laugh.

The bed was a mess.

"Calum—when was the last time you washed your sheets?"

"Last week. Why?"

"I don't know, it just smells like *eau de stripper* in here."

He threw a pillow at me. I crawled into bed, sliding as far to the edge as I could so I wouldn't crowd him, and snuggled down.

"Someone I know?"

"Do you really care?"

"Not really, but it's fun to torment you. Are you going to see her again?"

"Can you please drop it so we can sleep? If I knew you were going to give me the third degree, I would've kept you on the couch." He ruffled my hair before turning his back to me.

"Well, she obviously can't have anything on me. Can she unintentionally open portals?"

He smiled over his shoulder at me. "She's definitely no Master of the Universe." And with that, he turned off the light.

BLU 22

The next few days were a flurry of activity as we planned the reconnaissance missions to the Jurisdiction building. In light of what happened to Willow and Jack, the Captain had determined it was too dangerous for the trainees—they just didn't have the experience to survive something like this—but with the spy still unaccounted for, and Jack still injured, the rest of us were left trying to plan for missions meant for three times as many Team members. But it didn't matter that we had limited resources. The missions needed to be completed. If that meant that I got less sleep and needed more coffee than normal, so be it.

We gathered all the intelligence we could, but considering Jack, our spymaster, had been caught off guard, we didn't know how close we could even get. A single person was less likely to get caught than a group, so Styx would be the first to go in. The whole mission would be dead in the water if we couldn't figure out the extent of their ability to block our tech. Then the rest of us would follow, in staggered missions, to gather more intel. The longer these recon missions took, the more kids we would need to rescue—not to mention the horrors they would have to endure in the meantime. I had personal experience with those horrors, and I didn't want anyone else to experience them if I could do something about it.

The mood was dark. There was a strong chance that the minions had recognized Jack and radioed that intel before he killed them. The security might have been increased. On top of that, Willow's life still hung in the balance, making the mood that much darker. And there was always the possibility that Jyston was leading us into a trap. Even Ink had lost his perma-smirk, which was disconcerting.

The plan was clear: Ink would drive Styx to the perimeter of the camp's security. She would try to detect how far out the anti-tech reached, and see if there was a way to disable it. Best-case scenario, she'd be able to disable all the anti-tech and bring some back to the Compound to study. Worst-case scenario—well, we didn't talk about that.

When the time arrived, we were assembled in the Captain's office, waiting for Styx. Ink was pacing back and forth in his new body armor, unable to sit still. The armory had created it specifically for these missions: black combat pants with their new lightweight armor sewn in, and a skintight black shirt that had the same armor on the front, back, and down the arms. The armory had been working on this design for a while, and the armorers hoped it would provide us some protection against minions without limiting our mobility or stealth.

Ink struck an imposing figure in the new gear. The shirt strained against his muscled body, and the pants fit snugly against his legs. He wore his sword down his back, daggers at his sides, and a palmbox on his belt. I saw Silver eyeing him in awe; gone was the flirtatious man who exuded sex and laughter. This person standing before me was a killer, and for the thousandth time, I was grateful he was on our side.

Styx finally walked in, the Captain went over the plan one more time, and they headed out. Dev, in the tech building, kept the Captain on ear comms for as long as they lasted, and I was to be on backup just in case everything went to shit—if this week was any indication, it would. If all went to plan, they should be back at the Compound in three hours. Until then, all I could do was wait.

Almost three hours to the minute later, my ear comm came on. It was Dev.

"They're back. Meet at the Captain's office in an hour, after Styx gets out of the infirmary."

"What? Dev, why the hell is she in the infirmary? Is she OK? You can't just say shit like that!"

"Sorry, Blu." He sounded stricken. "I'm still getting used to this. Sorry. She's fine—just some minor burns that need treatment."

"Thanks for letting me know. I'll see you in an hour." I figured I wouldn't pester the medics if Styx really was OK, and I could wait to ask my questions until we were all there. I went to the mess hall for the third time today to grab a donut.

Ink caught up with me on the way to the Captain's office, looking disheveled but uninjured.

"Want to talk about it?"

"You know that I try to stay positive, B. I think we have the best team in the world, and there isn't much we can't do. We've gotten out of scrapes, pulled off miracle missions, taken down huge chunks of Jurisdiction, and we still keep going. But what we saw today—we're fucked."

"Why is this time so different?"

"The whole thing is a deathtrap. They have every inch of that place covered in security. Pressurized spikes that come out of the dirt, for fuck's sake. Anti-tech that reaches over a mile from the building itself. Just from where I was, I saw multiple guard patrols, guard towers, and security cameras, and I was over a mile away. It was a miracle I wasn't caught, and the only reason Styx isn't dead is because she figured out the trap on the anti-tech before it blew her head off. I'm not sure how we're going to pull this one off, B." He ran his hand through his hair.

"That seems like a ridiculous amount of security to keep people out of a children's training camp."

He nodded. "That's what we thought. They might be hiding something else there. Something big."

I grabbed his chin and made him look at me. "Not to sound cheesy, Ink, but we've handled the impossible before, and whatever it is, we'll handle it together, OK?"

"I can't handle another Hastings, B."

"I know, I know. But we have to keep trying, even if we're the only ones left. If we don't—who will?"

FARA 23

The next morning came all too early. I woke up to Calum's alarm, trying to remember where I was. When I opened one eye, I saw Calum staring at me.

"What?"

"Why are we getting up so ungodly early to go to the gym?"

"Because it's good for me. I need a swimsuit bod. Plus, maybe it will keep my Hulk emotions under control. Did I open any portals last night?"

"Not that I saw, and Agent Hanlon didn't call."

Relief flooded through me. I had made it through a night without opening a portal. Now to figure out why. But first, coffee and the gym.

A quick scan, and the two guys were nowhere to be found. Hopefully, whatever Jay had said to them would keep them at bay for a little while longer.

Adora's car was not at the gym. I knew she had the day off, so I was hoping she was sleeping in.

"See you at work?" I asked Calum as I got out of the car. He nodded and grabbed my arm.

"Make sure Millie walks you out to your car if you see those guys, OK? You know where the spare key is for my apartment?"

I thanked him, kissed him on the cheek, and headed into class.

A painful hour later, Millie stopped me on my way out.

"Fara? Can you come into my office?"

Her office was actually part of the locker room. Millie had placed a desk and filing cabinet in one of the communal showers. Despite the unusual accommodations, there was nothing out of place; neat piles of paperwork stood on her desk. Everything about Millie was about neat and compact power. Even her eyes seemed to drill into me as she began speaking.

"You killed it today. Whatever you were channeling, keep it up."

I nodded my thanks, waiting to see if there was more. Millie stared at me for a full minute, her jaw working, like she was debating what to say.

"I need you to hear this. It's something that's been on my mind since you joined my gym. What I'm about to say isn't easy to hear, but I respect you enough to say it."

I didn't know where this was going, but I respected her enough to listen.

"I'm not sure who told you that you weren't supposed to be loud or bold. I'm not sure what circumstances in your life made you believe that your purpose is to be as small and silent and accommodating and convenient as possible. But today, I saw a glimpse of what is buried deep inside you. Today, I saw a warrior in you. Let her out. You deserve it."

She paused, and I could see that she was internally debating whether to say whatever was next on her mind. She took a deep breath and continued.

"You look tired, Fara, and I worry about you. Adora told me about your apartment. Did they ever find who did that?" I shook my head. "Bastards. I am here whenever you need someone, for whatever you need. There's a cot back here if you need a place to stay, or I have a guest room. If things get bad and you don't know who else to talk to, you can come to me. You don't have to face it alone."

The tears started running down my cheeks—that this warrior, this amazing lady was reaching out to me and saw something in me that no one else saw. I felt something break loose inside, something that had been tamped down for so long, I didn't realize it was there. It wasn't big, it wasn't much, but it was a spark. Baby steps in asserting myself? A piece of kindling ignited? My parents were amazing people, and they tried to do what was best for me—what would keep me safe. But in their attempt to keep me out of harm's way, they stifled a part of me. And maybe that part of me was the key to getting this portal-opening thing under control. Or maybe it was the key to finding myself in this whole mess.

I reached across Millie's desk and gave her an awkward hug. She looked taken aback, but gently patted my shoulder and continued when I finally sat back in my seat.

"I'm going to waive your gym membership fee for the next few months, until you can get back on your feet again. Don't argue with me—I can see it in your eyes. Just pay it forward when you can." She gave me a small smile, a rare treat. I mumbled my thanks and headed for the door.

"Oh, and Fara?" she called after me. "That guy who was living with you was never good enough for you. Never. You need someone who treats you like you treat people. There are so many fish in the sea, should you choose. What about Calum?" She raised an eyebrow at me and let out a belly laugh when my face turned about fourteen shades of red. She waved me off and I walked out of her office, feeling better than I had in forever.

Calum was already gone when I got to his apartment. The two guys were nowhere to be seen, so I scurried inside and got ready for work in record time. I threw on what remaining clothes I had and rushed through putting on my makeup, hoping it was enough to satisfy Douche's obsession with women's appearances. I raced back out to Voldemort and drove to work as fast as the bungee cord would allow me—all the while wondering why the radio was turning on and off at random intervals. Great. Just another thing I needed fixed. Maybe I should just scrap the POS and get a bus pass. As if sensing my intentions, Voldemort's radio turned on and blasted the song "Don't Leave Me This Way." I had to laugh. With all the weird shit that was happening to me, it wasn't a long stretch to think that my car was communicating with me through the radio, like Bumblebee. I gently patted the dash and put it in park, looking around to make sure I wasn't followed, and rushed into The Grill.

As soon as I entered, Douche intercepted me, Hewitt not far behind.

"You're late."

"I know. I'm sorry. It's been hard, with my apartment—"

"I don't want excuses, I want punctuality. Consider this a warning. Again. If this continues, no matter your *living* situation, you will be replaced. The Grill has been open for five minutes already, and you already have a customer in your section. It's the same guy as before. I am not your personal messenger service—but maybe this time he'll actually order something."

Barrington Park was here? Oh no, no, no. Could I avoid this? Bribe Hewitt to take the table? Even if I did, it seemed that Barrington Park would stop at nothing to get my attention. And maybe if he talked to me, I could verify that the two guys who were following me belonged to him and get him to call them off. All while trying to serve him drinks. No problem.

I got my apron and gathered myself as much as I could as I approached the booth where Barrington Park was sitting. I had to stem my panic so that I didn't accidentally open a portal in the middle of lunch rush.

From afar, I could see he was somewhere in his late fifties or early sixties. His hair was dark, with salt and pepper throughout, and was perfectly styled, not a piece out of place. He was wearing a sport coat over his fit frame, and even from this distance I could tell it cost more than all my clothes combined. His nails shone like he'd recently had a manicure, and when he moved his arm, I could see some sort of diamond-encrusted watch on his wrist. He looked up as I approached, and his eyes were striking—such a pale blue that they were almost translucent. They held not an ounce of warmth. While Jay's eyes screamed *predator*, Barrington Park's eyes murmured something much more sinister. The way he was looking at me was disconcerting, as if just by looking at me, he could tear out my soul. But in a moment, that expression was gone, replaced by a bland smile. If it weren't for the fact that his smile didn't meet his eyes, I would have thought I'd imagined the chilling expression. No doubt about it—this man was lethal, even if he was going to try to be genial. He was a powerful man who was used to getting his way by whatever means necessary, and for the hundredth time this week, I felt how totally out of my depth I was.

I plastered my best smile on my face. "Good afternoon. Mr. Park, right? I heard you were looking for me?"

He smiled again, and again it did not reach his eyes. "Yes, but please, call me Barrington. You are a very hard girl to track down, Miss Bayne."

"I'm sorry. Things have been a bit crazy—"

"Yes," he interrupted. "I did hear about your apartment. Tragedy. Hopefully nothing of value was stolen?"

My heart stopped. How did he know about my apartment? It had to be the two guys—but why say that if it was him? I was not good at this spy thing.

"Not that I'm aware of, Mr. Park. I'm not sure why you want to talk to me, but I have to work. Can we set an appointment to talk later?"

"Oh, don't worry, Miss Bayne. I took the liberty of renting out your entire section for the next hour so that you and I could speak without being interrupted. And I will also compensate you for your time—triple what you would have made in tips in that hour."

Triple what I would have made? That kind of money could put Voldemort's nose back on—or get my apartment cleaned up! This guy was giving me all the creepy vibes, but money was money. At least if I was still here, I was safe. But why didn't Douche tell me that this guy rented out the space? Unless Douche was going to pocket the money. I would have to make sure I got paid.

"Now that the formalities are out of the way, please, have a seat." He paused as he waited for me to slide into the booth. This close, I could almost feel the power radiating off him. While he kept a pleasant look on his face, his very presence was menacing. I took a deep breath—no use getting panicky now and opening a portal.

"Miss Bayne, I would like to talk to you about an interesting job opportunity I have for you."

I blinked. Job opportunity? I wasn't sure how I thought this conversation would go, but that was *not* the direction I was ready for. My face must have given me away because Barrington chuckled and shook his head.

"Not what you were expecting? I'm not sure how much you know about me or my company, so before I get to the reason of why I'm here, I'll start at the beginning—if that is alright with you." I nodded, and he continued.

"I have always been interested in the science of communication—that's why I founded Specter COMS, Inc.

My company works with governments and organizations around the world to expand how—and where—they can communicate. We work with NASA on communications with the space station and the rovers on Mars. We work with private companies that send unmanned submarines deep under the sea. We work with governments to help simplify communication with their populations. We want people to be able to communicate to whomever, whenever, by whatever means they choose."

He stopped and smiled a beatific smile that radiated trust and confidence, like he had given this speech a thousand times, and now was at the part where I was supposed to say or do something that he wanted. But just like with Jay, silence did not intimidate me, and I could sit here quietly all day. I wanted him to keep going and get to the part where he tells me why he is stalking me, and confirms that the two guys are his employees. His smile slipped just a bit as he waited for me to respond. I kept my face blank. We sat like that for a while, each second his smile slipping just a bit more. Finally, he spoke first.

"You must be wondering what all that has to do with you."

I nodded but still did not say anything. I needed him to show his hand, and I was worried I would say the wrong thing. Better to stay quiet and wait. His smile slipped even more.

"A girl of few words. I can respect that. I'm not going to beat around the bush, then. I believe that you have in your possession a device that, quite frankly, will change the communication landscape forever. I want to buy the device from you. Then I would like to hire you to work with me and my scientists to study it. I will pay you handsomely for both."

My mask must have cracked because his smile widened. If what he said was true, he didn't realize I was causing the portals—he still thought that I had a device and had figured out how to use it to create the portal. How to respond? I had to play this carefully.

"Mr. Park, while I appreciate your time, I don't have any device—"

"Miss Bayne, we have irrefutable evidence to the contrary."

"I don't mean to be rude, but your evidence must be mistaken. I don't have anything like what you're talking about."

"I think you do."

"Mr. Park, I really don't know what you're talking about."

And just like that, his own mask slipped. His eyes drilled into my skull, and he slammed his hand down on the table hard enough to make me jump and turn the heads of other customers. I shrank down in my seat.

"Do *not* lie to me, Miss Bayne! You will find me far less amenable. I know that you have the device, and I know you know how to use it. I will get the device and your help one way or another."

"Is that why you are having two guys follow me?"

His silence answered for him. Seriously, this guy was a scary fruit loop. He was going to get what he wanted, whether I wanted him to or not, and I had a sinking feeling that he had more resources than even Jay's department. I was royally fucked, but I wasn't going to give up yet.

"Miss Bayne, I will pay you one million dollars for the device. I will then pay you an annual salary of $500,000, plus living expenses and bonuses, should you accept my job offer. You will have your pick of lofts to live in, clothes to wear, cars to drive, servants to see to your every need. Anything you can dream of, I can make happen for you. It is a more than generous offer for a waitress with a high school education. All you need to do is work with us on getting the device to work."

I nodded, speechless. That sort of money wasn't even real to me—it was like Monopoly money—and he'd offered it without breaking a sweat. Unfortunately, I didn't have the device. I just had me. And I was not about to sell myself to this guy, even if the price was amazing. He had let slip an interesting piece of information. Whatever device he had in his possession—whatever he'd created all those years ago—he couldn't get it to open portals. Which was why he needed me with the device. Otherwise, why go through all this hassle? In theory, he could just kill me and take the device he thought I had. He must consider *me* critical in opening the portal. Little did he know how right he was, but for the wrong reasons.

There was no way I was accepting his offer, but I was afraid if I turned him down right now, I might not live to see tomorrow. I needed time for Jay to come up with something—or for me to get this under control.

"Mr. Park, your offer is more than generous. You have given me a lot to consider. Give me some time to think about it?"

He stood up and put money on the table. The meeting was over.

"I'll give you twenty-four hours to decide. I'll be waiting." He leveled me with a stare that chilled me to the bone, and walked toward the door. On his way out, he looked over his shoulder.

"Miss Bayne, do not make the same mistake your mother did when I gave her a similar offer. It did not end well for her."

My stomach dropped. What did he mean? He'd offered her the same deal, and she turned it down? Did he do something to her? I sat down and put my head in my hands. He had threatened me, that was obvious. I was in deep, deep shit. I grabbed the money—there was $400 on the table. At least I could buy some groceries for Calum's place. I got up to finish my shift. It was going to be a long day.

"He said what?" Calum stopped chopping the onion and turned to look at me. I leaned on the doorframe of his kitchen and sipped my beer. Our shift had been so busy that I hadn't been able to talk to him after Barrington Park left.

"He said to not make the same mistake my mom did. It was definitely a threat."

Calum went back to chopping onions. "That's fucked up."

"Yeah, tell me about it. He's offering me stupid amounts of money because he thinks I have a device and can use it."

"You aren't thinking about taking him up on the offer, are you?"

"To be honest, I thought about it for a minute. It would be nice not to be broke, for once. And to have a chef."

"You have a chef." Calum laughed as he grabbed a pepper and started chopping it. He made the best stir-fry, and my stomach started to rumble.

"You know what I mean! But no, I'm not going to sell myself so that the scariest guy I've ever met can have access to alternate universes and possibly take over the world. You remember what my mom did—she lied to everyone to keep the power away from the baddies. I can't turn around and give it to them."

"Have you told Agent Hanlon?"

"I texted him on my way here."

I put silverware and drinks on the coffee table, and we were just sitting down to eat when there was a knock at the door. Calum got up and indicated that I should hide in his bedroom while he answered the door. I ran into the room with my plate, shut the door, and waited, trying to listen over my chewing. I heard Calum open the front door, then Jay's voice rumbling. I was about to leave my spot but then paused. I needed to be sure Jay was by himself before coming out. Even though I trusted him, I didn't trust his organization, and what if he was here against his will with someone from the department? How paranoid had I become? I was straining to listen for another voice when the door opened. Jay was staring at me, my fork halfway to my mouth. He raised his eyebrows at the tableau: just a girl in a bedroom with her plate of stir-fry. Under any other circumstances, I would have been mortified. All I could muster was a shrug.

"Tell me more about your conversation with Barrington Park."

I nodded as I walked out of the bedroom, chewing my dinner. Calum had already taken a perch on the couch, plate on his lap. I noticed that he'd made a plate for Jay as well; forever a good host.

I related everything that Barrington had said, Jay nodding and looking increasingly worried.

Calum asked, "Do you think Barrington had anything to do with Fara's mom's death?"

"Anything is possible," Jay replied. "Did they ever figure out what caused the crash?"

I knew the answer all too well, painful as it was. "The official report was reckless driving. According to witness statements, my father had been driving erratically, too fast for the road conditions. Witnesses said they saw him lose control of the car, and he crashed through the guardrail. The officer at the scene believed my parents died on impact, but the car exploded and burned everything, so it was just a best guess."

My throat closed and my eyes started to sting. I remembered getting the call from the police, my disbelief that my parents had died and that I was totally alone. The loneliness that ensued as I worked my way through wrapping up their affairs. The realization that they were never coming back. The grief that still reared its ugly head every now and again.

At the time, I'd had a hard time believing the reports. It didn't make sense. My mom and I had teased my dad relentlessly about driving like an old man, always below the speed limit, always blissfully unaware that the cars around him were speeding past. I was so angry that the one time he drove fast, he crashed. I felt so much guilt—maybe if we hadn't teased him so much, they wouldn't have died.

Calum put down his fork and rubbed my shoulder. I shrugged him off, but with an apologetic glance. I needed to start dealing with my emotions, one way or another, and pity wouldn't help.

"If it means something to you," Jay said, "I'll try to dig up the police file on their deaths. If Barrington Park had anything to do with it, it was probably wiped from the official record, but I can poke around. Do you really want to know, though?"

I thought about it. What would I do if I found out Barrington Park had something to do with my parents' death? Would it change my decision about working for him? No, it wouldn't, but it would deepen my resolve in never letting him get his hands on the device—or me, for that matter.

"If he had anything to do with their deaths, I want to know. Because if he did, I'll kill him."

Both Calum and Jay's eyebrows rose into their hairlines at that. I guess that was more forceful than they were used to from me—but then again, they had never seen me dealing with the possibility that my parents had been killed. New territory for everyone.

"OK," Jay said, "I'll do that later. Right now, we have a bigger problem. Fara, I'm supposed to bring you in to the department's offices for questioning tomorrow. I'm actually here unofficially, to warn you."

Oh shit. A thousand questions crowded their way into my mouth at once, and my panic was making a meteoric rise.

"What does that mean? Do I need to hide? What do they have planned? Can you stall them again?"

"I can't stall them any more than I already have without bringing more attention to you. If they think we're working together, then the questions go from interested to full interrogation of us both—and I can't risk it. For you."

Jay looked me in the eye. "Since I haven't told them about your . . . ability, they are still under the same assumption that Barrington Park seems to be—that you have a device your mother left you and have figured out how to use it. I am hoping that if you go in and act as if you don't know what's happening, I can convince them that it was a malfunction. We would just need to make sure that you don't accidentally set it off while you are there."

"What time are you supposed to bring me in?"

"I can arrange it so that it works as well as it can for you."

"I'm really doing this."

"I know it's not ideal, but I can't think of any other way. On the bright side, as long as the government is questioning you, then you are safe from Barrington Park."

"Great! I'll be safe from a megalomaniac because I'm being *questioned by the government*. Excuse me if I don't jump for joy at the prospect."

Calum snorted, but Jay studied the floor, saying, "Fara, if I could avoid this I would. But I promised you that I would keep you safe, and I *will* keep that promise. If questioning goes awry, or if you feel like you are losing control, I will get you out of there. I won't let them keep you against your will."

He looked up at me again, and I held his gaze. He was putting his career on the line for me because he believed it was the right thing to do. The least I could do was work with him to make this questioning as painless as possible.

"Alright, I'll come with you to be questioned—but I need your help to prepare."

"We can start now."

"Fine. I work tomorrow night, so can we go after I go to the gym in the morning? I want to work out as much fear as I can before going with you. Obviously, I can't afford to accidentally open up a portal when I'm insisting I don't know what they are talking about, so I need to do as much as I can to keep calm." Jay agreed that he could make that work.

The three of us practiced interrogating me until I felt like I was as prepared as I could be. Jay seemed to be most concerned about the assistant and her role in the questioning, but since he didn't know much about her, we couldn't really prepare for it. We were just going to have to wing it.

It was late by the time we were done. As I walked Jay to the door, and he looked down at me, his face unreadable, he opened his mouth to say something but stopped.

"What?"

He let out a breath, concern in his eyes. "My department has ways of tracking people, and they won't hesitate to use them if they think you can be of use to them—no matter the cost. So just remember your promise. If things go badly tomorrow, don't worry about anyone else. You run away, and you don't look back. And you stay gone so that no one can find you."

"Do you think tomorrow will go to shit?"

"I don't know. I would like to believe that my superiors are reasonable, but the assistant is an unknown factor. I just want you to be prepared."

I was trusting that tomorrow would go as planned, and I was hopeful that we would be able to convince the government that the first activation of the device had been a fluke—that I wasn't someone of interest. But in that moment, it felt as if the weight of it all was pressing down on me. What if they kept me forever? What if it all went wrong? I felt the fear grip me, and without thinking about it, I grabbed his hand. After his initial surprise, he turned to me and grabbed my other hand. It was my turn to be surprised.

We stood there, neither of us saying anything. I could feel something shifting between the two of us, so I stood perfectly still, willing the moment to continue. I wasn't sure what I wanted, but I knew that I wanted to continue . . . whatever this was. His presence was like a balm for my nerves. He was a rock-solid wall I could lean on, hide behind, take comfort in. I drew in a breath to say something—anything—that would let him know how much I appreciated all that he was doing, but before I could get the words out, he bent his head toward mine, eyes questioning, movement tentative. When I didn't back away, he closed the distance, his lips gently touching mine. Those gorgeous lips were finally kissing me, and I felt it all the way to my toes. We lingered in the kiss for just a moment, then Jay pulled back, resting his forehead on mine, eyes closed and smiling.

"I've been hoping you would do that for a while now," I said. He kissed me again. His lips were warm and so painfully gentle, as if he were afraid he'd hurt me. I lifted onto my toes so that my hands could reach up to grab his neck, to pull him closer to me—to let him know I was more than OK with how this was going. I could feel my body responding to his touch, my core heating up, and I allowed myself to feel all of it. I had forgotten what this felt like, and I reveled in it. My arms tightened around his neck, and his arms wrapped around me. In this moment, right now, I was so happy.

"Well, I guess we know another one of Fara's emotions that opens portals," Calum said wryly as the device started to beep uncontrollably.

I turned my head and saw another window, but as soon as I realized what had happened, I clamped down on my emotions, and the portal closed with a hiss. Calum shrugged and walked into his studio.

Jay looked down at me with a smile. "If I knew that was all it took for you to open a portal, I would have done that a long time ago." I couldn't help but grin at him, but then his face got serious.

"Tomorrow, that can't happen, OK? Do whatever you have to do to suppress it, but we need to keep your ability secret." I nodded and put my head on his chest, listening to his heartbeat and taking deep breaths. He spoke into my hair. "When this is all over, I'd love to take you out to dinner."

I smiled into his shirt. "Let's get through tomorrow first. But yeah—I'd like that."

He kissed me on the forehead, looked into my eyes, nodded once, then left.

I shut the door after him and walked into Calum's art studio to find him prepping a canvas for his next painting. I knocked on the doorframe, and he looked up, and we stood there in silence. I wasn't quite sure what he was thinking, but I was hoping he wasn't going to make a big deal about what had just happened.

"What is it?" I asked him as he indicated I should perch on the stool by the door.

He busied himself with his paints, not looking at me at all. "I'm just worried."

"I'm worried too."

"Obviously not worried enough."

"What's that supposed to mean?"

He glared at me. "Fara, you understand that you just made out with a guy who is going to take you into questioning *with the government* tomorrow, right? You don't know his intentions—he could have kissed you so that you would go easily with him for questioning. He could be using your kindness, your vulnerability. And you are so sweet, so trusting, that you just accept that he's a good guy because he says he is. You shouldn't be with him like that. It's not safe."

"Let me remind you, Calum, that the three of us planned for me to go in with him tomorrow. *Before* he kissed me. I was going anyway; I didn't have a choice."

"But now you'll go because he asked, not because you don't have a choice!"

"Does it matter why I go?"

"He's using you, Fara!"

Something in me snapped. I might not be gorgeous. I might not be educated. I might not be thin or stylish. But I was kind. I was funny. I was empathetic and loyal. And I had to trust that I could handle whatever was thrown at me. Even if Jay was using me, I could handle that too. If Calum chose to see the worst—that Jay only wanted to use me—then that was his problem, not mine.

"Is it really so hard for you to believe that he likes me because of *me*? That he could possibly find me attractive or smart or funny on my own? Not because he needs something from me—but because he genuinely likes me? Is that so hard for you to comprehend? Just because you think of me as a stupid little sister incapable of making my own decisions doesn't mean the rest of the world sees me that way!"

Calum's shoulders drooped. "Is that what you really believe I think of you?"

"I think you've been protecting me for so long that you've forgotten I'm a grown-up. I've been *letting* you protect me for so long that I've forgotten I'm a grown-up too. Calum, do you think I haven't already considered his motives? Why would someone like him be interested in someone like me, other than to use me to get what he wants? I'm an average-looking waitress who can't even keep a deadbeat boyfriend. Men knock me off my barstool to talk to women like Adora. People like Hewitt relish harassing me because I won't stand up for myself. So why would a gorgeous guy like Jay, who didn't know I even existed before a few days ago, all of a sudden want me? Of course I've considered it! But at some point, I have to believe that I'm worthy of affection. I have to believe that I have more to offer than opening portals. I want to believe it's just because of me. And more importantly, if he is using me, that I trust myself enough to deal with that too!"

I walked away, taking deep breaths. I was angry at Calum, but mostly at myself. How did I get to this point in my life? I tried to calm down. I couldn't afford to open another portal, so I lay down on the couch, willing myself not to cry. Remembering Jay's lips on mine—hoping that what he said was real—and that what I felt was real.

Calum didn't follow me, and I was grateful. I didn't want to talk to him about this anymore. Eventually I must have dozed off, because I woke up to Calum gently brushing the hair off my face.

"I'm sorry," he said quietly. "You're right. I do trust you. But it is because you *are* such a beautiful, amazing human being that I worry about you, not because you aren't. He would be stupid not to fall for you—even if I don't like it."

My anger at Calum deflated, and I grabbed his hand. "Don't worry. He asked me out for after this is all over. It's all business until then—and until I have my own place. If I'm honest, it felt weird kissing someone else in your apartment. I won't be repeating that."

"Yeah, the only person who should be kissing you in my apartment is me," Calum said with a wink, kissing the top of my head and heading to the bedroom. "Coming?"

BLU 24

I walked into the Captain's office with Ink, trying to regain my composure after our little heart-to-heart. If Ink was feeling defeated, it had to be worse than what we had imagined. I looked around the table, and everyone except Willow was there. Styx was seated, both hands wrapped in bandages, and she had a nasty cut above her eye. Her face was grim but determined—which seemed to be the general mood in the room.

Once Ink and I were seated, the Captain began. "We have some good news and some bad news. I'll start with the good news, since it won't take long: Styx was able to bring back a piece of Jurisdiction's new anti-tech, and once this meeting is over, she and Dev are going to be working around the clock to see if they can figure out how it works or, at the very least, how to disable it."

We all nodded appreciatively at Styx. From what Ink had said, taking that piece of anti-tech almost killed her. This was a huge win for the Team—but no one was smiling. We were waiting for the bad news.

"Styx, why don't you take over?"

"The bad news is, the prison's fortification is tighter and more advanced than even our worst-case predictions. It is a fucking nightmare. They have guard towers throughout the forest surrounding the building. They've also buried pressurized stakes into the ground at random intervals that have a nasty habit of impaling someone going for a stroll, so staying on the ground and hiking to the fence surrounding the building would be disastrous. The fence itself has some sort of current going through it—like nothing I've ever seen before—along with the standard razor wire."

"How did they build this without us knowing?" Jack said. "How did we not see or hear about it, or...something?"

"My guess is because no technology, other than Jurisdiction's, seems to work out there. Any sort of spying would have to be done in person, and . . ." she held up her hands for emphasis, ". . . as you can see, that's a nightmare."

"How far does the anti-tech reach?"

"At least a mile outside of the building."

What? That was going to royally screw us in so many ways. "So, unless you can figure out how to disable it, we'll be going in blind."

Styx nodded. "Yeah. That's not all. They have security cameras stationed throughout the forest and then at regular intervals on the fence. We can only assume that they have security cameras in and on the building, but we couldn't even get close enough to see. Finally, they have regular patrols on the main road, which seems to be the only entrance or exit."

The Captain joined in. "Which leads us to the next mission. While Dev and Styx work on figuring out this new anti-tech, we need to see if there are any back roads or maintenance roads that we could use to get in and out, and avoid getting impaled, preferably." She turned to Ink. "This mission is for you. Blu can drive and will be on backup if things go poorly. I will leave the planning up to the Team, with a word of caution. We know that we can get close enough to see the building— Jackrabbit and Willow proved that—but at what cost? So, stay away for now, if you can. Assume that palmboxes and comms will be useless."

We agreed to meet the next morning to begin the logistics of this mission. Since I was the only one who hadn't been to the building site yet, I had the most catching up to do, but even then, the planning wouldn't take long, especially given that we couldn't rely on technology. It was going to come down to good old-fashioned reconnaissance, and Ink was the best there was.

◆ ◆ ◆

The next morning, I felt, more than saw, a pair of pants aimed at my face, so I reached out from under the covers and snatched them out of the air, much to Ink's displeasure.

"You're no fun at all," he said, throwing yesterday's socks at me.

I pulled the covers back over my head. "I am fun—starting in about two hours with a few cups of coffee. Right now, I'm homicidal, so you might want to leave."

He lingered, absently taking pieces of clothes from the piles strewn about and examining them before setting them back down. I watched him for a while, not sure he was even really paying attention to what he was doing. He'd always been like this; he had so much energy that he walked around and touched stuff, always getting into things. It made me smile, until he found my "good" underwear shoved under a pile of towels.

"Where were these when we were dating?"

"I'm saving them for someone who would appreciate them."

"I would have appreciated them."

"You were a teenager, Ink. You just appreciated that I let you touch my boobs."

"Fair enough. I brought you coffee."

"And that is why I still keep you around." I got up and started walking to the bathroom.

Ink grinned. "Ah—those are the underwear I remember."

"For your information, I dress for me, not for you—or anyone else, for that matter. If I wanted to wear grandma underwear every day and they made me feel sexy, then I would. If I wanted to wear a black thong, I would. If I wanted to go commando, I would. None of those things are for you, or for any other man. So stop thinking that what women wear is for your pleasure. If they are worth your time, they're dressing for themselves."

Ink shrugged and continued to smile, taking a good long look at my ass. Hopeless. At some point I needed to knock some sense into him, but first, coffee.

Ink finally left, and I finished getting ready. I was running behind because I couldn't find my favorite shirt in the piles. I wondered if Styx had borrowed it again—and then wondered why she would, since all black shirts look the same—and then wondered why *I* cared since, well, all black shirts look the same. I eventually found something marginally clean, grabbed my coffee, and headed to the Quad for training.

After getting my ass thoroughly handed to me by the Captain during training, I helped some younger trainees with dagger throwing and hand-to-hand combat, and then headed to the mess hall to snag some food before we met to plan the mission. On my way, I ran into Styx, who seemed to be heading in the same direction. Her hands were still bandaged, but the swelling from the cut above her eye was slowly going down. She was wearing a black shirt too.

"Hey—is that my shirt?"

"Good morning to you too," she huffed. "I stopped borrowing your clothes when Ink told me I'd never fill them out like you did."

"He seriously was not dumb enough to say that."

"Yes, yes he was."

"Did you kill him a little?"

"Just a bit."

"Good. A black shirt is a black shirt. How are the hands?"

"They hurt like a bitch, but at least I can still use them. It could've been a lot worse. I disabled the self-destruct mechanism that would've taken my head off. I'll take a few minor burns over death."

"Good perspective. Self-destruct? They're really serious about keeping the anti-tech secret. Ink and I have been talking, and there seems to be a completely absurd amount of security around this building, for what it's supposed to be. Do you think there's something else going on?"

"I don't know, but until we can get closer and get this anti-tech stuff figured out, we won't be able to find out."

We got food at the mess and caught up on the latest Compound gossip. I normally don't pay any attention to any of it, but the way Styx described the Team's dalliances made me laugh uncontrollably.

"She literally fell asleep outside of Ink's door, waiting for him to let her in—and he wasn't even there!" Styx said through a snort.

"She should've known better. Where was Ink?"

"Rumor says he was with the girl from the armory. Second time he's stayed with her. It might be serious?" She waggled her eyebrows, which made me roll my eyes.

"With Ink? Please. He probably came back from armory girl's place to find the other girl in the hallway, only to bring her inside for a pre-training 'workout.' No wonder he was in a mood this morning."

Styx looked at me over her coffee mug. "You know he won't settle down unless it's with you."

I laughed. "We've been over this. It's not happening. Seriously. You're crazy for even suggesting it! I don't feel that way about him and vice versa. We're too much alike! He's brash and outspoken and ruthless, just as I am. He honestly needs someone who balances him out. Someone sweeter. Kinder, maybe."

"So, someone who's you but not?"

I laughed but didn't say anything. She raised an eyebrow at me. "Any more run-ins with your boyfriend?"

"Will you stop calling him that? Run-ins? You mean other than the last time, when he held a dagger to Silver's neck?"

She smiled. "So, he really knew who you were at the masquerade? And he still went along with your ploy and flirted relentlessly with you? That's some crazy shit." I nodded in agreement, packing up my stuff to go.

She continued, "I mean, all kidding aside—he told you where the plans for the building were, *knowing* that you are part of the Team. I sort of get why he doesn't turn you in, if he thinks it helps keep Dagna off his ass. But why help us?"

I had been asking myself that question on an endless loop for days, and I was no closer to the answer. Why go along with my ruse if he knew who I was? Why help us? Or was it even really help? If he knew that this building was already constructed and that we would eventually find it . . . was it a trap? Did he know that we would try to rescue the kids, regardless? I was no closer to the answer, but at this point the why seems superfluous. We needed a how—and I couldn't let him be a distraction until I had more information.

FARA 25

I slept fitfully, although I thankfully did not open a portal. Eventually, I gave up on sleep and quietly watched Calum next to me. He wore shorts, his bare chest rising and falling in the quiet rhythm of sleep. In the dark I could barely make out his tattoos, beautiful artwork from his own collection and rendered on his skin. They were such a part of who he was, I hadn't really noticed them in a while, but while he was asleep, I could stare at them—at him—without being self-conscious. He was beautiful, and for a moment I wondered what it would have been like to be in a relationship with him; what it would have been like in another world where we hadn't started out like siblings, where he would kiss my lips and not the top of my head. Would we have been a good romantic couple? I would have liked to believe so, even if we were too much alike, but circumstances being what they were, it wasn't possible to know. And now, with Beck gone and the thing with Jay, well, it didn't make sense to even wonder.

Dawn approached, and with it the events of the past few days went through my mind. Today I was going to be questioned by my own government, whether I wanted to be or not. Although I was trying to put on a brave face, I was petrified. I had to convince them I was of no interest. I had to believe that they were not the bad guys, that I would make it out of this and go back to my life, whatever that was. If I could get through this, I could focus on getting my apartment back in shape. I could maybe go on a real date with Jay. I could live *normally*.

But was that what I wanted? The past few days, while horrible and stressful, were liberating, in a way. I was able to do something unexplainable. I was able to open doorways to new worlds and, theoretically, step through them. Did I want to shove this talent down? It was this amazing thing that I was going to hide. Calum and Jay believed that hiding my ability was for my own protection—and I thought I agreed with them. What good was opening portals? Could I help people with it? Could I help myself? A tiny voice in my head said to take the chance and explore; to be brave. But I couldn't risk being captured and, as Calum reminded me, being put in a state of sleep forever to serve whatever bad guy's nefarious purpose. I knew it was the prudent thing to do—to suppress my ability. But a little piece of me wished I didn't have to.

Knowing that sleep was not going to come to me, I got out of bed, giving Calum a kiss on his forehead. I realized that there was a weird stillness about this moment, like it was a picture that I needed to remember. As though I might not see him like this again. I shook the feeling off and looked through my things; none of my workout gear had survived the Great Apartment Massacre. I sighed and put back on the same leggings I had been living in for the past few days and looked for any tank top I could find. I eyeballed the tank top I had grabbed from the portal and quickly debated whether to wear it. I knew it should probably be studied and whatever, but a girl needs to be cool when she works out. I shrugged and put it on—and although a little snug around my middle, it fit. Huh. I sent a silent thank you to whatever creature had let me borrow the shirt—and hoped that he/she/they/the alien ninja was not upset by its absence. A black tank top was a black tank top, after all.

I quietly made coffee and while it brewed, I grabbed a bag and put a change of clothes in it. If Jay was going to pick me up at the gym, then I would just shower there—no need to come back here. Coffee done, last donut and clothes in hand, I made my way to the gym.

"I've been so worried about you, chica!" Adora exclaimed as I walked through the door. "How are you? How's your apartment? I heard about Beck. What an asshole! I'm going to start telling everyone I know that he's terrible in bed. Ugh! But on to better things. Like, how's the hot agent man?" She waggled her eyebrows at the last one.

I laughed. I couldn't tell her what was going on, other than they were taking me for questioning, and I was a terrible liar—so I needed to distract her with part of the truth.

"Hot Agent Man's name is Jay, and he asked me on date . . . after he kissed me."

She squealed and danced around on her toes, trying to hug me at the same time. "Where did he kiss you?"

"In Calum's apartment."

"No! I mean, on the neck, cheek? The hooha?"

I laughed again. "On the mouth."

"Ohhhh! And what did Calum say about that?"

I rolled my eyes, and then Millie walked out and told us to get our asses in gear. I reminded myself why I was there—to work out any overpowering emotions so that I didn't open a portal by accident during my questioning, or during rush hour, for that matter. I pushed myself during class and was a sweaty, tired mess by the time I was done.

After class I went back out to my car to grab my clothes for a shower, checking my phone. There was a message from Jay saying he was running late and would just meet me at Calum's place in an hour. So much for planning.

I was typing a reply when someone grabbed my arm. I looked up, startled, to see it was a giant guy in a suit. Reflexively, I wrenched my arm out of his grasp and ran back toward the gym. Once my brain caught up with my body, I screamed. Adora came running out.

"What the fuck?"

"Bad guys—run!"

We made it into the gym, and I slammed the door behind us, but I was too late—the guy got his foot in between the door and the doorframe and ripped the door out from my hands. He grabbed me again and I kicked him, hard enough that he let go. I started to run to the back of the gym, Adora behind me. Millie stepped out of her office at the commotion.

"What's going on?"

"Some baddies are trying to get Fara," Adora said as we raced past her, hurdling benches and avoiding lockers on our way to the rear exit.

"In here, quickly, girls. I'll check the back door," Millie said, pushing us behind a wall and heading toward the back door.

I heard the door open and a deep, rumbling voice, then a crash. I peeked around the corner and saw Millie was facing another giant guy in a suit, whom she had somehow already disarmed.

"We just want Miss Bayne. She comes with us, and there's no problem."

"Fara, do you want to go with this guy?" Millie asked me.

"Uh. Not really."

"You heard the lady. She's not coming with you."

He shrugged and lunged at me. Millie intercepted him and then the fight was on. The man was twice her size and half her age, but she was having none of it. They were moving so fast it looked staged, Matrix style, and I would have been in awe if I wasn't feeling so terrible that she was getting hurt because of me. I had always known that Millie was a badass, but this just proved it. She was bleeding from her nose, but with a final move, she took him down face first, pinning his arm behind his back.

"Run, Fara!"

"I wouldn't do that if I were you." I whipped around. The first goon was holding a gun to Adora's head, his arm around her chest. "If you move, she dies. You need to come with me, Miss Bayne."

"She won't be going anywhere with you, dickface," Adora spat at him, but he ignored her. He was calm and professional—not like those hotheaded goons you see in the movies. This guy, like his partner, was deadly.

"Miss Bayne, my orders are to take you with me. I do not want to hurt this young lady here, but I will, if it's the only way to convince you of my sincerity. You need to come with me right now."

"Don't listen to him, Fara. Run!"

I froze. What the hell was I supposed to do? Should I run and leave Adora and Millie to their fates? Should I go with them, hoping he wouldn't hurt my friends? I couldn't live with myself if something happened to Adora or Millie because of me.

"Let her go and I'll go with you."

Adora shook her head, tears streaming down her face. The man nodded once and shoved her away, pointing the gun at me.

"Miss Bayne, with me please."

I palmed my phone into Millie's hand as she let the other guy up. He was bleeding from his forehead. "Agent Hanlon," I mouthed to her, as the guy grabbed me by the arm and marched me out the back door to the sedan that had been following me for days. Barrington Park wasn't going to take any chances with my answer—he was going to take me in, regardless. He probably knew I was heading to the government's offices today and wanted to get to me before that happened. I just hoped that Millie and Adora got my meaning, and Jay could come find me. If not . . . I didn't want to think of the consequences. If not, I had no hope.

We had been driving northwest out of the city for some time—at least thirty minutes was my best guess. I looked out of the window at the gray sky, and I tried to recognize something—anything—to get my bearings. If I didn't know where I was, I couldn't get back home when I escaped. And I would escape. I had to keep telling myself that. It was cold and rainy, and I shivered a bit in my tank top and leggings, wondering for the thousandth time where we were going and what was in store for me.

For the first part of the journey, I had yelled, screamed, kicked, and punched the glass that divided the front and back seats, all to no avail, and with no reaction from the two guys I had named Agents Smith and Johnson (it seemed to fit their Matrix vibe). I had tried to ask them questions, threaten them, and anything else I could think of—but they didn't react to me at all. Agent Johnson drove, while Agent Smith bandaged his head, then fiddled with the technology that was inside the car.

While from the outside, the car looked like a regular sedan, the inside was a different story. There was no way to open the back doors from the inside, even though I tried every so often just to see. How many times had someone been trapped like I was? I didn't want to go down that road. It would only make me freak out more.

In addition to being set up for kidnapping, it appeared that the car was decked out with hundreds of thousands of dollars' worth of technology. There were dials and screens everywhere, and I could only guess what they did. Barrington Park didn't mess around with his toys—if that was who hired them at all. All I had were questions and zero answers. I shivered again.

We passed corn and soybean fields, with the occasional roadside gas station. We were on a typical country highway in the Midwest, but I continued to pay attention anyway in the hope that I could find my way back home. Maybe when they let me out of the car, whenever that would be.

Eventually, the car turned off the highway onto a long, gated drive. A security guard opened the gate and let us through. I waved frantically at the security guard, trying to pantomime that I had been captured against my will, but either he couldn't see me in the back with the tinted windows, or he was paid not to care. Either way, my gesturing did nothing except chip away at my hope.

The drive was tree-lined, beautiful, and, I estimated, at least half a mile long, which meant that whatever our destination was, it couldn't be seen from the road. As we rounded the drive's last bend, our destination came into view. If I weren't scared for my life, I would have been impressed. The house was a huge white monstrosity, complete with columns and a circular drive that sat on top of a large, well-manicured lawn. I didn't know much about architecture, but this reminded me of a plantation in Georgia, not in the middle of the Midwest. Why would someone build this mansion here?

Agent Johnson stopped the car in the circular drive, and Agent Smith opened my door. We were in the middle of nowhere. What were the odds I would survive if I ran away right now and didn't get caught? Sensing my hesitation, Agent Smith reached into the car and hauled me out, my fantasy of escaping this moment short-lived. He dragged me up the stairs toward the front door, which was flanked by the two guards.

I was yanked into the foyer, and I took in as many details as I could. It was just as grand as the outside of the mansion, with its marble floors, a giant chandelier, and a double staircase that led up to a mezzanine. My parents were not poor, but this sort of grandeur was not something I was accustomed to. Even though my life was in danger, a small part of me was marveling at the beauty of this place. Another part of me thought that the beauty couldn't even begin to cover up the corruption that had allowed me to be dragged up here against my will and held by a man with no accountability. That small piece of me won out, and I tried to squirm out of Agent Smith's grip. He held on tighter. I would have bruises by the end of this. Hopefully, that was the worst I had to deal with.

"Welcome."

Barrington Park was standing at the top of the stairs, peering down at me. He gracefully descended, like an old-time movie star, an elegant—and deadly—figure in his sweater and slacks.

"Barnes, please release your grip on Miss Bayne. We don't want her to get the wrong impression of our hospitality."

Agent Smith (he would forever and always be) released my arm, but stayed close enough to touch me. He was such a giant of a man that I barely came to his elbow, and his hands were so enormous that he could snap my neck without much of a thought. Escape seemed less and less likely through speed or power; I would have to use cunning and gather as much information as I could. Or at least that's what I told myself, to stem the rise of panic.

"Mr. Park, why have you brought me here?"

"Consider this job training."

"But I haven't accepted your offer yet."

"Come, come, Miss Bayne. We both know what limited options you have in your professional life, so don't pretend you aren't going to accept. But before we get into all that, Barnes will show you to your accommodations."

I struggled frantically to keep the panic down. I couldn't afford to open a portal right now. I needed to stay calm and focused. I had no experience in how to escape kidnapping—they somehow skipped that subject in high school—but I had hope that with enough information, something would come to me. Or that Jay would miraculously find me . . . wherever I was.

Agent Smith took me through some sort of formal living room (I'm sure the room had a fancy name, but to me it just looked like a room no one used), up a back staircase, and into a wide corridor with plush green carpet. On either side of the hall were doors, almost like a hotel. Agent Smith stopped in front of one of them, unlocked it with a key, and gave me a less than gentle shove inside.

As I righted myself, I looked around at the huge room. It was a bedroom, complete with a giant four-poster bed and a bay window overlooking the grounds. There was a writing desk in the corner and a plush chair next to the window. A door to my left led to a bathroom, which I would explore in a minute. The suite was bigger than my apartment, the furnishings lovely, the view magnificent. I hated it.

Agent Smith locked the door behind me, leaving me in my gilded prison. I tried the windows, none of which opened. Bulletproof glass? I wasn't sure, but it was very thick, and honestly it didn't matter—I couldn't break them anyway. And even if I could, I was two stories off the ground. Fire code be damned, apparently.

The weather outside mirrored my mood and hampered what would have been a beautiful view. The rain had stopped, and a misty fog had settled on the grounds. The lawn from the front of the house wrapped around to the side and fed into a garden—the kind you read about in English literature classes. The green of the new buds on the flowers was barely visible, but I'm sure it was lovely in full spring. Beyond the lawn were the trees. Since this was the Midwest, I wouldn't call it a forest, exactly, but the trees were dense enough that even without their full leaves it gave the impression of cover. If I ever escaped, that was where I would make a run for it and potentially hide. It was better than the open space of the lawn. I shivered again—not *if* but *when* I got out. I had to remind myself of that.

I looked around the room in earnest, trying to see if there was anything, anything at all, that could help me out of this predicament. While the accommodations were more luxurious than a five-star hotel, there was no doubt that I was a prisoner. I opened all the drawers, and other than a Bible (really?) there was nothing. Not even dust.

I opened the closet and got quite the shock; it was filled with clothes, all in my size. I looked through the collection. They were expensive, beautiful, and nothing I would ever wear. Matching pantsuits, skirts, and dresses of every color imaginable—a far cry from the cheap T-shirts, jeans, and leggings that were my usual uniform. What were the chances that Barrington Park would put me in a room that just so happened to have a wardrobe full of clothes exactly my size? I didn't believe he did anything by coincidence, but the alternative—that he bought these clothes in anticipation of my arrival and even knew my size—was too much for me to contemplate. In the meantime, I was freezing and grabbed a long, gray cardigan that probably cost more than my entire wardrobe. I needed to be warm when I escaped, and a pantsuit wasn't going to do.

I don't know how long I had been staring out of the window, when the door opened. Agent Smith stood in the doorway and motioned for me to come with him. I sat on the chair and stared at him, not saying anything. It was a little act of rebellion, but it was enough that he strode across the room, grabbed my arm painfully, and yanked me to my feet.

"Hey!" I said, struggling to get out of his grasp. "I just want to know where you are taking me! I know you can speak. Just tell me and I'll go with you quietly."

He didn't say anything and continued to drag me through the room. His silence made me more afraid than I had been since this nightmare started. He could be taking me to be tortured or killed or any of a number of horrific things. I started to struggle for real—kicking and screaming with everything I had. He backhanded me across the face so hard that my teeth rattled, and I could taste the copper tang of blood in my mouth. I felt the sting, then the slow spread of pain across my cheekbone. That was going to leave one hell of a bruise. I straightened up, planted my feet, and stared him in the eye. He might beat me senseless, but I was going to make a stand and take back as much control as I could right here. I wanted to know where I was going. It might seem like a silly thing to plant my flag over, but without knowing, I couldn't prepare, and without preparation, I might not make it out. I wiped the blood off my mouth with the back of my hand.

"Please, just tell me where you are taking me, and I'll go with you."

"Mr. Park has summoned you for lunch."

I nodded and indicated with my free arm that he should proceed. He half walked, half dragged me to a dining room on the other side of the foyer. The table probably seated at least thirty people, but there were only two places set, and Barrington Park sat at the head of the table, at one of them. The other setting was next to him, which was the direction Agent Smith dragged me. As we walked in the room, Barrington looked up from his phone.

"Well, you look quite the mess. What happened?"

"Ask Agent Smith," I replied icily. Well, as icily as I could without crying.

He turned his gaze to Agent Smith. "What happened." Not a question—a demand.

"She would not come willingly."

"Because he wouldn't tell me where we were going!"

Agent Smith gripped my arm tighter and I winced.

"Barnes, release Miss Bayne, at once. When she asks you a question, you will answer, and other than escorting her to wherever I ask that you bring her, you will not lay a finger on her. Do I make myself clear?"

Agent Smith nodded once and released my arm.

"That's all, Barnes," Barrington said. He motioned for me to sit next to him.

"My employees are not used to questions," he said, by way of explanation.

"People just do what you say without question?"

"Yes," he said simply and started to put food on his plate, food that I hadn't noticed was already on the table—enough to feed me for a week. Meats and sides, sauces and salads. It was a feast. I was starving, but was afraid to eat it. What if he'd drugged it? What if it was poisoned? Although, that wouldn't make any sense—he could have killed me outright a dozen times and hadn't. Still, I couldn't afford to be drugged and accidentally open a portal.

As if reading my mind, he took a bite of the food. "It's perfectly safe, Miss Bayne. I took a great deal of care in retrieving you relatively unharmed. It would make no sense to kill you now. And sedating you would defeat the purpose of you working with me."

He wanted me awake, and that gave me hope. As long as my ability was a secret, I might get out of this alive. I just needed to convince him that his information was wrong and that I was of no consequence. My stomach audibly rumbled, and I served myself a bit of everything. I would need my strength for whatever plan to escape I came up with, and starving myself wasn't going to help.

I dug into my food, and after a minute I looked up to see Barrington studying me, like I was a code to crack. Finally, he said, "How did you do it? How did you figure it out?"

Let the games begin. "Figure what out?"

"How to work the device."

"What device?"

"The device that your mother gave you."

I looked up at him. This was the second time he had mentioned my mother. It also meant he didn't know Jay had the device. He thought I had it.

"How did you know my mother?"

"We can discuss that later. The sooner you help me, the sooner you can go back to your life—such as it was."

"Mr. Park, as I told you at The Grill, I don't know what you are talking about."

"Miss Bayne, I find that hard to believe. Your mother gave you a device before she died—or it would have been in her personal effects that were passed on to you."

"I swear, I don't have any sort of device, and my parents didn't leave me anything but debt. They've been gone years, so it's not like I could have missed the—"

"Enough!" He slammed his hand on the table. "It was *mine* and belongs to me. Tell me where it is, now!"

I shook in my chair, trying to make myself as small as possible. Immediately his face went back to the bland smile he had been wearing since I arrived. What the actual fuck? That sudden change alone was enough to freak me right out.

His normal manner of speaking resumed. "Miss Bayne, I have a similar piece of technology that can track when the device is used. It tracked it to your apartment, then to your friend's apartment when you were there. I know you have it and I know you can use it. My offer still stands. I will pay you for the device and hire you onto my team. Go back to your room and think about it, and you can give me an answer at dinner."

As if on cue, Agent Smith came back in to escort me back to my room.

"Miss Bayne, I will get the device and your services one way or another. I suggest you agree to my offer while I am still feeling generous."

With that, Agent Smith escorted me back to my room and locked my door. As I collapsed in the chair by the window, I replayed our conversation over and over in my head. He had claimed that the device was his.

Barrington Park was from another universe.

BLU 26

Styx and I met with the rest of the principal Team to figure out a general reconnaissance plan. The concept was simple: Ink and I would drive as much of the circumference of the building's land as possible, to see if there was any other way up to the building. It would also be helpful if it didn't have thousands of guards or pressurized spikes of death. If we found something, Ink would scout it quickly to get the layout, and then we would come back to the Compound to plan a more in-depth mission. If we found nothing, then we would come back and start over. Either way, the Captain reiterated multiple times, we were to come back and *not engage*. The Captain made sure that I understood that I was to burn nothing else down. Yet.

Ink and I put on our new armor, donned our other gear, and got ready to go. We had mapped out a different route to the building, hoping that by coming at it from another direction, we would get some sort of break in finding an alternative way in. Since the building was in the middle of a forest, and as far off the main roads as possible, it was a slim chance—but I was willing to try anything at this point.

We got into one of the Compound's trucks and started the drive. The sun was out, and the air was warming up; if we hadn't been heading toward a possible untimely death, I would have thought it was a lovely spring day.

"Take the next right," Ink said. We turned in to the forest, onto what looked like a hunters' trail. I was grateful for the truck's ability to go through mud and potholes as I navigated through the trees. This road was barely a trail and wasn't maintained at all. I had to wonder how Jack and Willow had even found this place in the middle of nowhere. I also wondered who owned this land, and if that could possibly help us.

"Hey, Styx, think the owner of this land's a sympathizer?" I chirped through my ear comm.

"Maybe they can get you in without dyi—"

The comm cut off. We were now within range of the anti-tech.

After another hundred feet or so, the trail took a quick turn, opening into a clearing that overlooked . . . more trees. It was a dead end. Disappointed, I pulled the truck into the clearing to turn around, hoping that there were no pressurized stakes waiting to impale us. As I started my three-point turn, Ink held up his hand to stop, and hopped out of the car—careful to stay on the tread marks we had just made. I rolled down the window and pulled myself out so that I was sitting on the truck's door, looking in the direction Ink was headed. There, in the midst of the trees was a small one-lane road. From our vantage point we could barely see it, but it appeared to lead toward the back of the building.

Ink climbed onto the bed of the truck to try to get a better look.

"Can you get me to the edge of the clearing? I want to climb higher."

I slid back into the truck and backed up to the edge of the clearing, hoping not to set off any spikes of doom. Once the truck had stopped, Ink picked a tree and started climbing. Moments later, he slid back into the truck.

"I think I figured out where the road starts, but I want to double-check."

I drove back the way we'd come, and after a couple of wrong turns, we finally found the road we'd seen from the clearing. We turned onto it, bumping our way through the potholes and avoiding trees until eventually it ran into a paved road—which was guarded by a gate and sentries farther ahead. That paved road seemed to be another way to the building.

I parked the truck under some trees, hoping that we were far enough away and under enough cover that the guards wouldn't notice us.

"I'm going to take a look," Ink whispered, sliding out of the truck.

I started to protest. We had information to bring back to the Team, which was what we had come for. But if Ink could get closer without getting caught, we'd have a better chance the next time we came for recon. I nodded once, and he vanished into the trees.

I tried to see where Ink had gone, but he blended so well into the tree cover that all I could see was nature. I fidgeted, tense. My instincts were telling me that something was off. I scanned my surroundings, but there was no one in sight and there was no noise other than nature sounds. I tried to place the feeling—it was like I was being watched. I looked around again and saw nothing.

"Well, as much as I would like to say I'm surprised to see you here, I've come to expect the unexpected with you, Blu."

I nearly jumped out of my skin as Jyston magically appeared from the trees and sauntered toward the truck, a smile playing on his lips. Although he had enough weapons on him to be a one-man army, he held his hands out, palms up, to show that he wasn't going to draw them—not yet, at least. I palmed my dagger and looked in the rearview mirror to see if he was alone. How the hell did he sneak up on me?

He stopped a few feet from the truck and smiled again, which was disconcerting. "If your friend keeps walking in the direction he is currently going, he will probably trip one of our more unpleasant security systems."

How did he know where Ink was? In fact, how had he known we were here at all? Had the sentries or security cameras caught us? The Second Counselor must have seen the question on my face, and grinned.

"I came to warn you that you have been spotted, and a host of Dagna's minions are on their way to intercept you right now. They are coming from the direction your friend is walking, so I suggest leaving the way you came."

He turned to walk away, back through the forest. I had to get Ink back to the truck, but I had so many questions that I needed answers. The Second Counselor, at least for now, was helping us. I had to take the risk.

"Second Counselor—wait!" I called after him. He stopped and turned around, eyebrows raised. "How did you know where we were?"

"Please, call me Jyston. That title just sounds so pompous out here, surrounded by all this nature." He gestured grandly, as if on a stage. "There are security cameras hidden in the trees on this road. When the security alarm went off, I volunteered to see what little birdie had tripped our wire. I had a hunch it was you. After all, I led you to the blueprints at that ostentatious party of the High Governor's. Plus, you seem to be the only one with enough impertinence to try to get a closer look." His smile widened.

"But why? Why tell me? Why warn me? Why let me know about all this?"

He covered the ground to the truck in three long strides and bent down so that his face was mere inches away from mine. My heart felt as if it would pound out of my chest—

from fear or excitement, I couldn't tell. He placed his hand on my cheek and looked into my eyes, searching. I waited for my instincts to kick in, to slit his throat or run away, but they didn't. For some reason, I knew, I just *knew* he wasn't going to hurt me. I'd dissect that feeling later. I left his hand on my cheek and looked into his striking gray eyes.

"You really don't remember, do you?" he murmured.

My breath caught. "Remember what?"

He shook his head as if the action would erase whatever memory he was reliving, and the sly smile returned to his lips.

"It's nothing of import." He released my face and took a step back, the moment gone. "Now, where were we? Ah yes. *Why* am I helping you? Can't I just give a beautiful woman my help?" The look on my face must have mirrored my disbelief because he laughed and continued. "That might be *a* reason, but not the foremost reason. Dagna outmaneuvered me for this building project, and I would like her to get payback. What better way than to help her enemy? It kills two birds with one stone—you do my dirty work for me, and it hurts her."

My mind was racing. "I thought you were overseeing this project. Are you saying Dagna's in charge of it?"

"I was. My original plans for the building were on display at the High Governor's house. Dagna found out about the plans and convinced the Counselor that this building had better uses, and he turned the project over to her. To be quite honest, I'm not thrilled with the direction she is taking it in. It was supposed to be an orphanage, modeled after the Compound. But she turned it into, well, it's not what I intended. And she also added a few *surprises* to its use. Those won't be on any blueprints."

He paused, letting the significance sink in. We were right—there was more going on in the building than we'd thought.

"As I've said, Dagna is a parasite who continues to use my brilliance for her own advantage. Losing this project to her hurt my ego, more than a little. So, giving you and your friends a little information was really of no consequence to me. What you choose to do with it will only benefit me, one way or another. Either you cause her a headache, which I consider a win, or you die trying, which will help Jurisdiction. Although, I rather hope you don't die for a while. I haven't had this much fun since I can remember." He winked at me, then looked up, head cocked like a wolf listening for his prey.

"Your friend returns." He turned back to me, a wicked smile crossing his face as he stuck his head through the truck window and kissed me quickly on the mouth.

"I certainly hope we keep running into each other like this," he whispered in my ear, then pulled back and said, louder, "She's not in danger, so please do not throw that dagger at me."

He slowly backed away from the truck, hands up, as Ink rounded a tree, muscles hunched, ready to strike.

"Ink, wait!"

Ink stopped, a look of confusion on his face as his arm dropped to his side, holding his dagger.

Jyston chuckled. "I always knew I liked you, Blu. Ink, is it? Ink, as I was telling the beautiful Blu, here, this road is heavily monitored. If I were you and wanting to sneak around, I would try the trail I just came down." He winked at me again, then backed away. "I trust you won't be throwing any daggers in my back as I leave. You'd best be off before Dagna's minions get here."

Jyston turned around and walked away, melting into the forest as Ink jumped into the truck. I turned it around as fast as I could and sped down the road. Big vans full of minions were pulling out from the maintenance road.

I pushed the truck as fast as it could go without killing us. I took the last turn out onto the main road fast enough to flip the truck over, but the good old truck held on and we sped away.

"Are they still back there?" I asked as I made another turn at breakneck speed.

"No. They let us go."

"Why?" All I could come up with was that they didn't want to catch us; they only wanted to keep us off the property and report back to Dagna. Ink didn't reply. He just kept clenching and unclenching his fists.

He finally turned his head and glared at me. "What the fuck, B? What happened back there?"

"You mean with Jyston? You left to scout, and the Second Counselor snuck up on me. I asked him some questions, which he sort of answered. Then you showed up, he gave us more information—and warned us about the minions. We need to get back to the Compound and tell the Captain what we found out."

"What *you* found out. And you conveniently left out the part where he kissed you."

I huffed, exasperated. "Because that's not the important part of what just happened, Ink!"

"He's the fucking enemy, B! You didn't punch him in the face or slit his throat, so you couldn't have been that upset by him putting his mouth on yours! Have you lost your mind?"

"No—but I seem to be the only one who hasn't. Look, he helped us today and we need to get back to the Compound and use the information he gave us. That is the third time he's helped me over the past couple of weeks! I don't know why, other than what he told me—which is that Dagna's trying to kill him and that any enemy of hers, which I am, is a friend of his. I don't trust him, Ink, and I'm not stupid, so stop thinking

I am—don't look at me like that!—I'm as trained a killer as you are, and a kiss doesn't change that! All I know is that he's the reason we know about the building in the first place. He's the reason I wasn't captured in the alley, he's the reason we now know there's a way into the building, and he's the reason we weren't just captured by Dagna's minions. I don't know why, but he has been helping us, so stop acting like an asshat jealous boyfriend and help me *think*!"

Ink looked out the window, and I let him sit in his silence. I could understand why Ink was freaked out by the kiss. If I was honest with myself, I was freaked out too—and a bit puzzled, and a tiny bit excited. But this mission was more important than any of that, and we now had information to give to the Team. It felt as if we had finally gotten a tiny opening to help rescue these kids, and I was going to do everything in my power to exploit it.

We drove the rest of the way in silence. As I pulled into the Compound, Ink put his hand on my knee.

"I'm sorry," he said. "It's just hard for me, B. You're my family—my everything—and you let him kiss you. The enemy, the guy we've been trying to take down our whole lives. I feel betrayed, but I'm not sure if that's right. I do trust you. I think you're brilliant—and if you didn't kill him for kissing you, then why should I think you should have? If you tell me that he is trying to help us, whatever the reason, then I have to believe you. I don't have to like it, but I believe you."

I put my hand over his and squeezed. "I hear you. I do. But right now we need to focus on how we can use what he told us to get those kids out. The Second Counselor's actions surprised me, but if what he said was true, then we might have a shot—a tiny one—at rescuing those kids and burning the whole thing down. I'll worry about Jyston after the mission is over, if I'm around to worry about him at all."

"You will be, Blu."

I shrugged. "You know the odds as well as I do. And this is the biggest mission we have ever attempted. I want to believe that this will be successful, and we will all get out of there alive, with the kids. But we may not, and I would prefer not to spend my last days fighting with you over something dumb like a kiss. OK?"

27 FARA

The afternoon dragged on, which was a weird sensation—I was simultaneously bored and afraid for my life. I took a hot bath and put my dirty clothes back on, not wanting to wear a pantsuit or dress. I looked at myself in the mirror and winced. There was a giant bruise across my cheekbone where Agent Smith had hit me, and both arms were ringed with purple and blue bruises from where he had dragged me here and there. My hair hung in wet waves down my back and smelled faintly of roses because of the high-end shampoo and conditioner that I'd used.

With nothing else to do, I sat in the chair by the window. At first, I gazed out and watched the security guards, gardeners, and other staff come and go, willing myself to stay awake. After a while, I noticed a pattern in the guards' movement and started to track where they went, how often, and how many at a time. I didn't know if I would ever get out of here, but if I did escape, knowing that information might be important, and so I watched and counted.

After what seemed like hours, my door opened. Agent Smith stood in the doorframe, taking up most of the space.

"Dinner," he grunted, indicating I should come with him. Not wanting another bruise, I followed him to the dining room.

The table was set as it had been for lunch, and Barrington once again sat at its head. He was studying something, and when I came closer, I realized it was a device. I tried to keep my face blank and immediately started pushing my emotions

down, taking deep breaths and doing anything I could think
of to stay calm.

He smiled that same bland smile as he started piling food
on his plate, and I sat down. I was starving—I hadn't eaten
much at lunch—and followed his lead.

"How do you like your accommodations?" he asked, as if
it were a dinner party.

"You mean my prison? It would actually be nice if I hadn't
been brought here under duress, beaten, and held captive."

He shook his head sadly. "You could have all this and more
if you just stopped fighting me. I'm not sure why you believe
I'm the enemy, Miss Bayne. I am offering you a much higher
salary than you could ever make as a waitress, accommodations
that will rival these, all the creature comforts of the world, and
still you resist."

Get information—that was what I was trying to do.

"Is this your house?"

"Sadly, no. It's lovely though, isn't it? It's the governor's
house. He and his family are in Europe, on holiday, and he
has given me the use of it and the staff for a time. Its location
serves my purposes."

"Do you think the governor would mind that you are
keeping a hostage here?"

"Come now, Miss Bayne—hostage is such a nasty word.
But to answer your question, I could shoot someone and not
lose his support, although I would prefer not to."

"Whose clothes are in my closet?"

"Ah yes. I had those purchased for you, since your normal
attire would not suit the position you are being offered. Will
you accept my offer?"

I swallowed the last bite of food and took a deep breath.

"Mr. Park, I can't accept your offer because I don't have
what you are looking for. You've kidnapped the wrong girl."

He sighed and lifted his device from the table, showing it to me. "This is what it looks like. Your mother had the original and passed it along to you."

"I promise she didn't. I'll even take a lie detector test or whatever to prove it to you. She never gave me anything like that!"

"Do not take me as a fool, Miss Bayne. Your mother was a brilliant woman; she figured out how to use this device and taught you."

"She didn't—"

"Miss Bayne, stop. Just stop. All evidence points to you. My offer remains open through this evening. Tomorrow, if you still refuse to help me willingly, I will have to employ more . . . forceful . . . ways of obtaining your services. I always get what I want, Miss Bayne. Always. I would very much like for us to be business partners, but I will get your cooperation one way or another. Sleep on it."

"How did you know my mother?"

"Her research ran parallel to my interest in expanded communication. The government gave her the device that is rightfully mine. They stole it from a person who had stolen it from me. It was no fault of hers that she was given something that didn't belong to her, but when I told her my offer, she responded in the same manner you have: a stubborn refusal to take my generous proposal. It was too bad that she died . . ." But the way he said that last sentence suggested that he thought the exact opposite.

"She died in an accident."

"Yes, she did. It just so happens that I am good at making accidents happen."

Barrington's words rang through my head over and over as I tried to keep myself awake in my room. I couldn't afford to lie down. With all the stress of the last few days, I would most certainly open a portal if I slept, and that was the very last thing I needed.

Though I was exhausted, it wasn't hard to stay awake. Between the revelation that Barrington had been responsible for my parents' deaths and his threats of forcing me to cooperate in the morning, I was working overtime to keep my emotions in check.

It felt like putting together a thousand-piece puzzle that was missing a handful of pieces. I made a mental list for the hundredth time of what I knew, and turned over each piece in my mind. I knew that he believed the device belonged to him. If that was true, then I also knew he came from a different universe—and if *that* was true, I knew that travel through the portals was possible and not just theoretical. With taking the leaves and the tank top, travel between universes had seemed a likely possibility, but the fact that Barrington was still alive multiple years later in this universe opened up a whole host of possibilities. But that train of thought led to even more questions. When did he arrive? Why was he here? It stood to reason that he needed the device to get back to wherever he came from, but if that was the case, how did he lose the device to begin with?

And then there was my mom. He wanted me to believe that he had something to do with my parents' deaths. If he had, then the desire I had to thwart whatever plan he'd concocted was fortified tenfold. I would make him pay in whatever way I could. Revenge was a very powerful motivator for getting my ass out of here and, well, doing something thwart-y.

And finally, there was his threat about tomorrow. How was he planning to force me to cooperate? My mind immediately went to torture, but in what form? Would he torture me into telling him where the device was? That path of thought was doing me no good. It just made the low thrum of dread in my stomach bloom into a full-blown panic attack, and I couldn't afford that right now. I needed to avoid torture, not just because I obviously did not want to be tortured, but because I wasn't sure I could keep from opening a portal if it happened.

I thought of all the tactics that could possibly be of use to me and threw most of them away. But one possibility seemed to rise to the top. What if I told Barrington the truth—that the government had the device? The more I thought about it, the more it seemed to be my best option. I had no loyalty to the department, regardless of my feelings toward Jay. If I gave up the location of the device, would he believe me and let me go? It was a long shot, but one I was willing to take.

I kept my vigil out of the window, trying to make out the figures moving in the dark. The guards kept their regular patrols, and the staff had all retired inside or gone home. At one point, it looked like a person was being dragged between two burly security guards, but I couldn't make out any details. Did they capture another poor soul? Now, there was a cheerful thought.

The night passed as slowly as I could ever remember time passing. Each line of thought led me to darker and darker places. What if he never let me go? What if he tortured me until I helped him? And if I helped him, what did that mean? It couldn't be good, whatever it was. What if I opened a portal by accident? As the thoughts circled, my feelings of helplessness and hopelessness became unbearable. Finally dawn broke. I got into the bath one last time to clear my head. I tried to remember what Millie had said, that I was a warrior deep down. I didn't feel much like one, but I needed to be strong and keep my emotions in check if I was going to make it through whatever this morning brought. I could only hope that Jay had somehow convinced his department to launch a rescue mission—for no other reason than they wanted me as badly as Barrington did.

I was out of the bath and dressed when the door opened. Instead of Agent Smith, it was Barrington himself, looking irritatingly dapper in slacks and a sweater.

"Good morning, Miss Bayne. Have you reconsidered my offer?"

"Mr. Park, as I said, I can't help you. I don't have it."

He nodded to me once. "Please follow me. I believe I have something to change your mind."

We walked down the corridor, through the mezzanine, until we came to an unmarked door. He opened the door, indicating I should proceed down the concrete stairway. We walked down the stairs in silence, with each step my sense of dread becoming almost unbearable. The stairs finally ended in another plain white door. Barrington opened the door and I walked through, close enough to smell his cologne—and something else, something cold and metallic, and it put me on edge. The door opened into a hallway with a single bare lightbulb hanging from the ceiling. To the left, the hallway had doors on each side and ended in what seemed like a dead end. To the right, it made a sharp turn, and although I could not see where it led, I could hear the clinking of dishes. The kitchens. Barrington brushed past me and went to the third door on the right. He knocked once and opened it for me to walk in.

As I did, I stopped dead. The room was large and bare, except for a single chair sitting behind a table in the middle of the room, under a bare lightbulb. Sitting in the chair, head hanging down and shackles on both hands and feet, was Jay. He raised his head to look at me. His face was a patchwork of bruises, cuts, and blood. His nose had been broken, and when he opened his mouth to speak, his teeth were caked in blood. I rushed forward to help him, but Agent Smith, who had been standing by the wall, grabbed me. I struggled and screamed and kicked. I needed to get to Jay and help him. His gray eyes met mine, and he slightly shook his head. He didn't want me to fight. Not yet, at least. I stopped struggling, and Agent Smith put me down.

Barrington spoke with a bland smile. "It seems that Agent Hanlon here took offense to your accompanying my men here and decided to take it upon himself to rescue you."

"More agents are on their way, Barrington," Jay said. "The government wants her as badly as you do. Even your contacts with the governor won't help you this time." He spat blood on the floor.

"I think you might be mistaken, Agent Hanlon. When I made the call to the senator's office this morning and explained that Miss Bayne had come with me willingly, he put a call in to your superiors. No one else is coming. I was going to be rid of you last night, but then it occurred to me that you could still be of use."

Barrington started to pace, and the look on his face changed to the terrifying one that I had glimpsed at the restaurant. This was going to be very, very bad.

"You see," he continued, "Miss Bayne is under the mistaken impression that my offer is one that can be denied. Even after I told her that I had her mother killed because she stubbornly refused to help me, Miss Bayne still refused. Even after I threatened her, she still would not tell me the location of the device. But then you came along—a white knight to save the day. And why would a lone agent be sneaking on the property if not to rescue his fair maiden?"

He nodded to Agent Smith, who walked over to Jay and punched him so hard in the face that I could hear the crack. Then Agent Smith put Jay's hands on the table. Agent Johnson held him down as Smith grabbed some sort of hammer from off the table. I realized what was happening and started to scream again and run toward Jay, but Barrington wrapped his arms around me, pinning me to his front and whispering in my ear, "Miss Bayne, this could all be avoided if you just tell me where the device is."

Agent Smith raised the hammer and brought it down with frightening precision onto Jay's finger, with a horrifying crunch.

"Get away from him! I'll kill you!" I screamed, thrashing against Barrington. His grip around me was like a vise, and his breath was in my ear.

"This could end now. Where is the device?"

I started to sob. Jay's finger was stuck at a terrible angle, his face bloody. I couldn't let them kill him. I would help them if it meant saving Jay. He seemed to sense what I was preparing to do and shook his head violently.

"Don't help them, Fara," he said. "These pieces of shit don't deserve your help." Agent Smith raised the hammer again, and it came crashing down on Jay's ring finger. He groaned, but kept looking at me, pleading in his eyes.

I couldn't take it anymore. I was shaking, tears streaming down my face.

"The government has it," I croaked. "They took it after the crash."

"But that can't be, Miss Bayne," Barrington cooed into my ear. "The readings are from where you are, not where Agent Hanlon has been. I hate to say I don't believe you, but I don't believe you." Crack—another finger broken.

"It's true, asshole," Jay ground out. "I had the device until yesterday. And now Fara's mom's traitorous assistant has it. Fara didn't know that."

"All too convenient," Barrington responded offhandedly. He nodded to Agent Smith, and the hammer came down, this time on Jay's wrist. He cried out and I started to panic. I could feel a portal opening. Somehow, this time I knew it was coming.

Jay was in such pain, and it was because of me. All my fault—my fault—my fault. I wanted this whole nightmare to be over. I wanted to run to him, kiss his injuries, and have him hold me and tell me it was OK. I would help Barrington. I would give him what he wanted if only he let Jay go. There was no way out of this, no way that I could see where we both got away, and if I had to choose between me and Jay, or me and Adora, or me and Calum, I would choose my friends every time. Jay must have seen the look on my face. He knew what was coming too.

"Fara," he said quietly, "don't."

I shook my head and stopped struggling. I would show Barrington what I could do, and they would let Jay go. I would stay as a prisoner if it meant that Jay would go free. Barrington let me go and I took a step away from him. I felt the portal opening. It was weird that I could recognize the sensation. I let it channel through me.

"Fara," Jay repeated, "remember your promise. Remember your promise to me. To Calum. Do it, and don't come back. Not until you have it figured out. Don't come back."

And what he was telling me to do hit me. He didn't want me to stop opening the portal. He wanted me to open a portal and jump through it. He was reminding me of the promise I had made because he wanted me to run. But I didn't want to keep my promise. I wanted to stay and make sure Jay would be OK. I shook my head. I couldn't go through with it.

"Fara," Jay pleaded. "Please."

A sob escaped my lips. I wanted to stay, but that wasn't what Jay wanted, and I knew it. He wanted to protect *me*, to keep me safe, but also to keep my power out of the hands of a terrible person like Barrington Park. He knew the consequences of my power in the wrong hands, probably better than I knew it myself.

"Well, this is all well and good, but whatever promise Miss Bayne made to you won't mean anything if you are dead. Barnes?"

Agent Smith raised his hammer again. Barrington had let me go completely now that I wasn't struggling, and he was focused on the hammer falling, a small smile on his lips. In the commotion, no one noticed the portal opening in front of me. I looked through it, making sure I wasn't about to jump into an ocean or some lava, and I could just make out a room with a hardwood floor on the other side. I wished for the window to get big enough for me to fit through, and it grew. Out of the corner of my eye, I saw Jay nod to me once and smile, as the hammer came down on his left hand with a crunch. He cried out, louder than the others. Maybe to create a distraction, maybe because it hurt more this time, I couldn't tell. But I knew that I couldn't wait for the portal to get any bigger. Barrington's attention would turn back to me in a second, and I had to take my chance. I didn't want to run, but I had made a promise, and as much as it killed me to leave everyone behind, I had to go. Maybe the new universe could teach me some tools that I could use to save everyone. At the very least, maybe I could learn to control this power of mine.

I pushed my hand through and turned to see Barrington reach for me. I stumbled out of his way and fell to the ground . . . on the other side of the window. As I looked up I could see Barrington's face through the window, looking at me with a combination of rage and confusion. As he reached his hand toward the portal, I forced myself to think "close" and it did, with a hiss.

I was in another universe.

I sat there, dazed, for a second, trying to get my bearings, and as I came back to myself, I could hear shouting. I looked up toward the source of the noise and froze. My heart was pounding. *No way.*

The person standing before me and shouting—was me.

From behind me, I heard a familiar voice. "You must be Fara. I'm glad to finally meet you."

BLU 28

I couldn't believe my eyes. A girl fell out of thin air onto the floor of the Captain's office, and she had my face.

"How did you get here?" I shouted since I wasn't sure what else to say. There isn't a standard response for when you see yourself sitting on the floor in front of you. She looked as surprised to see me as I was to see her.

The Captain came around the table. "You must be Fara. I'm glad to finally meet you."

The girl, Fara, looked toward the Captain. Her eyes were wide with shock.

"Can someone tell me what the fuck is happening?" Ink yelled. He was now standing between the Captain and the girl. She looked up at him, disbelief on her face.

"Calum?" she asked.

Ink paled, a first. "How did you know my name? Who are you?"

"But you can't be," she muttered, tears starting to slide down her cheeks. Watching myself cry was a strange experience.

"Fara," the Captain said calmly, "I think I have some answers for you—for all of you. But let's get you off the floor first. Can I get you some coffee?"

She nodded and struggled to get up. Ink reached to help her, and they stared at each other before he pulled out a chair and she sat down. I went back to my seat as did the rest of the Team, staring at this girl in disbelief and silence. She looked around the table, obviously in shock. The tears had stopped, and I noticed a huge bruise across her cheekbone and dark circles under her eyes. Whatever had happened, and wherever she'd materialized from, she was hurting and in trouble.

The Captain returned with a cup of coffee and set it in front of Fara. She took a sip and looked questioningly at the Captain.

"How did you know?" she asked her.

"About the coffee? It was a guess. It is how Blu drinks it. Two sugars and a splash of milk." The Captain looked at me, and the girl's eyes followed. We locked eyes for a moment and then she turned away. Her hair was long and hung in blonde waves down her back, as mine would if I let it be. Her face was rounder than mine, but her eyes—it was her eyes that were the biggest difference that I could see. While they were the same startling blue as mine, they held a compassion and a kindness that I didn't see in my own reflection.

The Captain sighed and said, "I know we were originally here to talk about what Blu and Ink learned on their mission, but obviously this incident takes precedence.

"I'm sure you are all wondering why a girl who looks just like Blu fell out of thin air and into my office. It is a legitimate question. It might make sense if Fara starts with her side of the story, and I fill in the gaps as we go. Fara, are you up for that?"

She looked around the table, and I was afraid she was going to faint, but her face smoothed out, like whatever emotion was causing her to panic just disappeared. She turned to the Captain first.

"Do you mind if I ask . . . is your name Millie?"

The Captain chuckled and nodded. "It is—but everyone here calls me Captain."

"How do you know her name? How did you know my name?" Ink interrupted. He seemed to be the most freaked out of any of us, and that was saying something.

"I know Millie at home." She paused, her eyes lined in silver as she looked at Ink. "And you are . . . Calum is—was—my best friend. You look different, but the same."

"And where is home?" Jack asked. When she looked at him, she recoiled, but then straightened herself out.

Before the girl could answer, the Captain said, "We will have plenty of time for questions—but let's start at the beginning of your story, Fara."

"How do you know my name?" she asked quietly.

The Captain smiled. "I knew your mom." The girl stared at the Captain in shock.

"I promise I will tell you about that and more in a minute," the Captain continued, "but in order to keep these folks here from going into further shock, I think you should begin. Can you do that?"

The girl nodded, wiping her eyes with the back of her hand and taking a deep breath.

"So, um . . . I'm not sure where to even start. I come from a different universe."

"Did I just hear you right?" Styx said. "A different universe?"

The girl nodded. "Do any of you know about the physics theory of the multiverse?"

We all stared at her blankly. I, for one, had no idea what any of those words meant, together or separately. When none of us answered, she gathered herself and told us her story. When she reached the part where she had escaped through the portal, tears started streaming down her face again. I could tell that she was dealing with the guilt of leaving someone behind, and it was eating her up inside. She hadn't wanted to run. I knew that feeling too well, and my heart went out to her. Ink, however, had a different reaction.

"Wait," Ink interrupted, "you aren't shitting us. You are from another universe? You've traveled between them already? So, you're like the Blu from wherever you're from? That's so fucking cool!"

Leave it to Ink to see the bright side. She smiled shyly at him, and before she could reply, Styx spoke up.

"How does the portal-opening work?"

She looked at Styx with affection, then caught herself.

"Adora?"

Styx looked at the Captain, who answered.

"Fara, there's a process here when someone comes to live, where I give them nicknames. Like Blu's name is actually Fara—although she might not remember it. Ink is Calum, Styx is Adora, Jackrabbit is Hewitt, and so on. I know it must be strange for you to see people you recognize from your own world sitting across from you."

"Who is Adora in your world?" Styx asked.

"She is another good friend of mine." Fara smiled at Styx, who couldn't seem to not smile back. "I recognize all of you, although you look a little different."

"All of us? That is . . . interesting," the Captain said.

Fara shook herself off and wiped her eyes. Watching emotions play across her face was strange, since it was my face too. It was weird looking at myself but having that person act independently. It wasn't just me—we were all staring—which was probably making the situation harder for her. I noticed Ink taking particular interest in her; behind that perma-smirk was real concern—the same kind I saw in his eyes when he talked to me.

"This must be really hard for you."

"It must be hard for all of you too," Fara countered. "A girl appears out of thin air, wearing your face, staring at the others like I know you. I'm sorry my problems landed in your laps—that I landed in your laps. I'm sorry to cause such a fuss." She seemed to curl in on herself, trying to make herself smaller—staring at her hands. I felt for her. But before I could say anything, Ink interrupted, his perma-smirk back.

"Blu, I am pretty sure I have never heard those words come out of your mouth." He looked at Fara and winked. "Blu here doesn't believe in apologizing."

"Only when it comes to you, asshole. You should apologize for just being you." I tried to smack him across the table. He blew me a kiss, and I flipped him the bird. Even in the weirdest times, I could count on Ink to be himself.

"There is no need for you to be sorry, Fara," Captain said, once Ink had settled back into his chair. "If my theory is correct, you are linked with our world in more ways than just magically appearing."

What? How could this girl be linked to our world, other than she obviously looked like me? This day could not get any weirder.

"I know this is probably the strangest thing any of us has ever dealt with, but I promise you, Fara, you are not in danger. And I promise you, Team, that Fara's arrival is a sign of a far greater threat than even the mission we are currently undertaking. I need to provide Fara a brief history of our world so that she can grasp the full impact of what I'm about to tell you. Everyone should probably get comfortable. We have a lot to talk about."

Jack got up and got coffee as the rest of us settled in for what was probably going to be a long meeting. Fara carefully avoided looking at us, pulling her legs onto the chair and hugging her knees to her chest. Did I look that small when I did that? Or was it because she looked so frightened that it made her look tiny? Ink's hand had settled on the arm of her chair, as if he sensed her panic too.

"About thirty-five years ago," the Captain began, "a young man named Harrison decided that he wanted to take over our world—or at least, that's how I imagine it. I'm not sure what prompted him to decide world domination was his calling, but he did."

She stood, grabbed Fara's empty coffee cup, and walked back to the coffeepot brewing in the corner.

"At the time, our government was a democracy, and through legal—and illegal—means, Harrison became president. But that wasn't enough for him, so through a series of presidential proclamations and administrative orders, he abolished the checks and balances of the government and anointed himself Counselor of the country, with all the powers of a dictatorship."

The Captain returned to the table and handed Fara a fresh cup of coffee. She took it into her shaking hands with a nod of thanks.

"Of course the people rebelled. After a few years of skirmishes, it appeared that the rebellion was winning against his supporters, and the Counselor was going to be deposed. The rebellion, which I was a part of, was excited at the prospect of reestablishing democracy. Unfortunately, little did we know that the Counselor's brother was on another mission. He was a genius in creating advanced technology like nothing our world had ever seen before. He created these."

The Captain pulled out a palmbox, and Fara gasped, her face turning white.

"That's the device!" she said.

A palmbox had somehow made it into Fara's world. Weird.

The Captain continued. "Yes, they are called palmboxes here. The Counselor's brother invented these, but in doing so he accidentally created something else. When he was testing the capabilities of the palmboxes, a window—a portal— opened up. Like the one you created, Fara."

"How did that even happen?"

"We don't know, Jackrabbit. All we know is what happened afterward and what we heard secondhand. The Counselor was desperate, and so when his brother brought him the discovery, he acted. He sent his brother through the portal to see what he could find. And what he found in the alternate universe were weapons schematics. He came back to build them. Those weapons changed the fate of the war, and of our world."

"Holy shit," Jack muttered.

Holy shit was right. Everyone knew that Jurisdiction had used massive weapons to conquer our country, and then the rest of the world, bit by bit, eventually establishing Jurisdiction's rule. But no one knew that the weapons came from a different universe. At least I didn't.

"Does the Counselor still have the weapons?" I asked.

"They used the last one over on the other continent, and when they went to make more, they realized that the schematics had been destroyed." The Captain smiled, with a hint of pride. The Team. Right then, I was so fucking proud of being part of it.

"Why didn't the brother just go get more?" Ink asked.

"He tried," Captain replied, "but when he went through a portal to get more weapons, the brother, Barrington Park, was trapped in another universe."

I didn't recognize the name, but Fara's face turned even whiter, and she started to shake. Ink instinctively put his hand on her arm, and she grabbed it, then must have realized what she had done and let him go.

"That's who kidnapped me and tortured my . . . friend," she said. "He's a big technology and weapons guy in my world. Super powerful and ultra-rich. But I don't understand—why is he trapped there? He had another device on him, which is why he could track me. Why couldn't he use that one to open a portal? Why did he need me?"

"A Team member followed him through a portal and stole his palmbox, which is why he became trapped. I'm not sure why his new palmbox won't open portals."

Styx's eyes lit up. "So if a Team member stole it, do we have it at the Compound?"

"Unfortunately, no. From what I learned later, the Team member couldn't get the palmbox to open a portal, so she couldn't get home. The palmbox is still in Fara's world."

"That's what Barrington must have meant when he told me someone stole it from him! Agent Hanlon told me that the government thought it was some sort of weapon, which was why they took it in the first place."

The Captain nodded. "Regrettably, your government killed the Team member in the process of taking the palmbox."

Fara paused, the remaining color draining from her face. "I'm so sorry—"

"No need to apologize, Fara. You didn't do it. Anyway, the fact is that once they had it, Barrington was trapped in your world."

"How did you learn about this?" I asked.

"Fara's mother told me."

FARA 29

I didn't want to hear what Millie/the Captain was about to say. This whole week had been one huge revelation after another, none of which were good. If there were infinite alternate universes, how did I choose the one that held Barrington's equally horrific brother? I guess in a week full of horrors, what was one more, right?

"Your mother appeared in my office about fourteen years ago, quite unexpectedly, just like you," the Captain said. "After a few tense moments, she told me her fantastic story. That is why I knew who you were, Fara, when you dropped in, unexpectedly—just like she did."

The Captain told the same story that Jay had told me about my mother, and how she had been asked to test the device—the palmbox. But she added something Jay hadn't known.

"One day an experiment went awry. When that happened, you and your mother were both exposed to something. She described it only as some sort of 'toxic light,' and she soon realized that the toxic light had somehow changed you both. She eventually understood that her emotions were triggering portals. In time, she was able to control it, as she could control her fear and anger. After a few tries, she was brave enough to step through the portal, and she ended up here."

Tears ran down my face as things started to fall into place. That was why my dad had been so adamant about not letting me go back to the lab—he was afraid something else was going to happen. And it was why my mom had worked with me for so long to keep my emotions under wraps. Even now, after all the stuff I had seen and done—sitting in a different universe, for god's sake—it still made me feel better that our theory was right and I wasn't just crazy.

"She visited a few more times," the Captain said, "and we became friends. She told me about you, Fara, and your world. The last time she came was about four years ago. She believed she was in danger. She brought me her research and told me that if you were ever to come here, I should give it to you."

From her desk, she pulled out a giant file folder and handed it to me. My mom's notes. She had hidden them in the one place the government could never get to. Another tear slid down my face, and I wiped it away. I had my mother's notes. When I got back home, I could give them to Jay. If Jay was still alive. If I ever got back.

There were so many questions I wanted to ask, so many things that were going through my mind, but my brain had shut down. It was like I couldn't handle any more, and so my body turned numb.

The Captain smiled kindly at me and said to the others, "Even though I know you all have a thousand questions, I think that's enough excitement for one night. However, before we go, I have one more thing that we need to address. Although she would deny it, Blu is a celebrity here at the Compound." Blu rolled her eyes at that, but the Captain kept going.

"It is going to be strange for everyone to have Blu's doppelganger walking around the Compound. Other than those in this room, I would prefer people not knowing where Fara came from—at least for now. We are still working on a . . . leak . . . here at the Compound, and I don't want anyone to know about Fara's special abilities. As she said, governments have a knack for wanting to exploit what she can do, so if Jurisdiction finds out about her, then she will be in just as much danger here as she was in her home world. We cannot let that happen. I am tasking each of you here to protect Fara like she is one of our own, because she is. With her abilities and insights into her own world, along with her recent information about Barrington, she will be an invaluable Team member. Do I make myself clear?"

She met each person's eyes at the table and waited for them to audibly agree. There was something formal about the action—like it was an oath. I wondered what that was all about.

"However, since we can't keep her locked up in a room—not that we would ever do that—we need a good cover story. Does anyone have any ideas?"

Jackrabbit was the first to speak. "What about planting a story that she's Blu's cousin? It's straightforward and simple. I can create a backstory for her, something easy to remember. She could have just escaped from being held by Jurisdiction, which would account for the bruising."

"OK, it's settled, then," the Captain replied. "Fara looks like she could use a rest, and I'd like her refreshed so she can join us for our mission debriefing, so let's push it to after training tomorrow, first thing. You are all dismissed, except Fara and Blu—please stick around, for a second."

Everyone got up from the table. Ink stretched, his shirt rising and showing that he had an amazing stomach; while my Calum was lean, Ink was ripped. He caught me staring and I blushed. He leaned down and whispered in my ear, close enough that I could feel his breath.

"See you soon, Fara."

My name on his lips sounded so different than how Calum said it. Ink said my name like he was tasting it, and it sent shivers down my spine. He was certainly trouble. He probably flirted like that with all the girls, so I wouldn't take

275

it personally. Was Calum like that with girls who weren't me? I didn't think so; he was as shy as I was. Nonetheless, it was weird to have someone who looked like Calum sound like that.

"For real, Ink," Blu said, smacking him in the arm, "the girl just fell into an alternate universe. The last thing she needs is someone who looks like her best friend getting all breathy sexpot on her, mkay?"

Ink didn't seem put off at all, and only grinned wider.

"I can't help it if I'm a sexy beast."

Styx called over her shoulder, "Yes, yes you can. C'mon, bad boy—we'll see them in a few."

I took a few moments to gather myself. My hands were shaking, and I held onto the coffee like it was my security blanket. I peeked at Blu out of the corner of my eye and wondered how she looked so calm. I also was admiring the purple hair. Maybe I would do that, someday, if Douche wouldn't fire me for it. If I got back.

When I got back.

The Captain sat back down at the table after grabbing coffee for herself and Blu.

"Thanks for staying. I just wanted to check in with you two. Fara—this has to be a lot to take in. How are you holding up?"

I appreciated the question, but I wasn't sure how to answer, as I thought back to the crazy things that had happened over the past few days. I had to stop a hysterical cackle from coming out of my mouth. How was I holding up? I shrugged. "To be honest, I'm a little freaked out, but mostly I don't want to be any more of a burden than I already am."

"Why would you think you are a burden?"

"I just landed here while you are obviously in the middle of something else."

"You are certainly not a burden, and you are more than welcome here. You can stay forever if you want, although I have a feeling that you will want to go back to your own life at some point. For now, recuperate here. I owe at least that to your mother; she was a good friend. Blu—how are you doing?"

Blu smiled. "I must admit it's weird, but I think I have the easier side of it. So there are multiple versions of me. But I think I'm going to like this version. It would really suck to meet myself and find out that I'm a bitch."

"Well, you are a bit of a bitch, Blu, but we love you anyway," the Captain quipped, and a laugh escaped both Blu and me. Our laughs sounded so similar that we stopped and looked at each other, then laughed again.

The Captain grinned at us. Once we were done, she continued. "The second reason I wanted you to stay is that I have additional information for you two. I will tell the rest of the Team soon, but in the meantime, I think you both should know this now. Fara, you and your mother are not the only people able to open portals; someone in Jurisdiction has figured out how to do it as well. Your mother suspected this, and she came to warn me about it."

All humor had left the room. Blu gasped, and my stomach dropped.

"How?" Blu asked. "How did she know?"

"I'll try to explain it as best I can, although I'm not an expert in this at all. How Fara and her mother traveled between our two worlds isn't technically a portal, although we call it that. It is a tear in the membrane that separates our worlds. They tear the membrane to step between worlds, and when the tear closes, it leaves the membrane a little weaker than it was before it was torn. If the membrane is torn around the same area multiple times, then the membrane becomes substantially weaker in that location. Following so far?"

We both nodded.

"About five years ago, Fara's mother realized that her ability to open portals/tears was becoming easier, but the instances in which she opened them unintentionally were also increasing. She had been able to control it for years, so the change troubled her."

She also realized that I was opening more portals in my sleep, the Captain told us. Being the scientist that she was, my mother began running tests on herself and on me while I slept. Then she came here to warn the Captain about what she had found. She said that someone in this world had figured out how to create portals, and the constant opening and closing of the portals was thinning the membrane.

"Because the membrane was becoming so thin, it was pulling on Fara's ability and making it harder for her to control it. Although Fara's ability is controlled by her emotions, her control of the ability is hindered when the membrane is thinner. Her mother warned that should Fara arrive in this world, that was a sign that the membrane holding our worlds apart had thinned to dangerous levels."

Once my mother had returned to my world, the Captain sent her spies in to Jurisdiction, to find proof, but they could never get anything solid.

"That is, until recently. Blu and the Team have been working on infiltrating a new Jurisdiction facility. Our intelligence indicated that the building is a prison for children, but the heightened security around the building doesn't seem to be in proportion to a prison, and we cannot figure out why. In addition, the security includes technology that is far more advanced than anything I have ever seen. How is it that Jurisdiction has created something so advanced, especially with Barrington trapped in Fara's world?"

The answer, she believed, was that the tech was from another world. Someone at Jurisdiction had been opening portals and coming back to this world with new technology, just like Barrington did.

"I believe that this activity is weakening the membrane just like Fara's mother warned us, and that Jurisdiction, under the Counselor's directive, has been able to open up portals to different worlds and bring back technology. I believe that the building we are trying to infiltrate is actually housing the technology."

"Technology and weapons?" Blu asked.

"Yes. My theory is that the Counselor has been trying to open up a portal to Fara's world over and over to rescue his brother, which is thinning the membrane. Fortunately for us, he's been unsuccessful. However, his portals *have* been successful, inasmuch as he's been able to get to other worlds and retrieve weapons, or their schematics."

My heart sank. This was so much bigger than just two universes colliding.

"I think that at first," the Captain said, "the Counselor just wanted to reunite with his brother, to bring him home, but now that he has this technology, and possibly weapons, I believe his plans are more nefarious. Once he figures out a way to open a portal to Fara's world, he is going to take his minions and the weapons, reunite with Barrington, and then launch an assault. He wants to take over all the worlds. I think he is targeting Fara's world next. He wants to finish what Barrington has already started."

"Why can't he open a portal to my world?" I asked.

"I don't know, but he must not have figured it out yet, because otherwise Barrington would not have kidnapped you."

Blu said what I was thinking out loud. "And that's why it's so important that Jurisdiction doesn't get their hands on Fara, since she is the link between our world and hers."

"Yes, Fara's arrival not only was foretold by her mother, but also sets off a possible chain of events that are catastrophic: the reuniting of the two brothers and the conquest of Fara's world."

"So," Blu said, "we need to get into that building for another reason—we have to destroy whatever horrible shit is in there before the Counselor figures out how to reunite with his brother. Before her world suffers the same fate as ours."

"Exactly. Fara, it appears that you now have a vested interest in our mission. If we cannot destroy the building with whatever is in there, then I fear for your home world. And since we have a spy in our midst, we are running out of resources. Those you have met this evening are the only people at the Compound who I can trust to help with this monumental task. I would like to add you to that list. Will you stay and help us?"

I sat quietly, trying to absorb what the Captain had said. How did I even begin to help them? They were talking of missions and things I had only seen in movies. These people sat with daggers strapped to their legs the same way I carried a purse. And although I had this amazing ability, I was still only a waitress with a high school education. I had already left Jay to die in order for me to escape. I wasn't cut out for heroics. I was no warrior.

Thinking of Jay made my heart ache. Was he still alive?

At that moment, I knew what I had to do. I reached deep down to the tiny place inside me that was starting to grow. It was a tiny flicker of fire, but it was there. I held it tight and looked across the table at the person who was me, but not. Even though we apparently had the same DNA, we were so different. She had been raised to fight for herself and others. She had been raised to be a warrior. I had been raised to push my feelings down. I had panic attacks at the thought of strangers, and let Hewitt harass me. Did I have what she had inside me too? The only way I was going to find out was if I tried.

"I will help you," I said, "but there's something else. I know I have no right to ask for a favor, but I'd like to ask for two."

"Of course you can ask for anything you wish, Fara," the Captain said. "If it is within our power, we will do it."

"Thank you. OK. The first favor is that while I'm here, I need to figure out how to control this portal ability so that I can eventually go home. But I also need other training. Weapons, fighting, whatever. I have a feeling I'll be at a disadvantage in this world without knowing some of those things. Plus, it might help me in my home world."

"We can start tomorrow," the Captain replied.

"Great." I took a deep breath. I wasn't sure they would agree to this next thing, but I needed to ask. "As for the second favor . . . as I told you, I left Agent Hanlon with Barrington when I escaped, and I'm afraid they are going to kill him. I'm going back to rescue him, and I could use your help."

Blu nodded. "Then we have work to do."

EPILOGUE
Midwest Territory, Present Day

He walked to the designated meeting place, just outside of the city center. He knew he was early, but he wanted to hide so that when his informant arrived, he could startle him by appearing from seemingly nowhere. Childish, he knew, but he liked people thinking he could appear out of thin air. It added to the mythos he had created around himself.

He saw his informant get out of his car and walk up to the meeting spot. The man put on his game face—the one that he had used for the past twenty years, the one that allowed him to move without question. Even when he hated what he had to become in order to survive, even when he was disgusted by what he'd had to do, disgusted by who clamored for his attention, he never allowed his role to waver—except with her. But she was a fleeting thought, a cool breeze on his mind. When he had exacted his revenge—revenge for the family lost to his enemies—he would stop the act and think of her. If he even remembered who he was, back before the game began. But today, he was what the informant expected him to be: cold, calculating, and deadly.

He put his hands in his pockets and stepped out from behind the rubble. The informant jumped, which pleased him. He needed the information the informant was providing and had risked everything to wrest control of the informant away from Dagna, in order to save the informant, to save the girl, but mostly to save hope—hope that one day he would be free of this role.

He forced a smirk onto his face. "You called this meeting. To what do I owe the pleasure?"

"She's here."

"The daughter?"

"Yes."

"Interesting. When did she arrive?"

"Just Now."

"Very well. You are dismissed."

"Sir—why is she important?"

He shrugged and walked away, fading into the darkness. But the answer to the informant's question hung in the air. He could taste it. The reason the daughter was important: she was the final piece of the puzzle. She was a necessary part of his plan to exact his revenge. To bring the world to its knees.

ACKNOWLEDGMENTS

Books are not created in a vacuum, and the list of people who have been instrumental in helping me realize the dream of publishing my first book is evidence of this. I could not have written *Running in Parallel* without the support and love of so many, and I count myself lucky every day to know such fine folks. So, in no particular order, thank you:

To my amazing friends: Andrea, Kirstin, Sarah, and especially Tiffané, for your countless hours of reading, re-reading, discussing, hand holding, and general consoling when I was convinced that I should quit writing, sell my stuff, and live in a yurt. I need to find a different term, since "beta reader" doesn't begin to cover how much you helped me, but regardless of your TBD superhero titles, I am more than grateful for your insights and patience in helping these worlds and characters come to life. To my editor, Kathrine Kirk, for shaping this book into being the best version of itself. I'm so glad that I found you—you really are the best! To my mother for the spark that created the idea behind *Running in Parallel*, but mostly for your unending love and support. To my kids for understanding when my office door was shut more than you wanted, and being proud of me anyway. But most of all, to my husband. For twenty years the idea for this book rattled around my brain, but I was too afraid to put it to paper. The five words you said— "Why don't you write it?"—changed everything. You gave me the space, love, and support to do just that, and for that I am forever grateful. I love you more than steak fries and cheeseburgers—combined.

Made in the USA
Columbia, SC
05 July 2021

41441483R00176